# ROCK CANDY MOUNTAIN

## VOLUME TWO

WRITTEN & DRAWN BY

# KYLE ✳✳✳✳✳ STARKS

COLORED BY
## CHRIS SCHWEIZER

DESIGN BY
## DYLAN TODD

PUBLISHED BY IMAGE COMICS INC.

## ROCK CANDY MOUNTAIN, VOL 02. FIRST PRINTING. APRIL 2018.

Published by Image Comics, Inc. Office of publication: 2701 NW Vaughn St., Suite 780, Portland, OR 97210. Copyright © 2018 Kyle Starks. All rights reserved. Contains material originally published in single magazine form as ROCK CANDY MOUNTAIN #5-8. "ROCK CANDY MOUNTAIN," its logos, and the likenesses of all characters herein are trademarks of Kyle Starks, unless otherwise noted. "Image" and the Image Comics logos are registered trdemarks of Image Comics, Inc. No part of this publication may be reproduced or transmitted, in any form or by any means (except for short excerpts for journalistic or review purposes), without the express written permission of Kyle Starks, or Image Comics, Inc. All names, characters, events, and locales in this publication are entirely fictional. Any resemblance to actual persons (living or dead), events, or places, without satiric intent, is coincidental. Printed in the USA. For information regarding the CPSIA on this printed material call: 203-595-3636 and provide reference # RICH – 783831. For international rights, contact: foreignlicensing@imagecomics.com. ISBN# 978-1-5343-0495-6

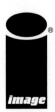

## *CHAPTER FIVE*

# "A hobo came a-walkin'."

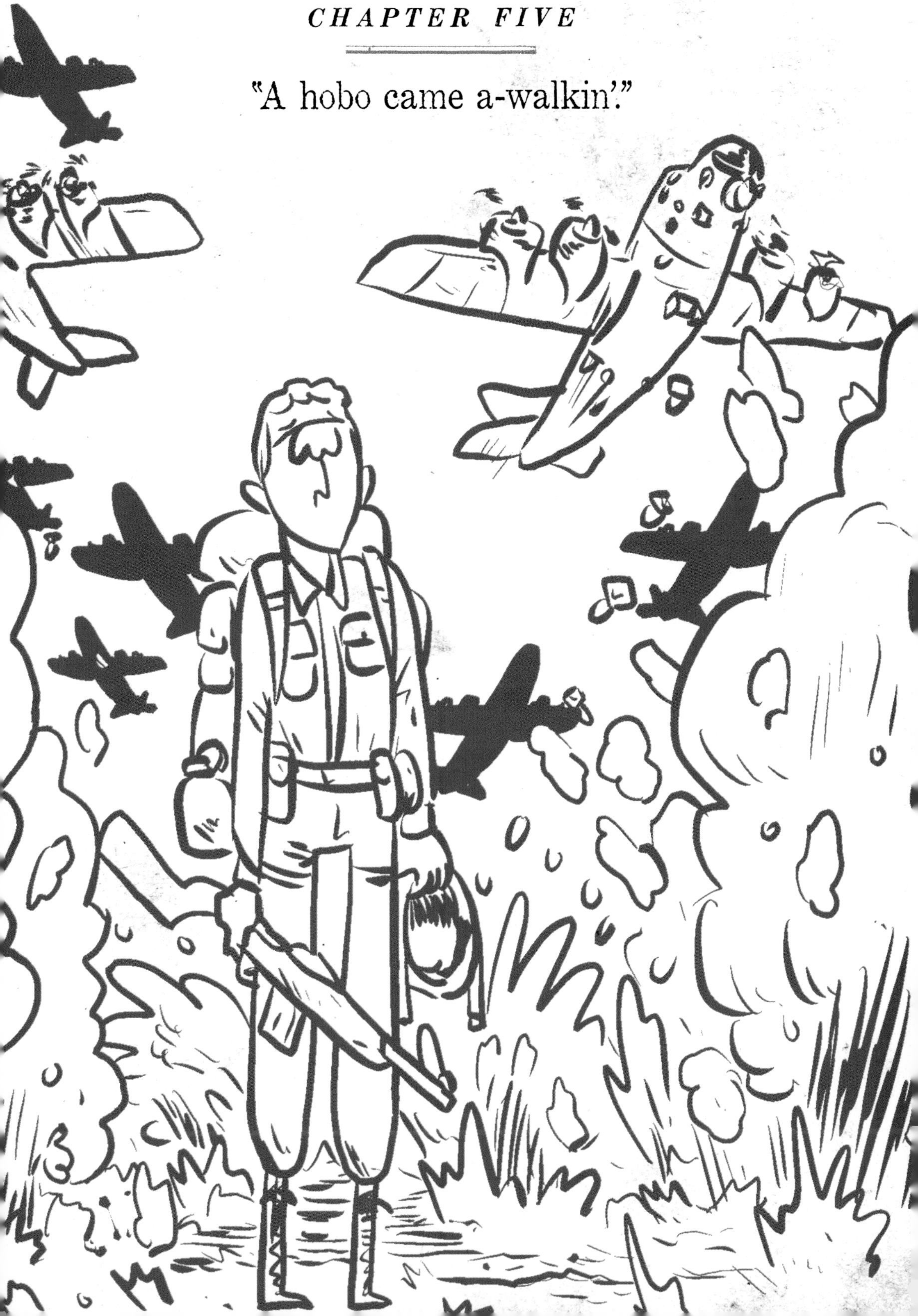

"danger."

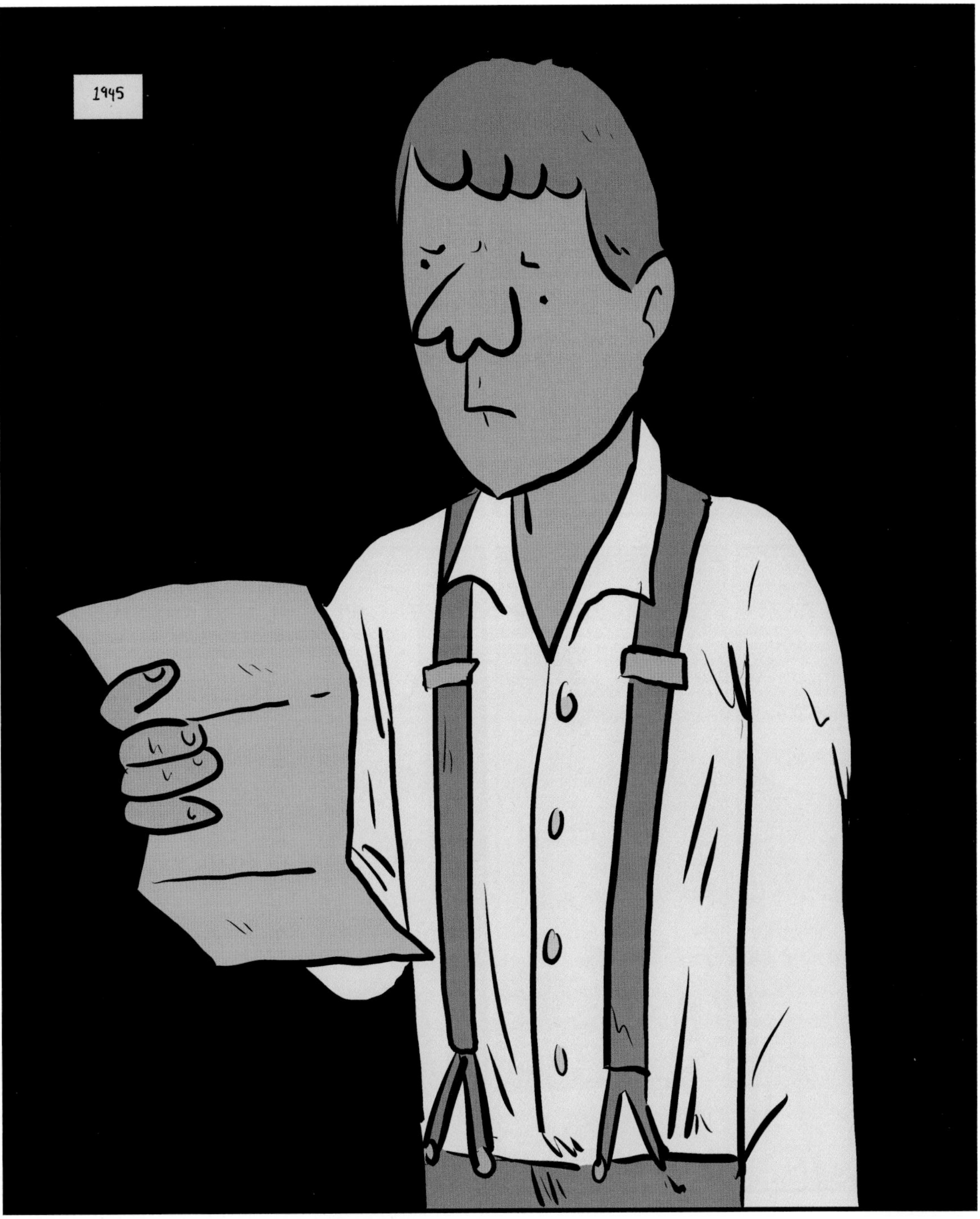
1945

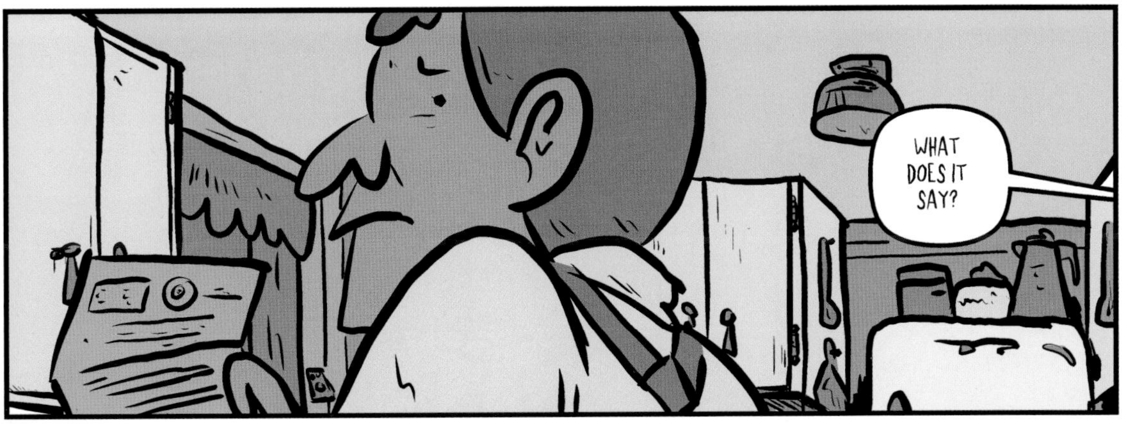
WHAT DOES IT SAY?

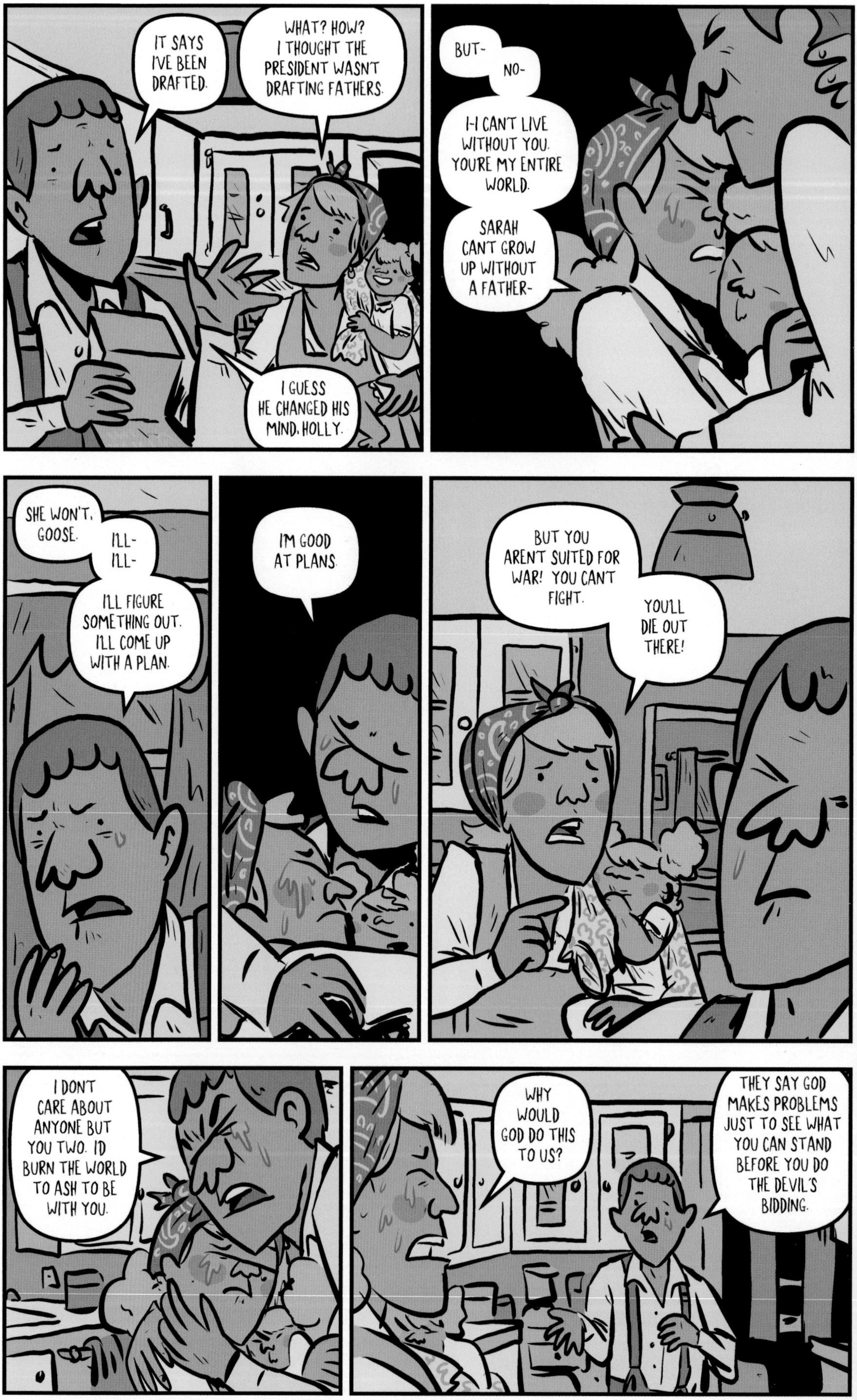
IT SAYS I'VE BEEN DRAFTED.
WHAT? HOW? I THOUGHT THE PRESIDENT WASN'T DRAFTING FATHERS.
I GUESS HE CHANGED HIS MIND, HOLLY.
BUT-
NO-
I-I CAN'T LIVE WITHOUT YOU. YOU'RE MY ENTIRE WORLD.
SARAH CAN'T GROW UP WITHOUT A FATHER-
SHE WON'T, GOOSE.
I'LL- I'LL-
I'LL FIGURE SOMETHING OUT. I'LL COME UP WITH A PLAN.
I'M GOOD AT PLANS.
BUT YOU AREN'T SUITED FOR WAR! YOU CAN'T FIGHT.
YOU'LL DIE OUT THERE!
I DON'T CARE ABOUT ANYONE BUT YOU TWO. I'D BURN THE WORLD TO ASH TO BE WITH YOU.
WHY WOULD GOD DO THIS TO US?
THEY SAY GOD MAKES PROBLEMS JUST TO SEE WHAT YOU CAN STAND BEFORE YOU DO THE DEVIL'S BIDDING.

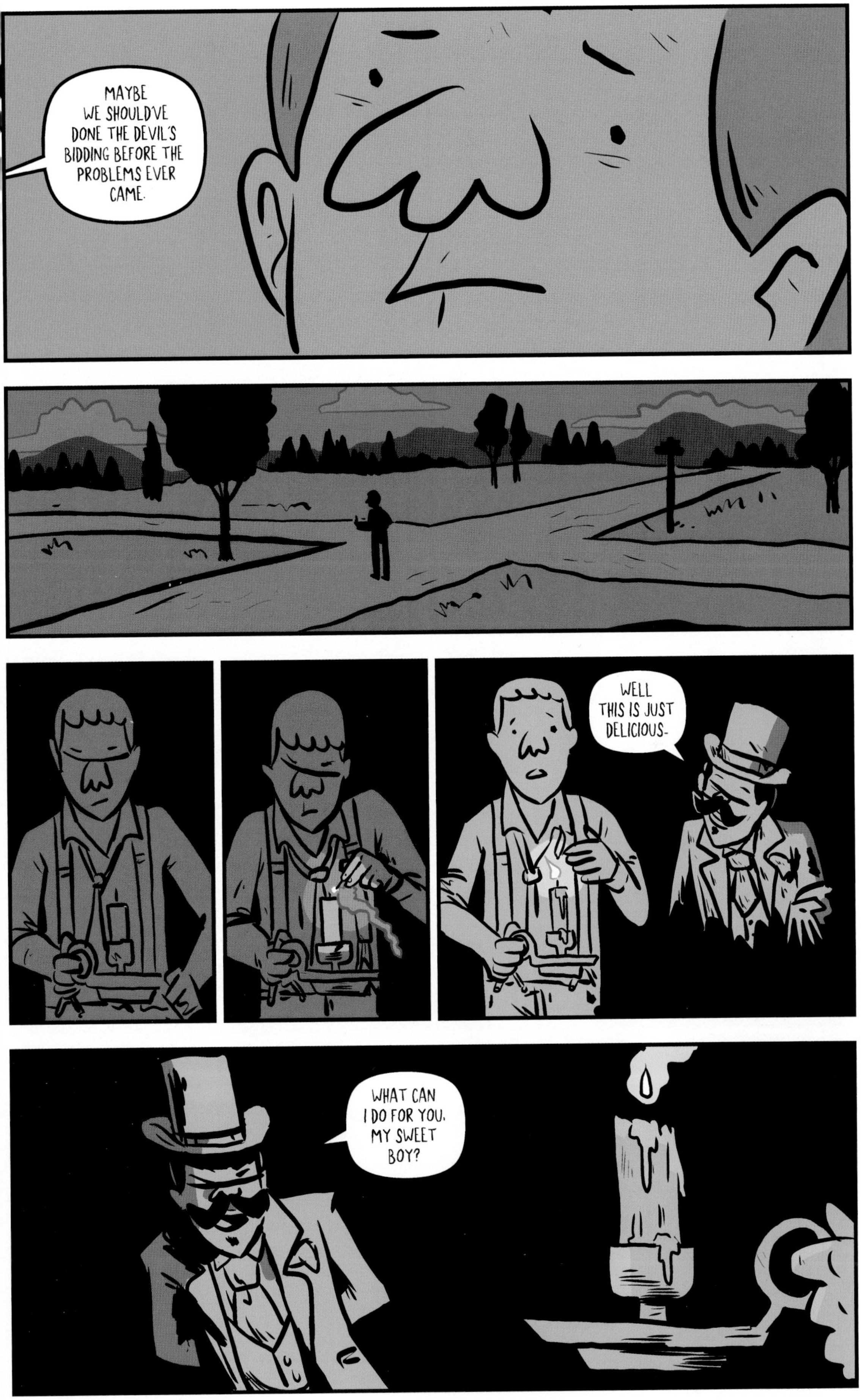
MAYBE WE SHOULD'VE DONE THE DEVIL'S BIDDING BEFORE THE PROBLEMS EVER CAME.
WELL THIS IS JUST DELICIOUS.
WHAT CAN I DO FOR YOU, MY SWEET BOY?

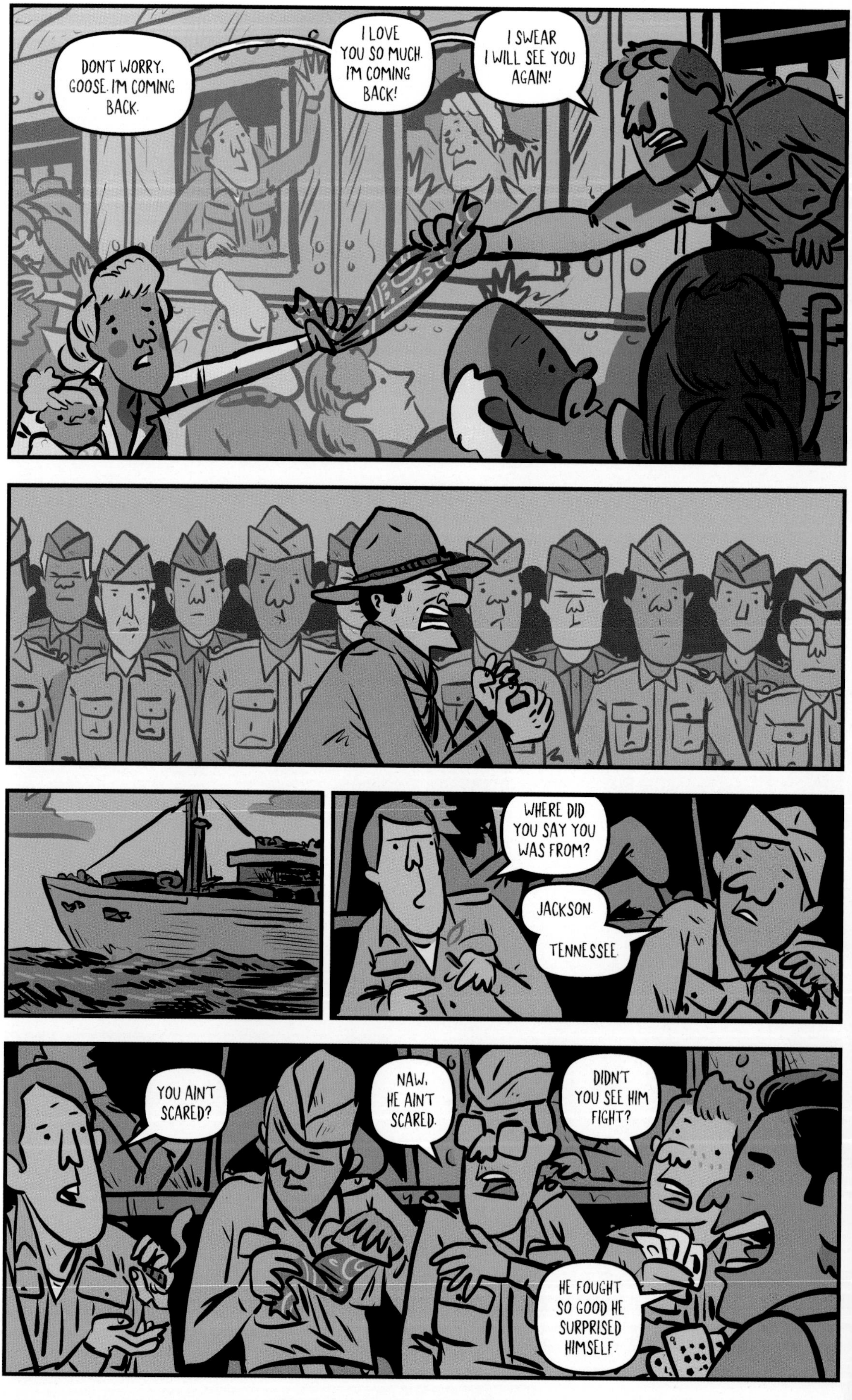
DON'T WORRY, GOOSE. I'M COMING BACK.
I LOVE YOU SO MUCH. I'M COMING BACK!
I SWEAR I WILL SEE YOU AGAIN!
WHERE DID YOU SAY YOU WAS FROM?
JACKSON.
TENNESSEE.
YOU AIN'T SCARED?
NAW, HE AIN'T SCARED.
DIDN'T YOU SEE HIM FIGHT?
HE FOUGHT SO GOOD HE SURPRISED HIMSELF.

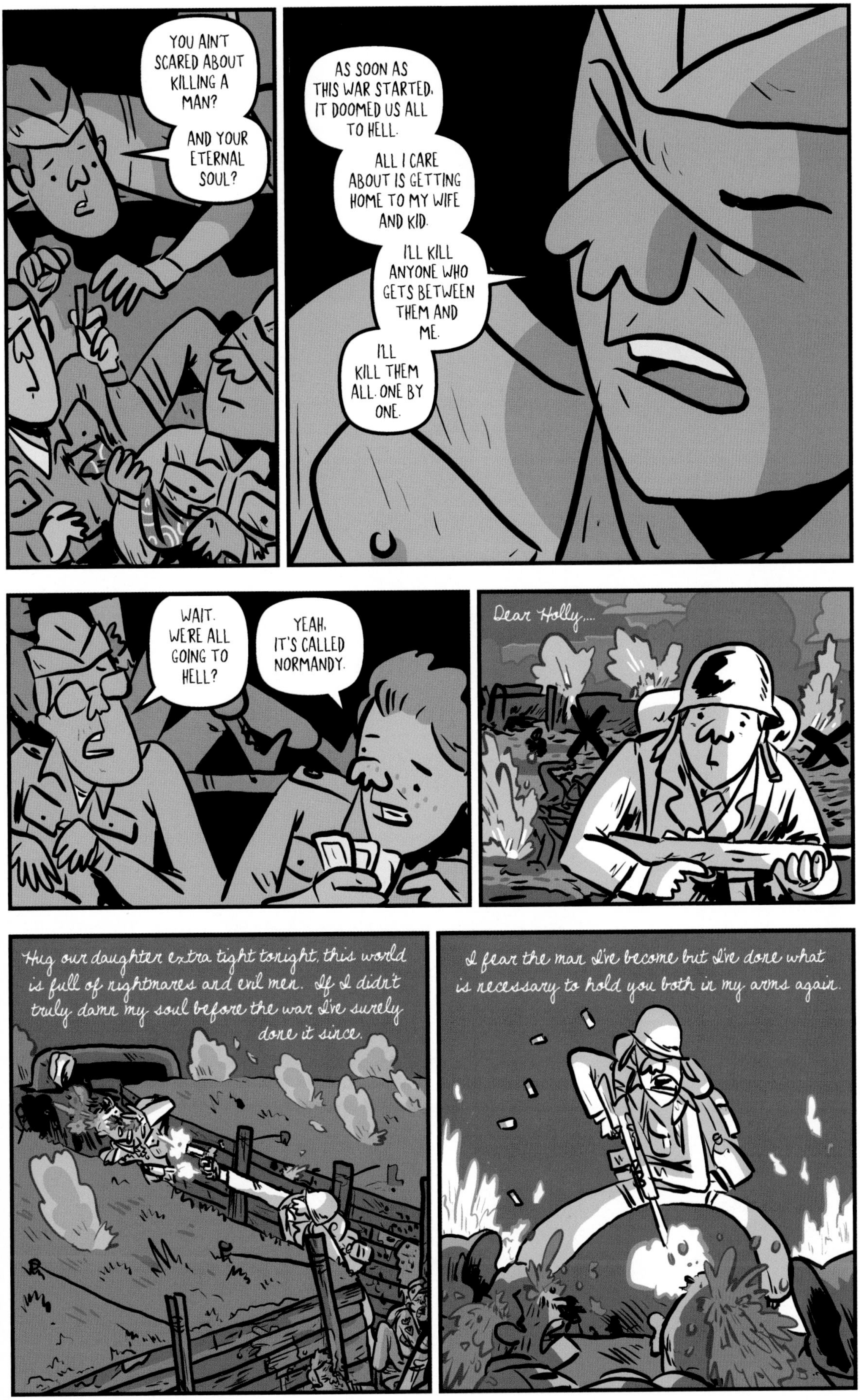
YOU AIN'T SCARED ABOUT KILLING A MAN?
AND YOUR ETERNAL SOUL?
AS SOON AS THIS WAR STARTED, IT DOOMED US ALL TO HELL.
ALL I CARE ABOUT IS GETTING HOME TO MY WIFE AND KID.
I'LL KILL ANYONE WHO GETS BETWEEN THEM AND ME.
I'LL KILL THEM ALL. ONE BY ONE.
WAIT. WE'RE ALL GOING TO HELL?
YEAH, IT'S CALLED NORMANDY.
Dear Holly,...
Hug our daughter extra tight tonight, this world is full of nightmares and evil men. If I didn't truly damn my soul before the war I've surely done it since.
I fear the man I've become but I've done what is necessary to hold you both in my arms again.

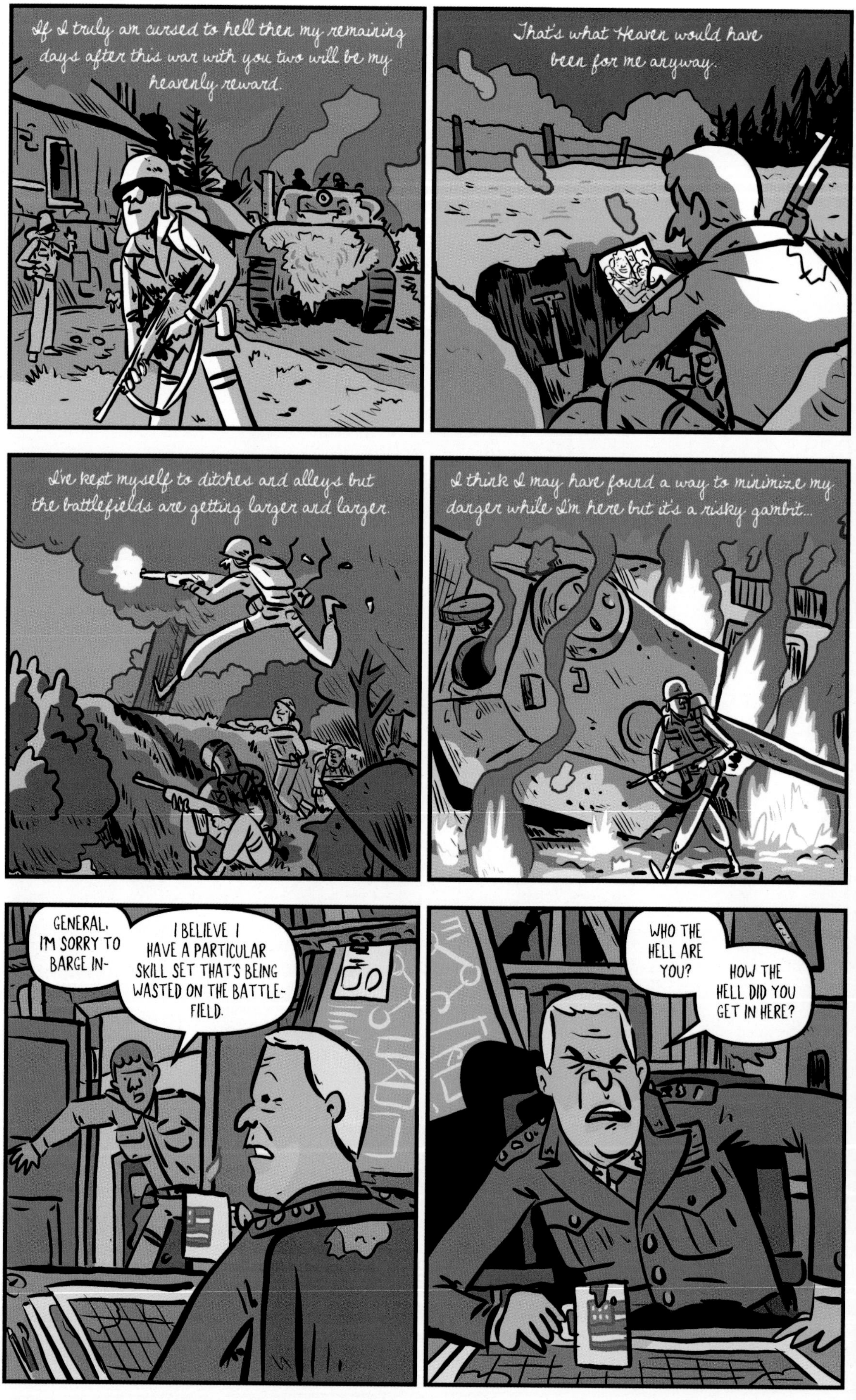
If I truly am cursed to hell then my remaining days after this war with you two will be my heavenly reward.
That's what Heaven would have been for me anyway.
I've kept myself to ditches and alleys but the battlefields are getting larger and larger.
I think I may have found a way to minimize my danger while I'm here but it's a risky gambit...
GENERAL, I'M SORRY TO BARGE IN-
I BELIEVE I HAVE A PARTICULAR SKILL SET THAT'S BEING WASTED ON THE BATTLE-FIELD.
WHO THE HELL ARE YOU?
HOW THE HELL DID YOU GET IN HERE?

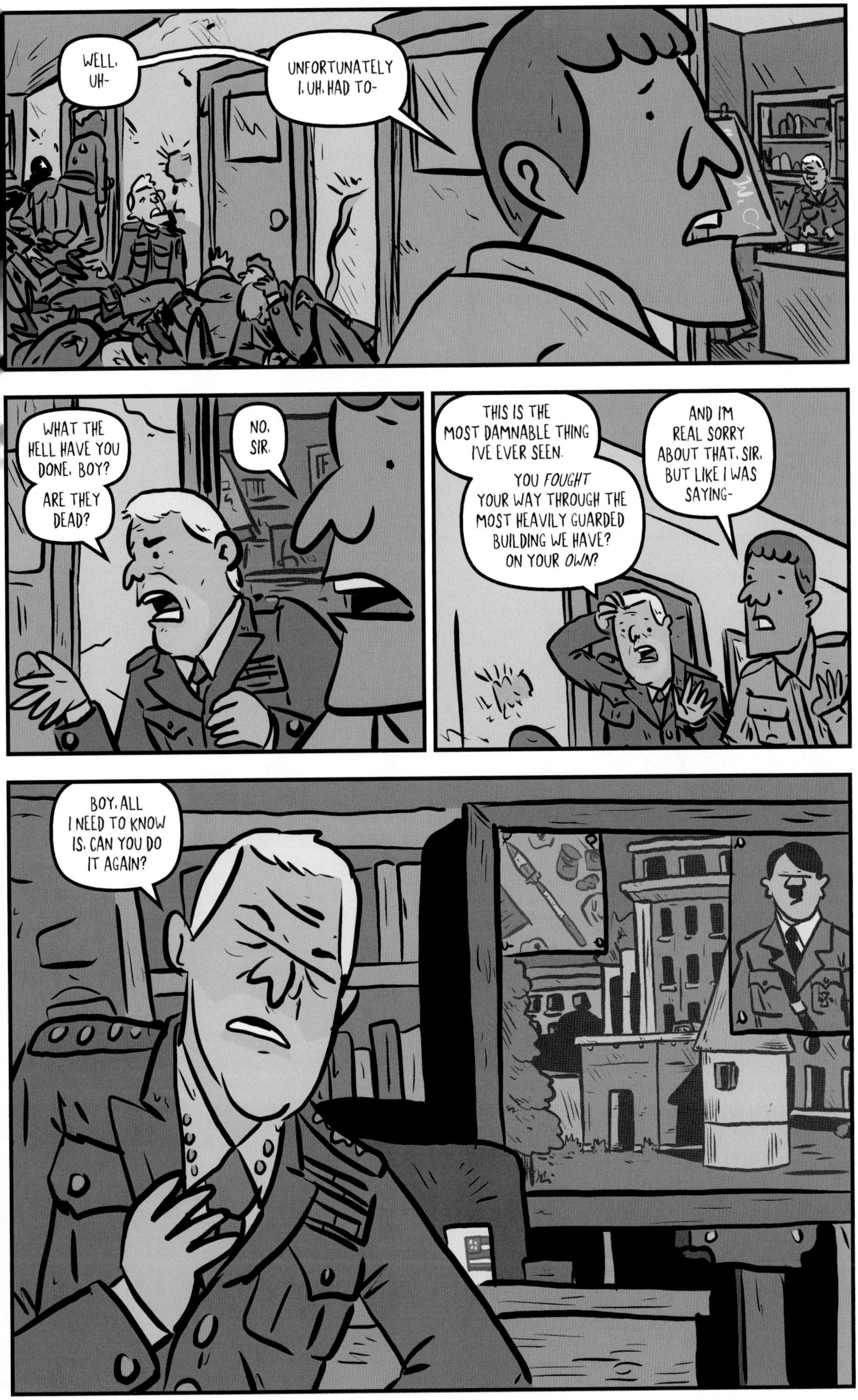
WELL, UH-
UNFORTUNATELY I, UH, HAD TO-
WHAT THE HELL HAVE YOU DONE, BOY?
ARE THEY DEAD?
NO, SIR.
THIS IS THE MOST DAMNABLE THING I'VE EVER SEEN.
YOU FOUGHT YOUR WAY THROUGH THE MOST HEAVILY GUARDED BUILDING WE HAVE? ON YOUR OWN?
AND I'M REAL SORRY ABOUT THAT, SIR, BUT LIKE I WAS SAYING-
BOY, ALL I NEED TO KNOW IS, CAN YOU DO IT AGAIN?

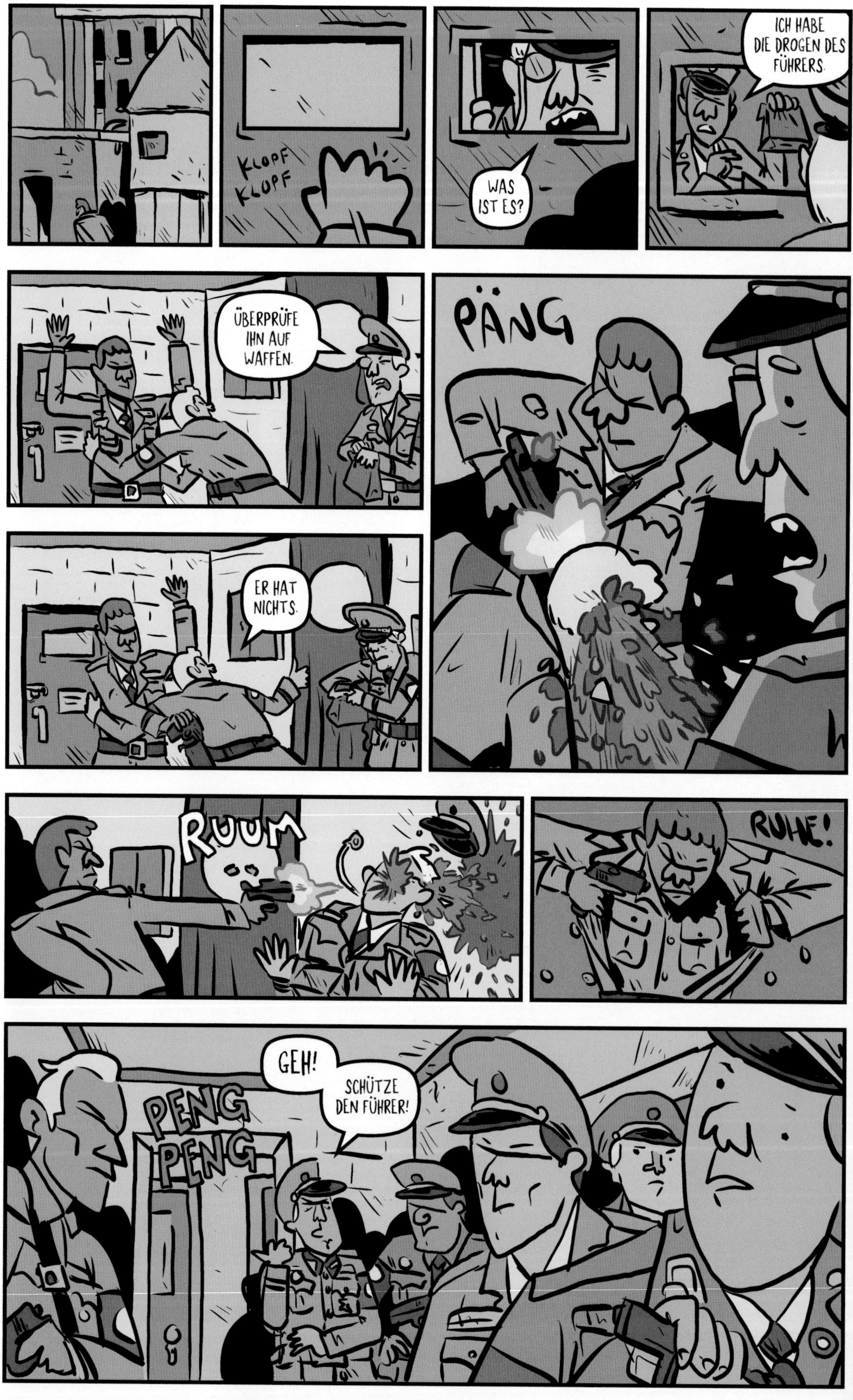
KLOPF KLOPF
WAS IST ES?
ICH HABE DIE DROGEN DES FÜHRERS.
ÜBERPRÜFE IHN AUF WAFFEN.
ER HAT NICHTS.
PÄNG
RUUM
RUHE!
GEH!
SCHÜTZE DEN FÜHRER!
PENG PENG

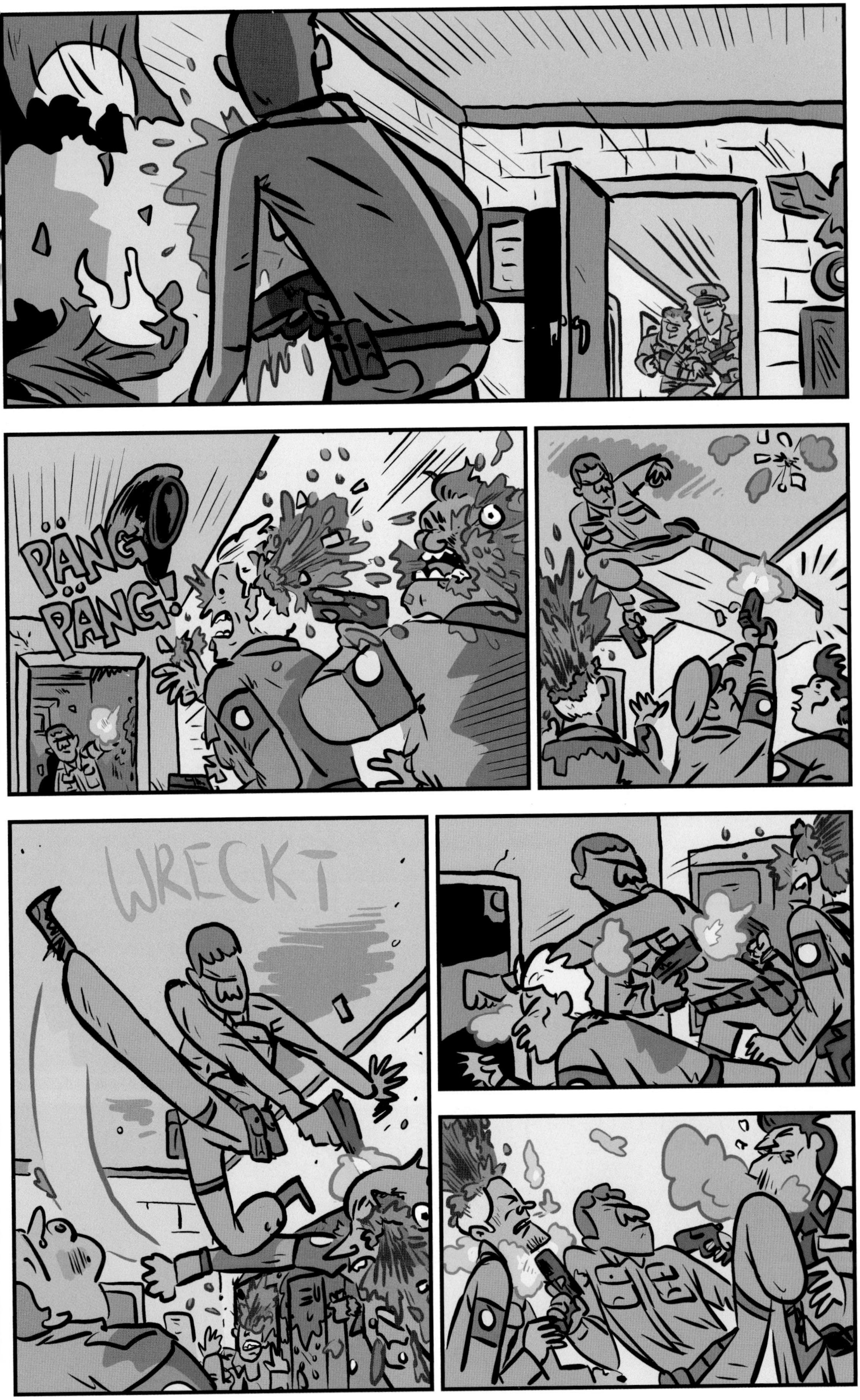
PÄNG PÄNG!
WRECKT

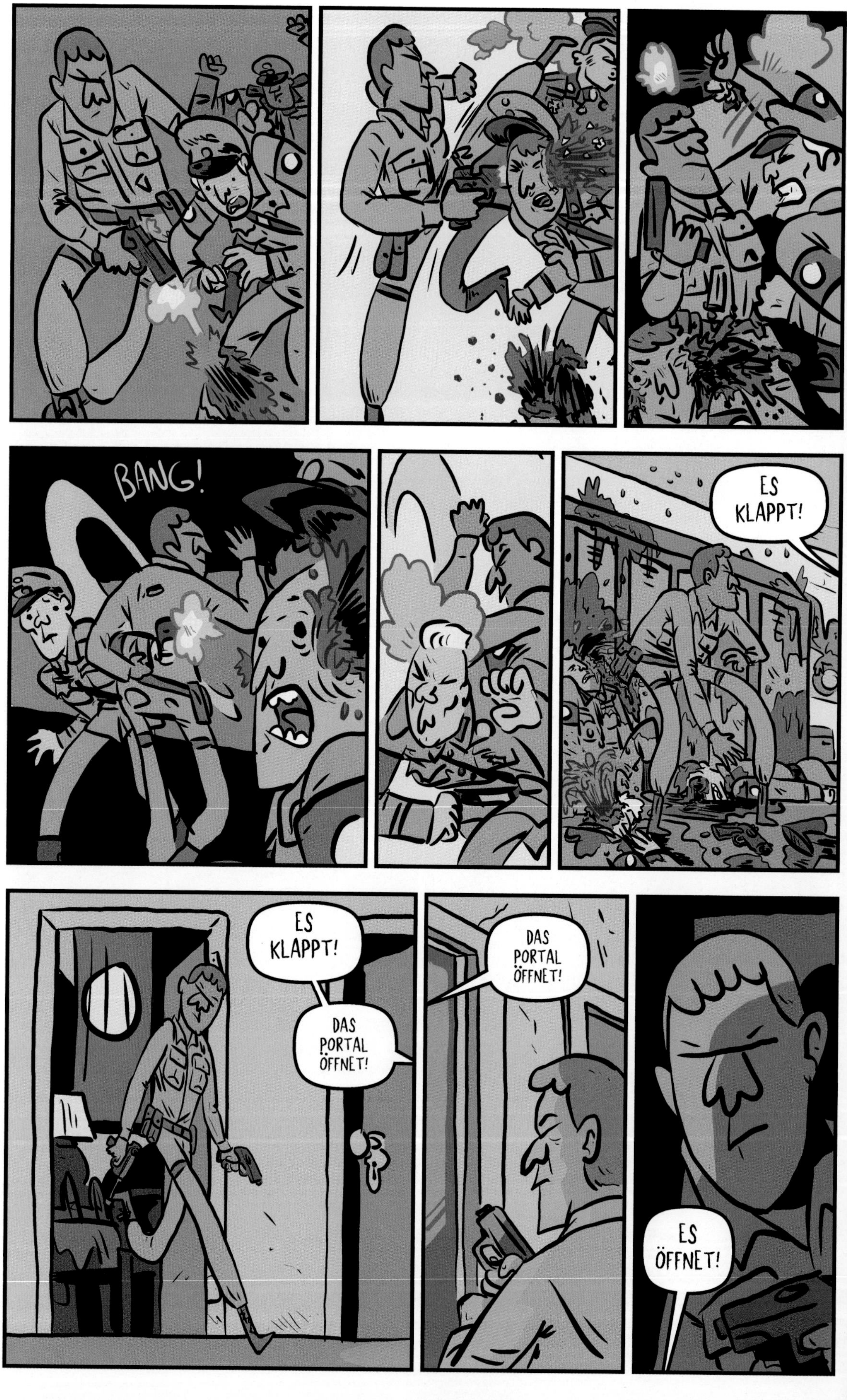
BANG!
ES KLAPPT!
ES KLAPPT!
DAS PORTAL ÖFFNET!
DAS PORTAL ÖFFNET!
ES ÖFFNET!

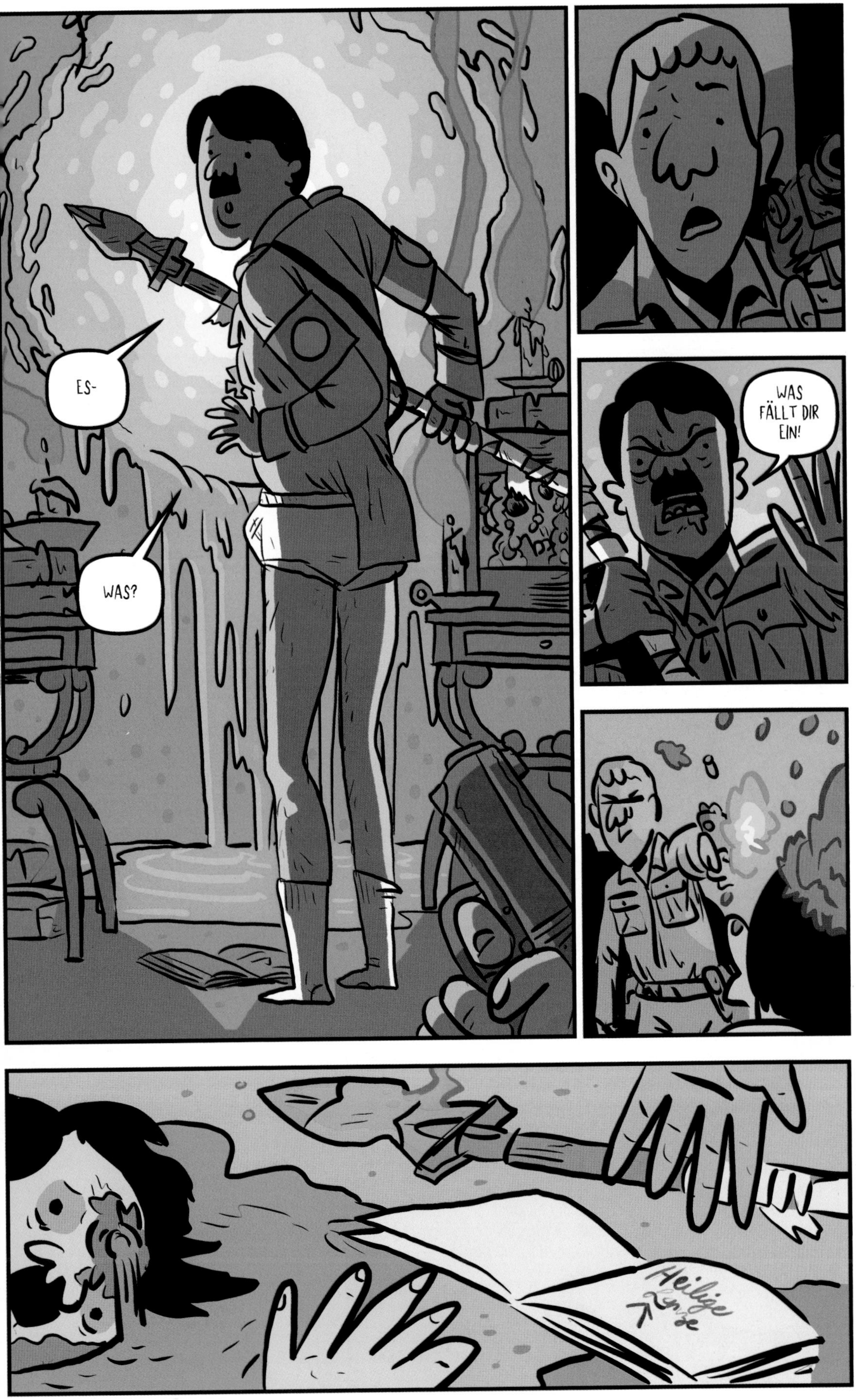
ES-
WAS?
WAS FÄLLT DIR EIN!
Heilige

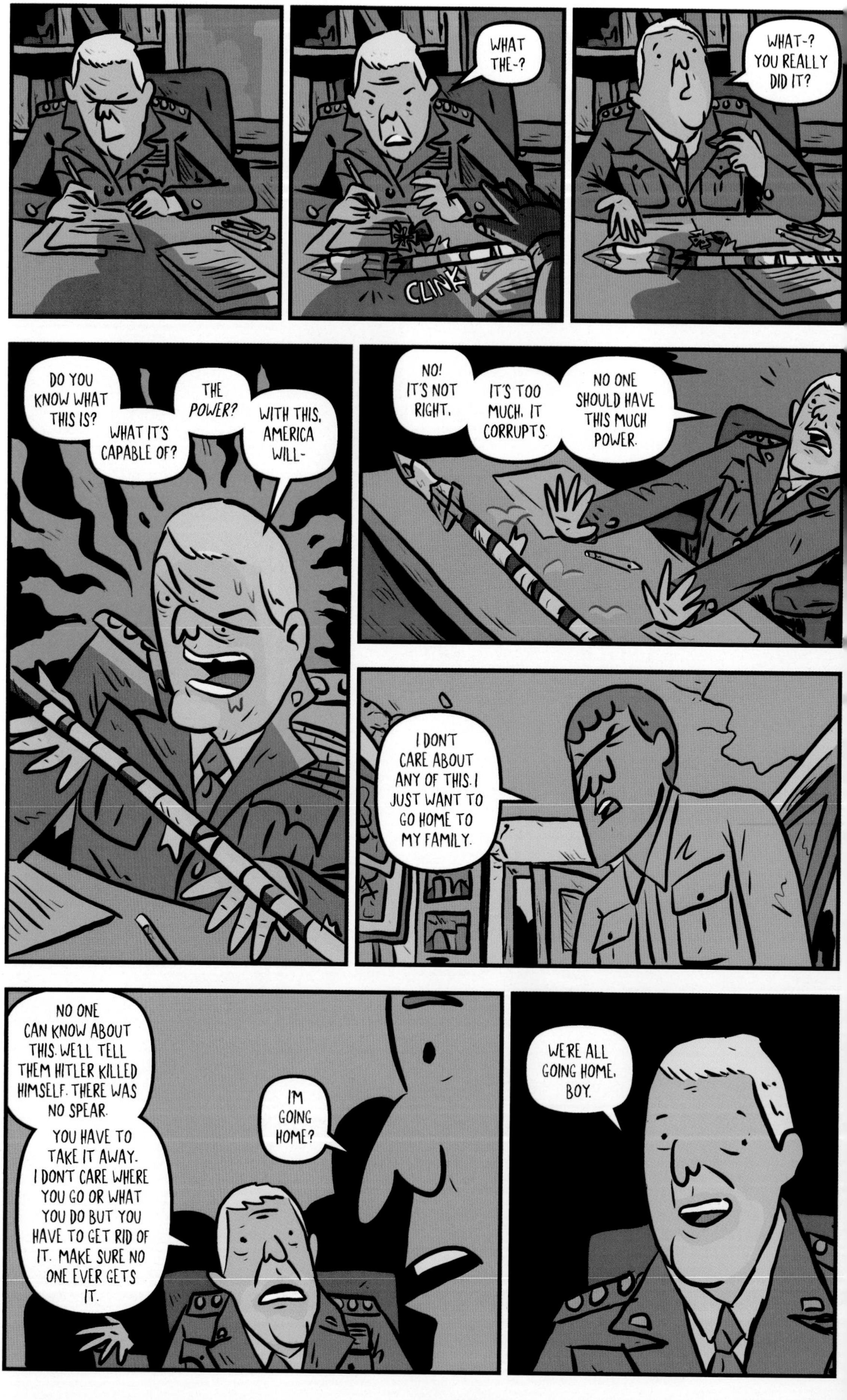
WHAT THE-?
CLINK
WHAT-? YOU REALLY DID IT?
DO YOU KNOW WHAT THIS IS?
WHAT IT'S CAPABLE OF?
THE POWER?
WITH THIS, AMERICA WILL-
NO! IT'S NOT RIGHT.
IT'S TOO MUCH. IT CORRUPTS.
NO ONE SHOULD HAVE THIS MUCH POWER.
I DON'T CARE ABOUT ANY OF THIS. I JUST WANT TO GO HOME TO MY FAMILY.
NO ONE CAN KNOW ABOUT THIS. WE'LL TELL THEM HITLER KILLED HIMSELF. THERE WAS NO SPEAR.
YOU HAVE TO TAKE IT AWAY. I DON'T CARE WHERE YOU GO OR WHAT YOU DO BUT YOU HAVE TO GET RID OF IT. MAKE SURE NO ONE EVER GETS IT.
I'M GOING HOME?
WE'RE ALL GOING HOME, BOY.

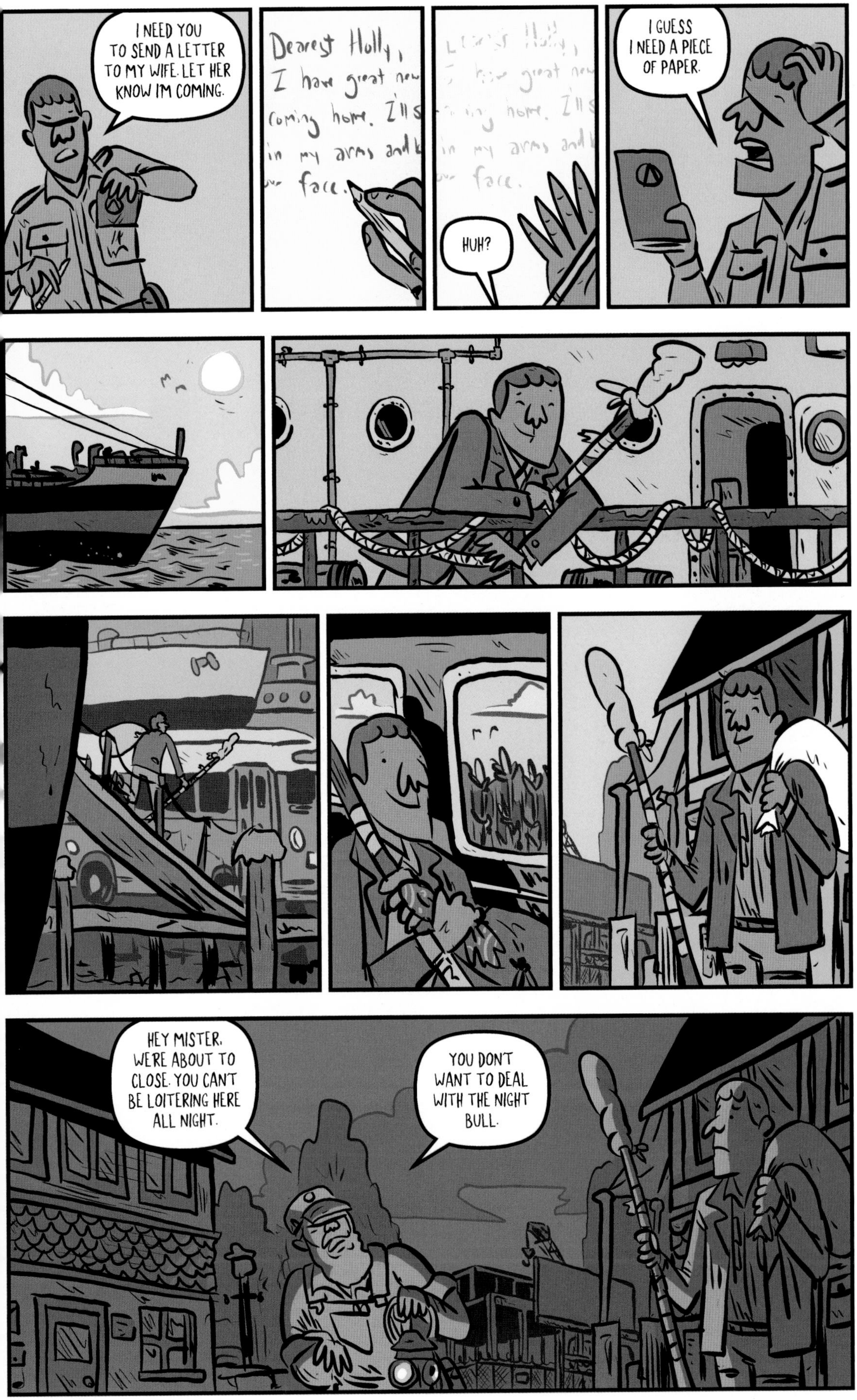
I NEED YOU TO SEND A LETTER TO MY WIFE. LET HER KNOW I'M COMING.
Dearest Holly,
I have great new
coming home. I'll
in my arms and
face.
HUH?
I GUESS I NEED A PIECE OF PAPER.
HEY MISTER. WE'RE ABOUT TO CLOSE. YOU CAN'T BE LOITERING HERE ALL NIGHT.
YOU DON'T WANT TO DEAL WITH THE NIGHT BULL.

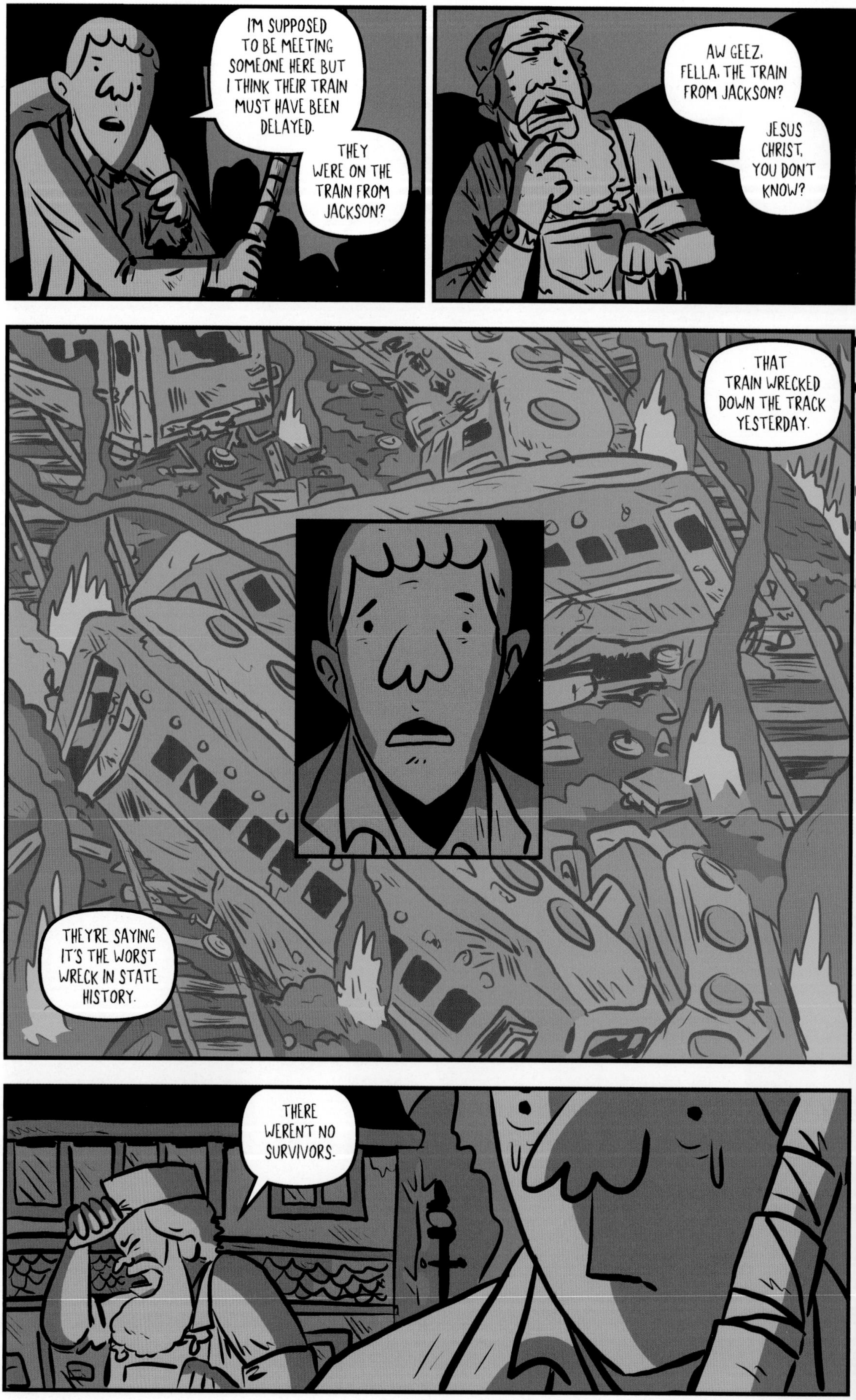
I'M SUPPOSED TO BE MEETING SOMEONE HERE BUT I THINK THEIR TRAIN MUST HAVE BEEN DELAYED.
THEY WERE ON THE TRAIN FROM JACKSON?
AW GEEZ, FELLA, THE TRAIN FROM JACKSON?
JESUS CHRIST, YOU DON'T KNOW?
THAT TRAIN WRECKED DOWN THE TRACK YESTERDAY.
THEY'RE SAYING IT'S THE WORST WRECK IN STATE HISTORY.
THERE WEREN'T NO SURVIVORS.

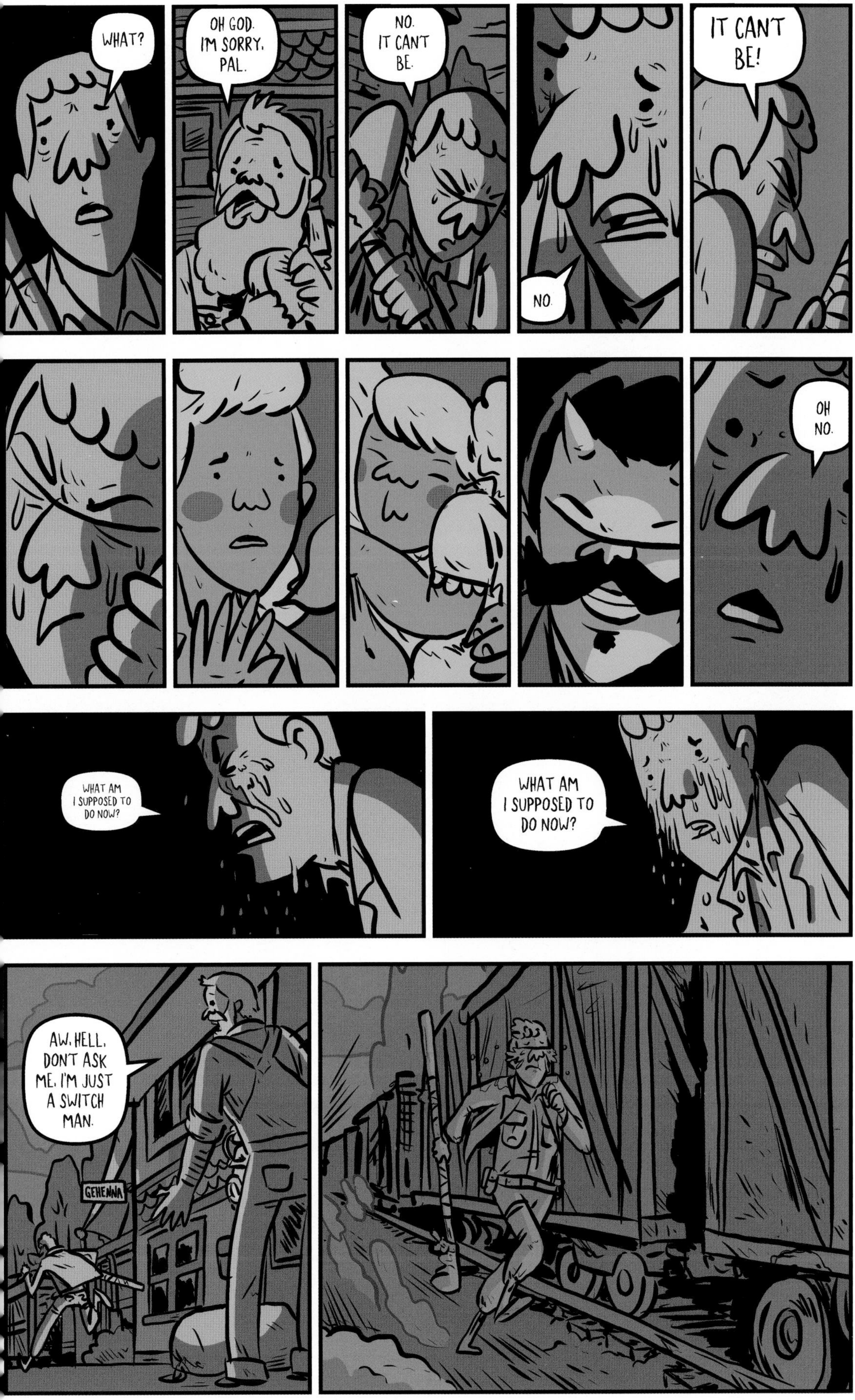
WHAT?
OH GOD. I'M SORRY, PAL.
NO. IT CAN'T BE.
NO.
IT CAN'T BE!
OH NO.
WHAT AM I SUPPOSED TO DO NOW?
WHAT AM I SUPPOSED TO DO NOW?
AW, HELL, DON'T ASK ME, I'M JUST A SWITCH MAN.
GEHENNA

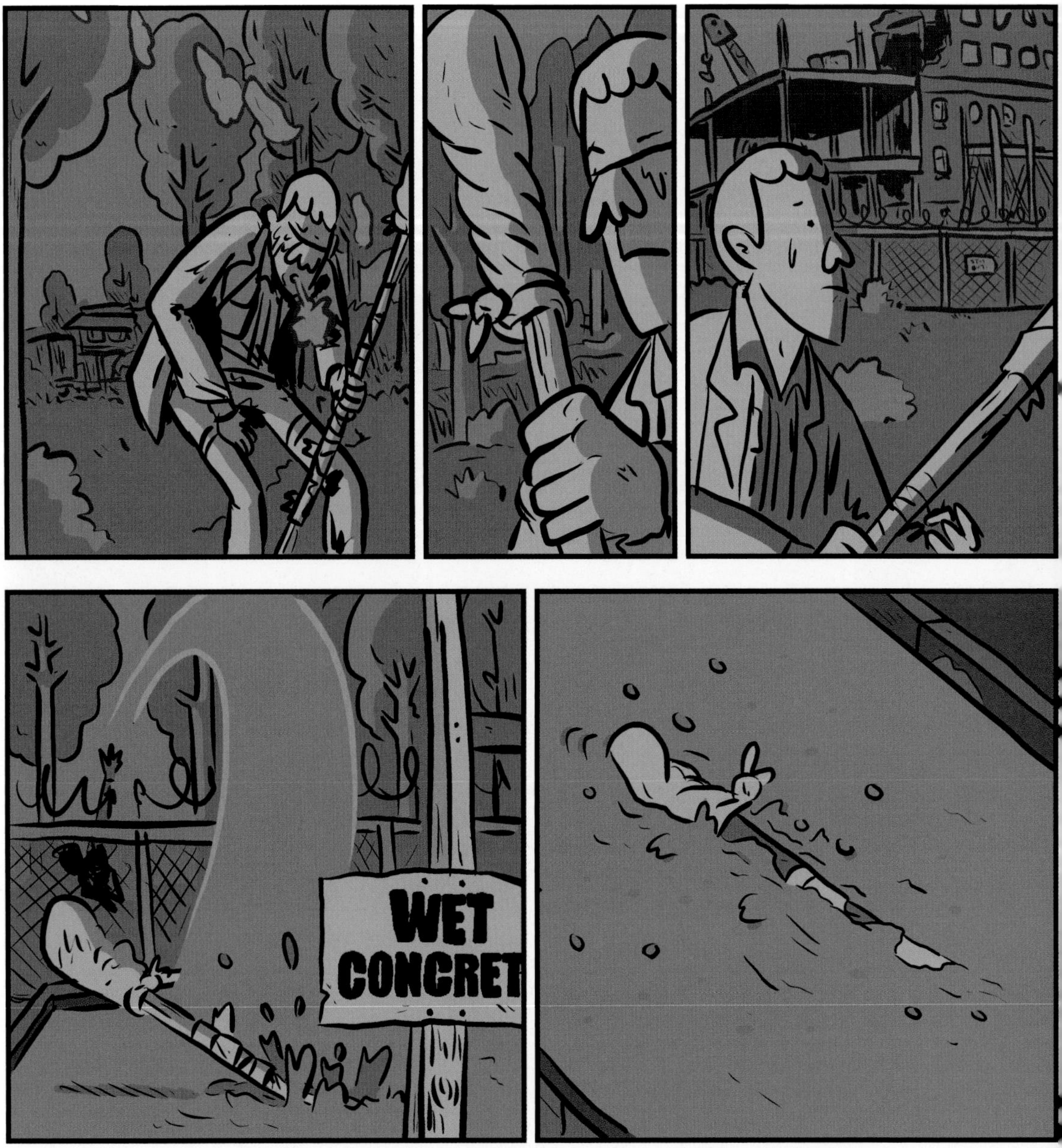
WET
CONCRET

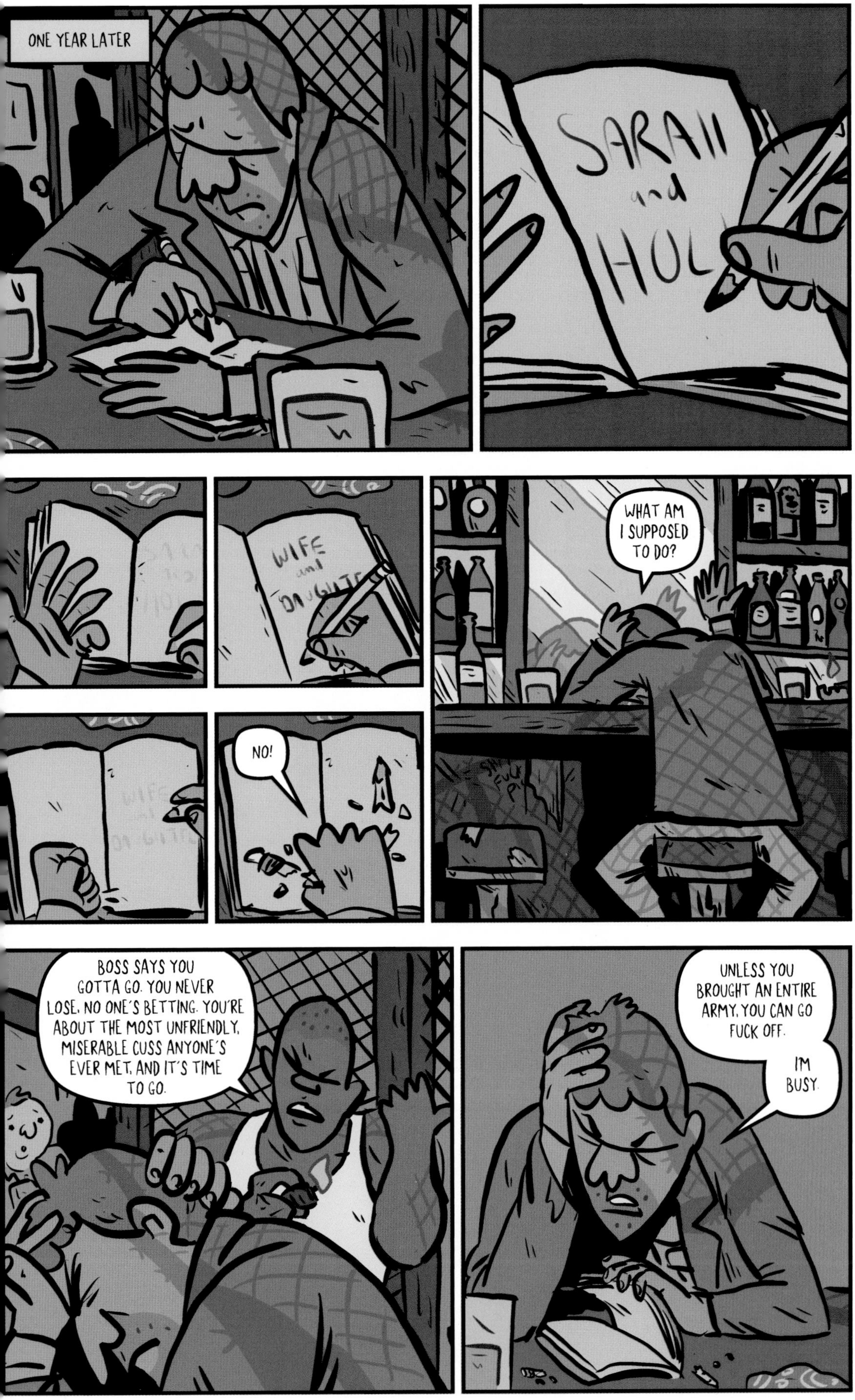
ONE YEAR LATER
NO!
WHAT AM I SUPPOSED TO DO?
BOSS SAYS YOU GOTTA GO. YOU NEVER LOSE, NO ONE'S BETTING. YOU'RE ABOUT THE MOST UNFRIENDLY, MISERABLE CUSS ANYONE'S EVER MET, AND IT'S TIME TO GO.
UNLESS YOU BROUGHT AN ENTIRE ARMY, YOU CAN GO FUCK OFF.
I'M BUSY.

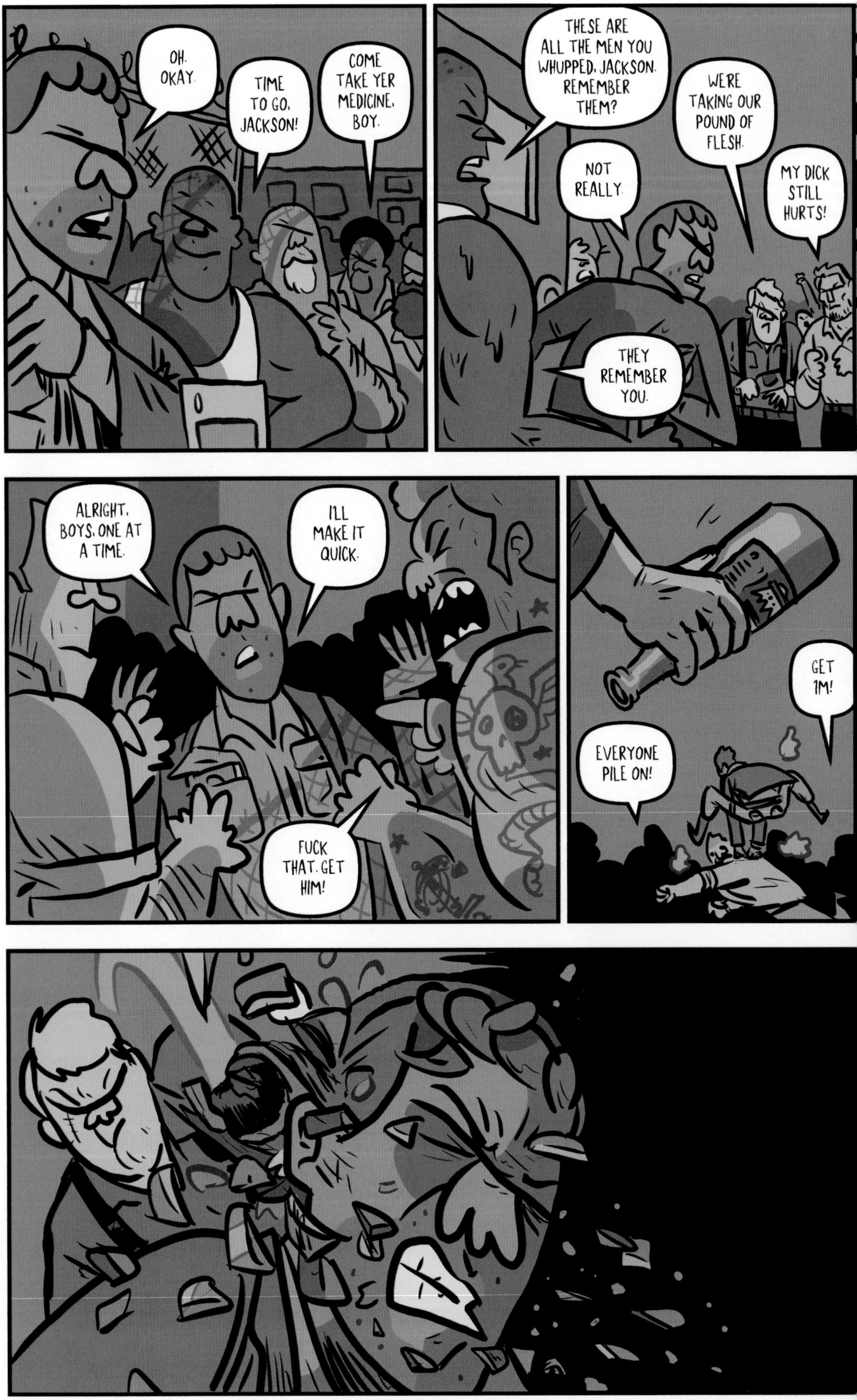
OH. OKAY.
TIME TO GO, JACKSON!
COME TAKE YER MEDICINE, BOY.
THESE ARE ALL THE MEN YOU WHUPPED, JACKSON. REMEMBER THEM?
NOT REALLY.
WE'RE TAKING OUR POUND OF FLESH.
MY DICK STILL HURTS!
THEY REMEMBER YOU.
ALRIGHT, BOYS, ONE AT A TIME.
I'LL MAKE IT QUICK.
FUCK THAT. GET HIM!
GET 'IM!
EVERYONE PILE ON!

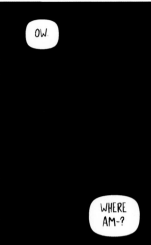

OW.

WHERE AM-?

HE'S WAKIN' UP, BANJO!

CALM DOWN, FELLA, WE'RE JUST TRYING TO HELP.

WHO?

WHERE AM I?

WHAT HAPPENED?

IT LOOKS LIKE YOU CAME DOWN WITH A CASE OF THE 'GOT FUCKED UPS.' MY DUDE.

I THINK YOUR FACE MIGHT BE ALLERGIC TO KNUCKLES.

WE SAW YOU GET WORKED OVER BY SOME THUGS.

THEY WAS WORKING A SQUARE DANCE ON YOU.

SO WE BROUGHT YOU TO THIS HERE JUNGLE TO CLEAN YOU UP.

WHY WOULD YOU HELP ME? A STRANGER?

A HOBO'S LIFE IS MEASURED IN THE NUMBER OF FRIENDS HE HAS.

ALRIGHT, YOU BUMS, SHOW ME YOUR HANDS.

BUMS?

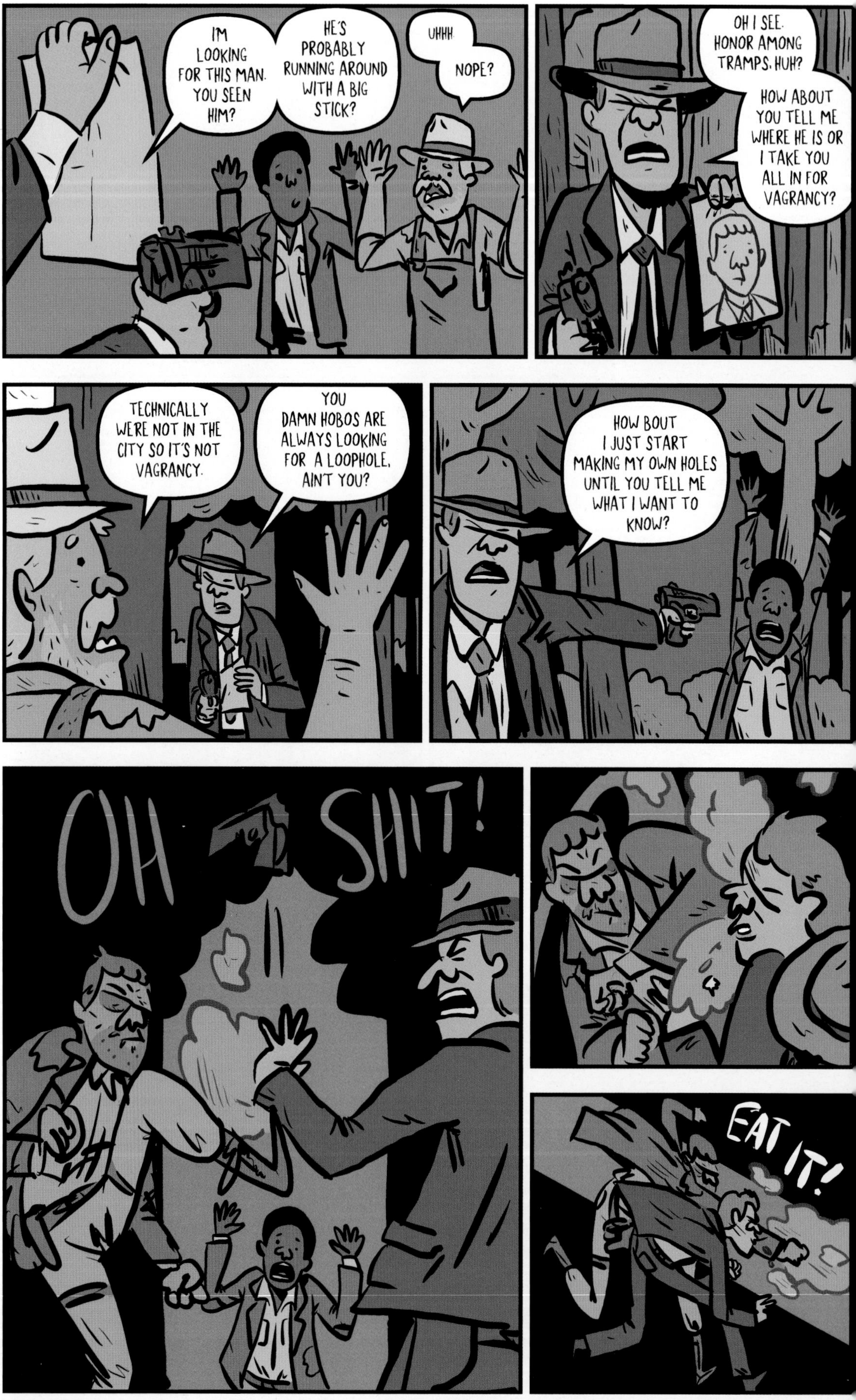
I'M LOOKING FOR THIS MAN. YOU SEEN HIM?
HE'S PROBABLY RUNNING AROUND WITH A BIG STICK?
UHHH.
NOPE?
OH I SEE. HONOR AMONG TRAMPS, HUH?
HOW ABOUT YOU TELL ME WHERE HE IS OR I TAKE YOU ALL IN FOR VAGRANCY?
TECHNICALLY WE'RE NOT IN THE CITY SO IT'S NOT VAGRANCY.
YOU DAMN HOBOS ARE ALWAYS LOOKING FOR A LOOPHOLE, AIN'T YOU?
HOW BOUT I JUST START MAKING MY OWN HOLES UNTIL YOU TELL ME WHAT I WANT TO KNOW?
OH SHIT!
EAT IT!

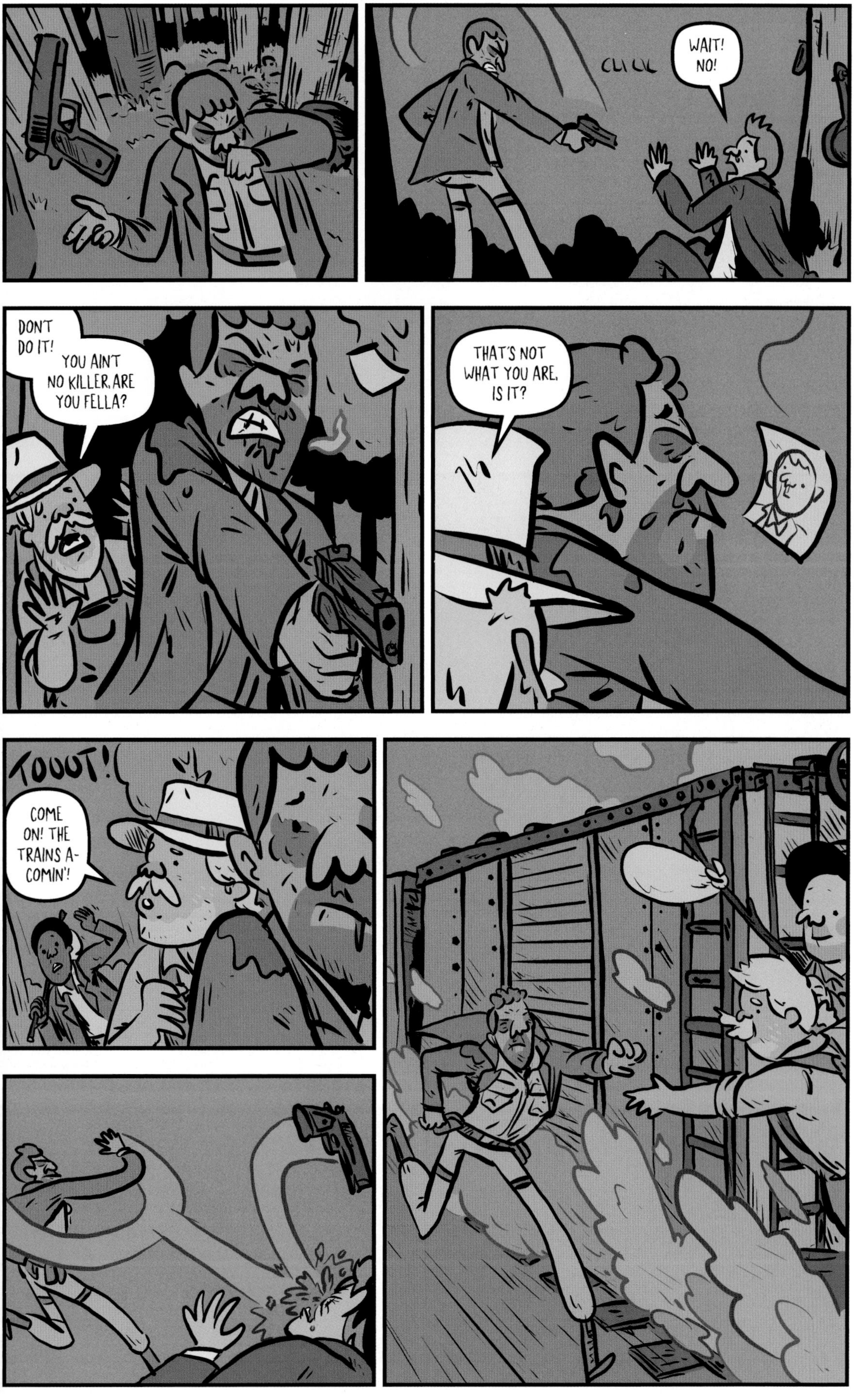
CLICK
WAIT! NO!
DON'T DO IT!
YOU AIN'T NO KILLER, ARE YOU FELLA?
THAT'S NOT WHAT YOU ARE, IS IT?
TOOOT!
COME ON! THE TRAINS A-COMIN'!

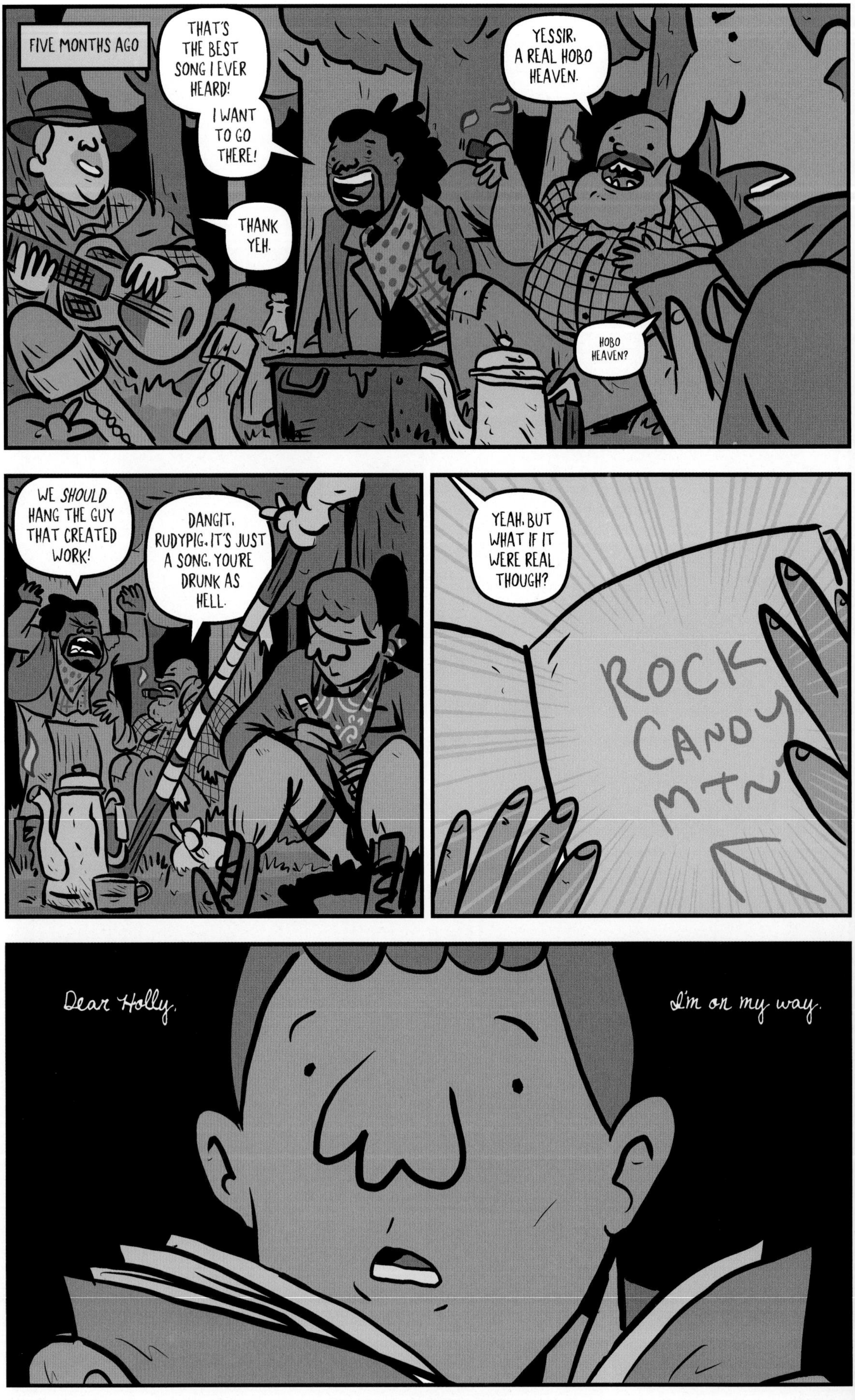
FIVE MONTHS AGO
THAT'S THE BEST SONG I EVER HEARD!
I WANT TO GO THERE!
THANK YEH.
YESSIR, A REAL HOBO HEAVEN.
HOBO HEAVEN?
WE *SHOULD* HANG THE GUY THAT CREATED WORK!
DANGIT, RUDYPIG, IT'S JUST A SONG, YOU'RE DRUNK AS HELL.
YEAH, BUT WHAT IF IT WERE REAL THOUGH?
ROCK CANDY MTN
Dear Holly,
I'm on my way.

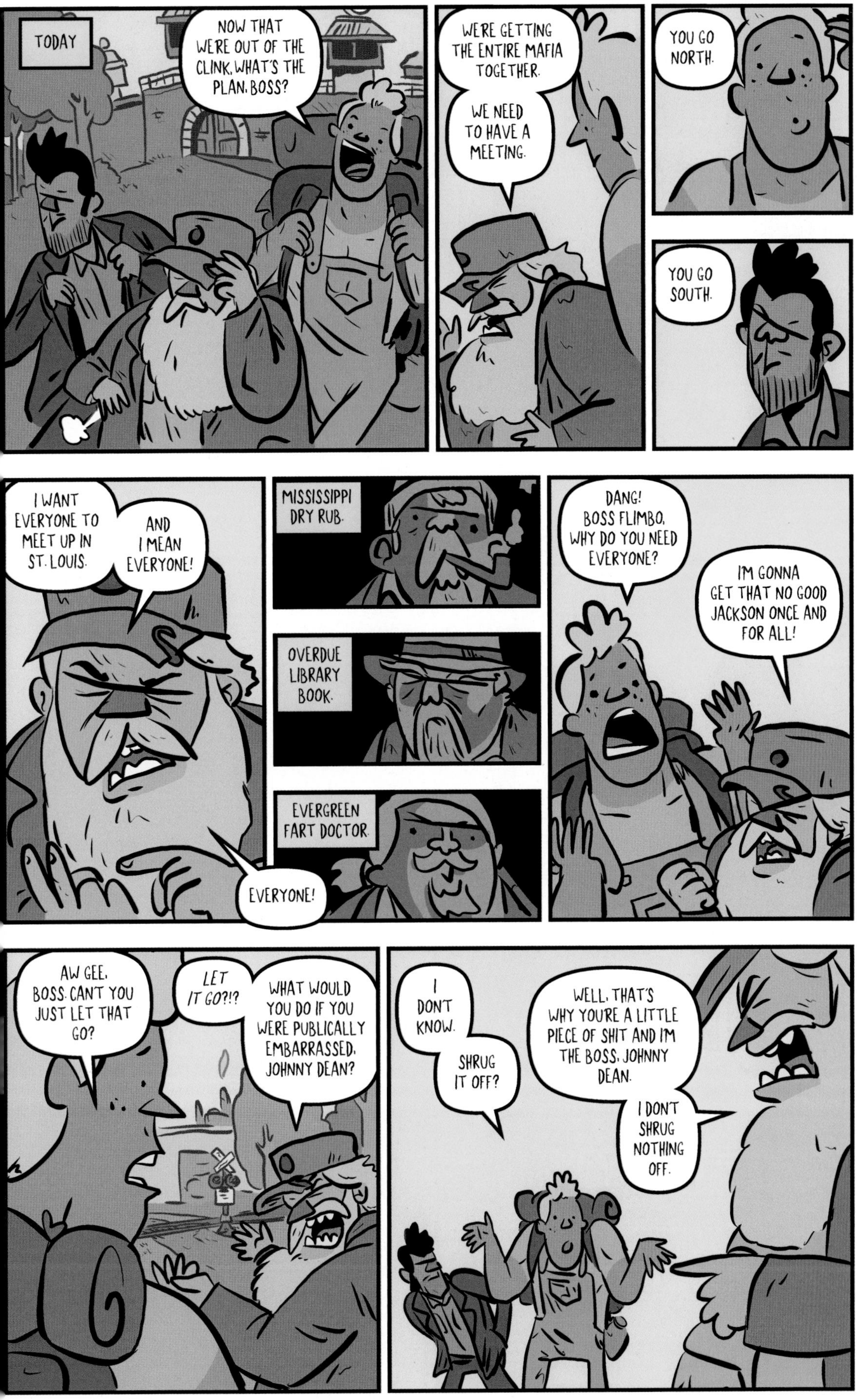
TODAY
NOW THAT WE'RE OUT OF THE CLINK, WHAT'S THE PLAN, BOSS?
WE'RE GETTING THE ENTIRE MAFIA TOGETHER.
WE NEED TO HAVE A MEETING.
YOU GO NORTH.
YOU GO SOUTH.
I WANT EVERYONE TO MEET UP IN ST. LOUIS.
AND I MEAN EVERYONE!
EVERYONE!
MISSISSIPPI DRY RUB.
OVERDUE LIBRARY BOOK.
EVERGREEN FART DOCTOR.
DANG! BOSS FLIMBO, WHY DO YOU NEED EVERYONE?
I'M GONNA GET THAT NO GOOD JACKSON ONCE AND FOR ALL!
AW GEE, BOSS. CAN'T YOU JUST LET THAT GO?
LET IT GO?!?
WHAT WOULD YOU DO IF YOU WERE PUBLICALLY EMBARRASSED, JOHNNY DEAN?
I DON'T KNOW.
SHRUG IT OFF?
WELL, THAT'S WHY YOU'RE A LITTLE PIECE OF SHIT AND I'M THE BOSS, JOHNNY DEAN.
I DON'T SHRUG NOTHING OFF.

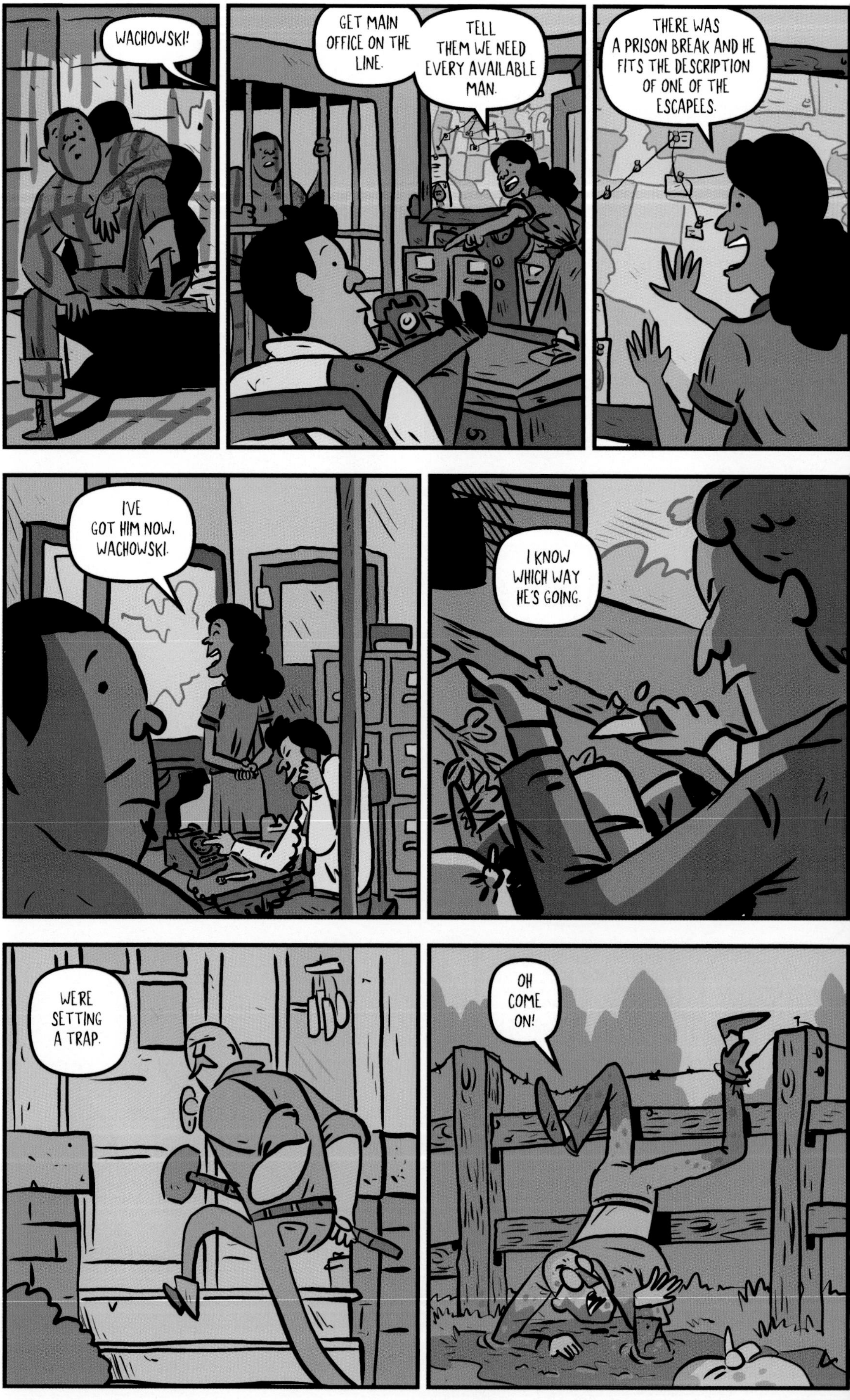
WACHOWSKI!
GET MAIN OFFICE ON THE LINE.
TELL THEM WE NEED EVERY AVAILABLE MAN.
THERE WAS A PRISON BREAK AND HE FITS THE DESCRIPTION OF ONE OF THE ESCAPEES.
I'VE GOT HIM NOW, WACHOWSKI.
I KNOW WHICH WAY HE'S GOING.
WE'RE SETTING A TRAP.
OH COME ON!

# *CHAPTER SIX*

## "Where the rain don't fall."

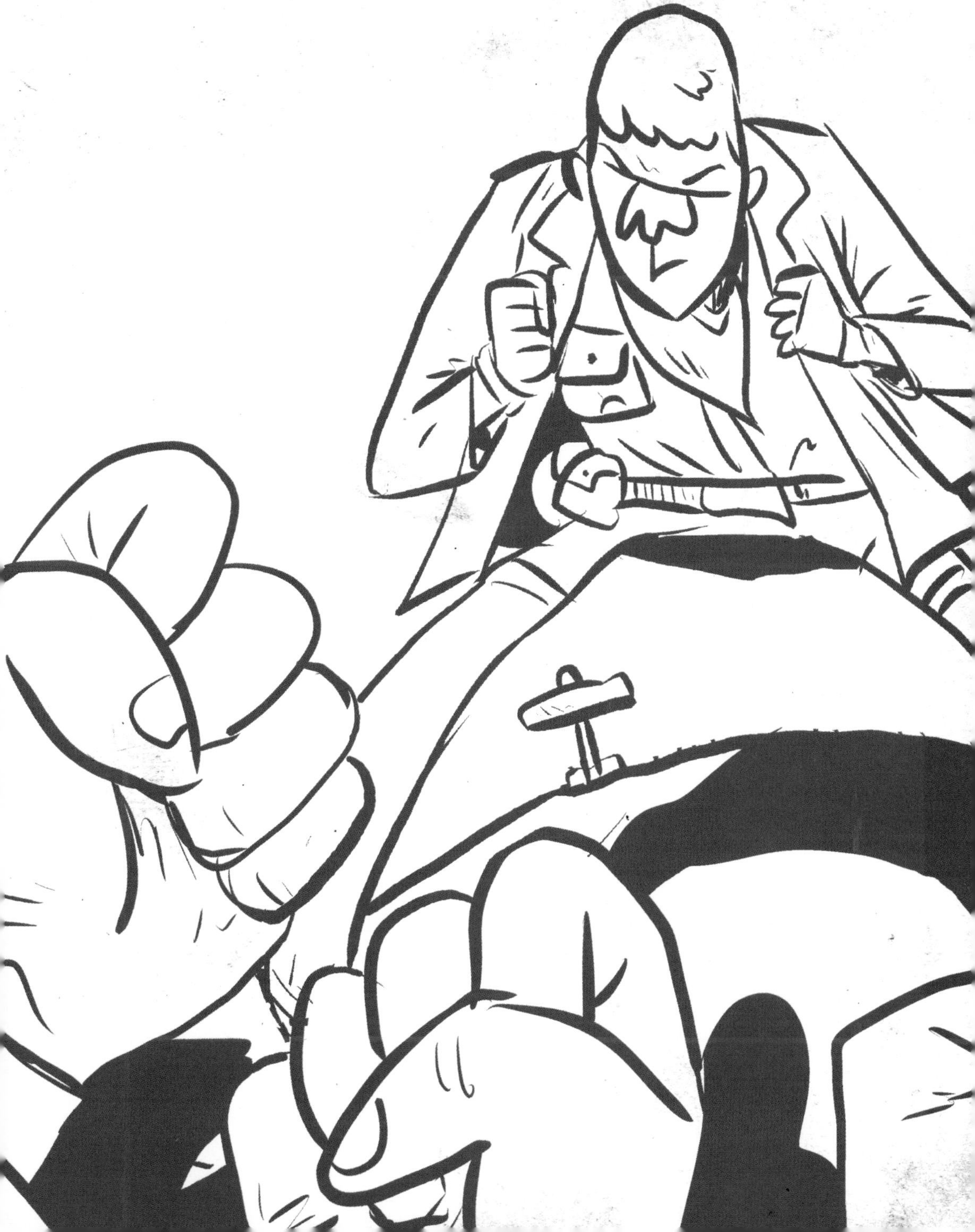

*"good place to
catch a train."*

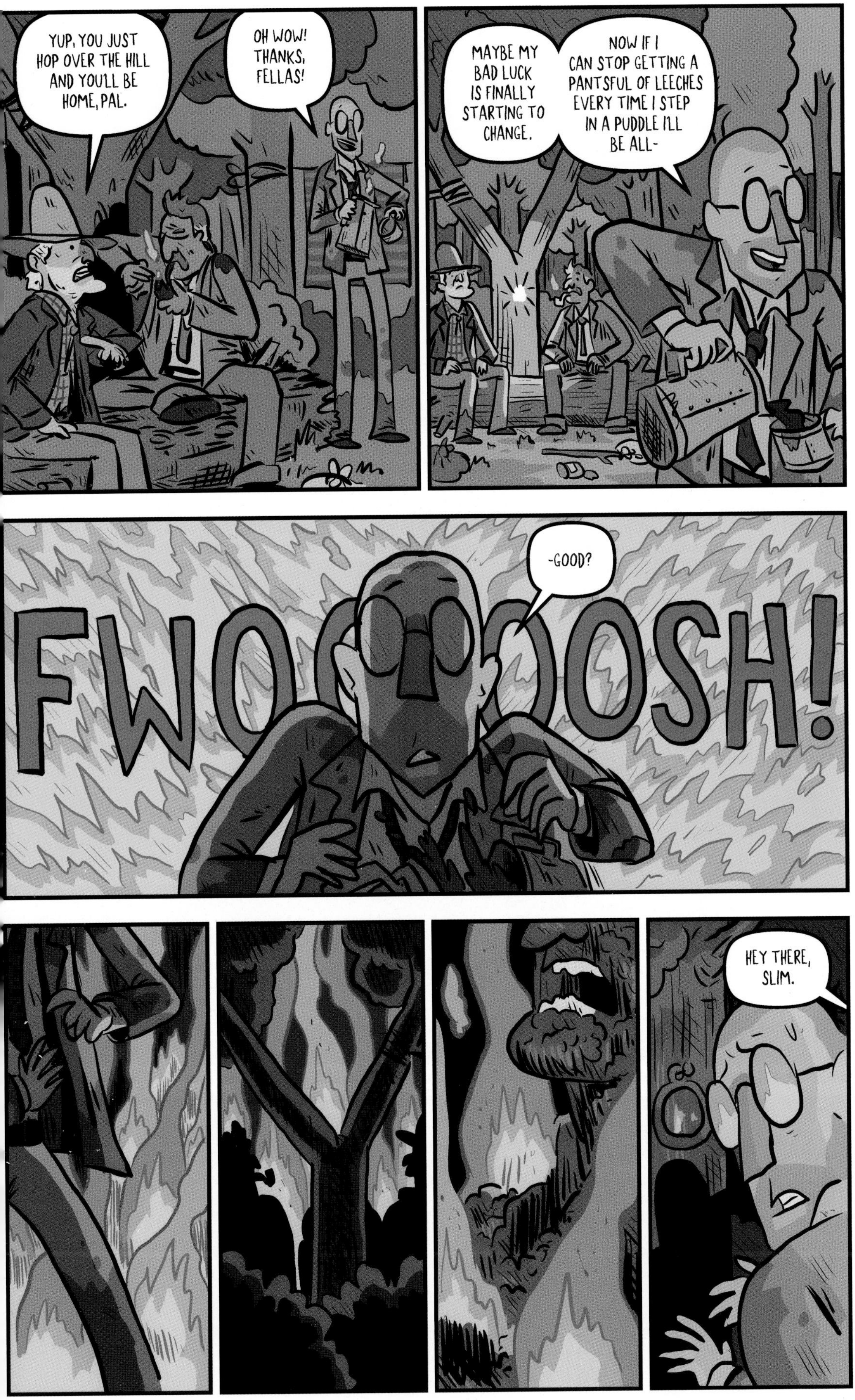
YUP, YOU JUST HOP OVER THE HILL AND YOU'LL BE HOME, PAL.
OH WOW! THANKS, FELLAS!
MAYBE MY BAD LUCK IS FINALLY STARTING TO CHANGE.
NOW IF I CAN STOP GETTING A PANTSFUL OF LEECHES EVERY TIME I STEP IN A PUDDLE I'LL BE ALL-
FWOOOOOSH!
-GOOD?
HEY THERE, SLIM.

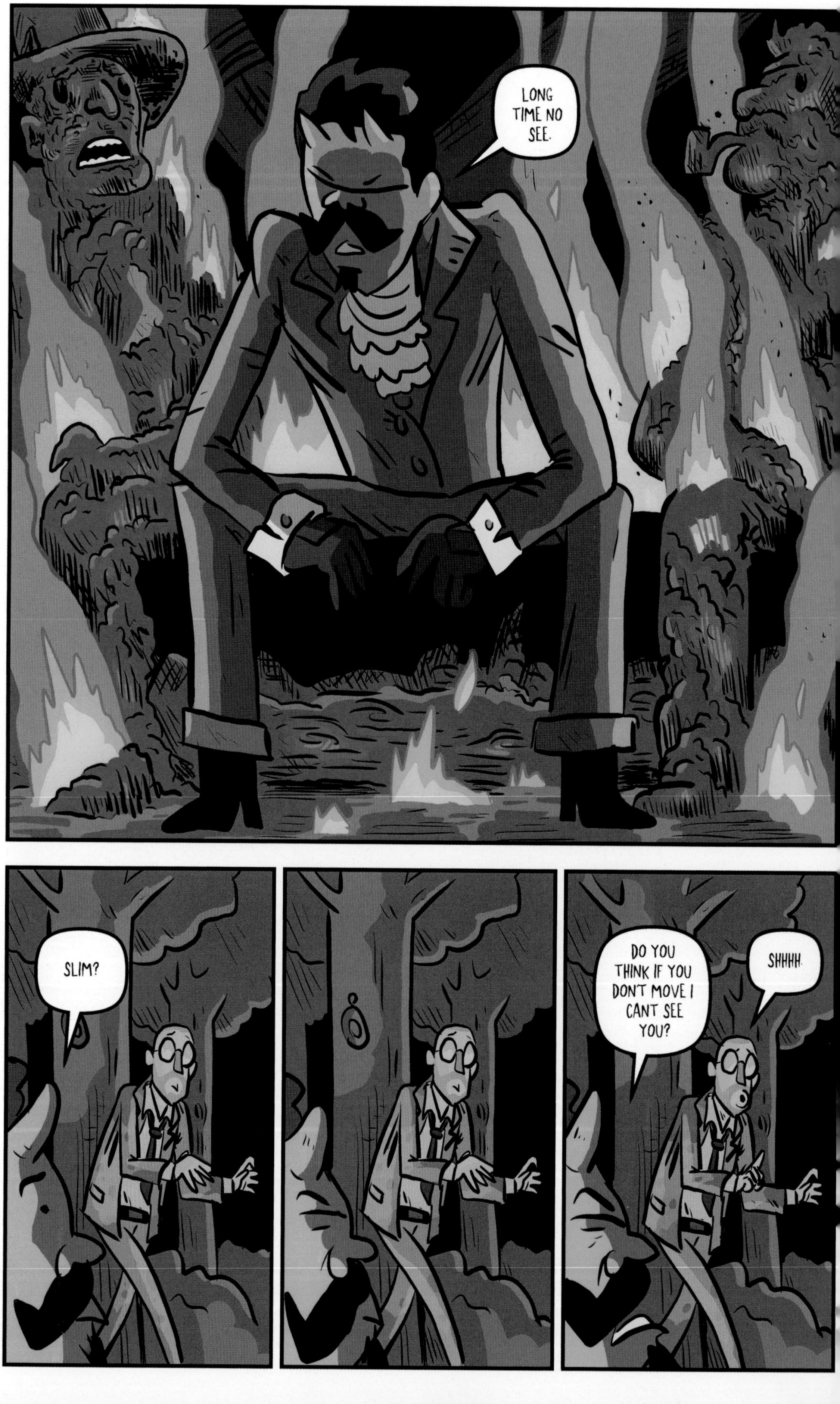
LONG TIME NO SEE.
SLIM?
DO YOU THINK IF YOU DON'T MOVE I CANT SEE YOU?
SHHHH.

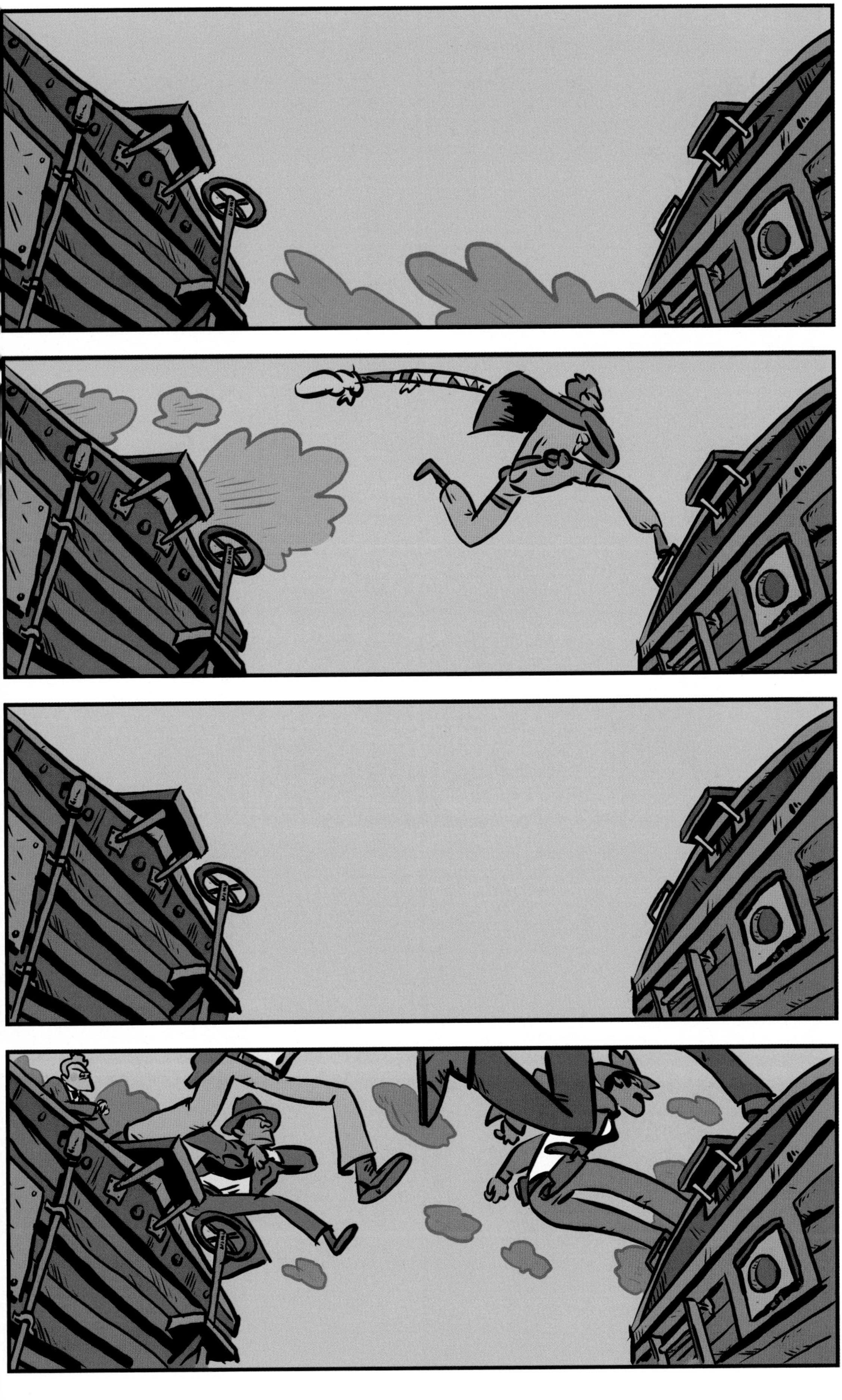

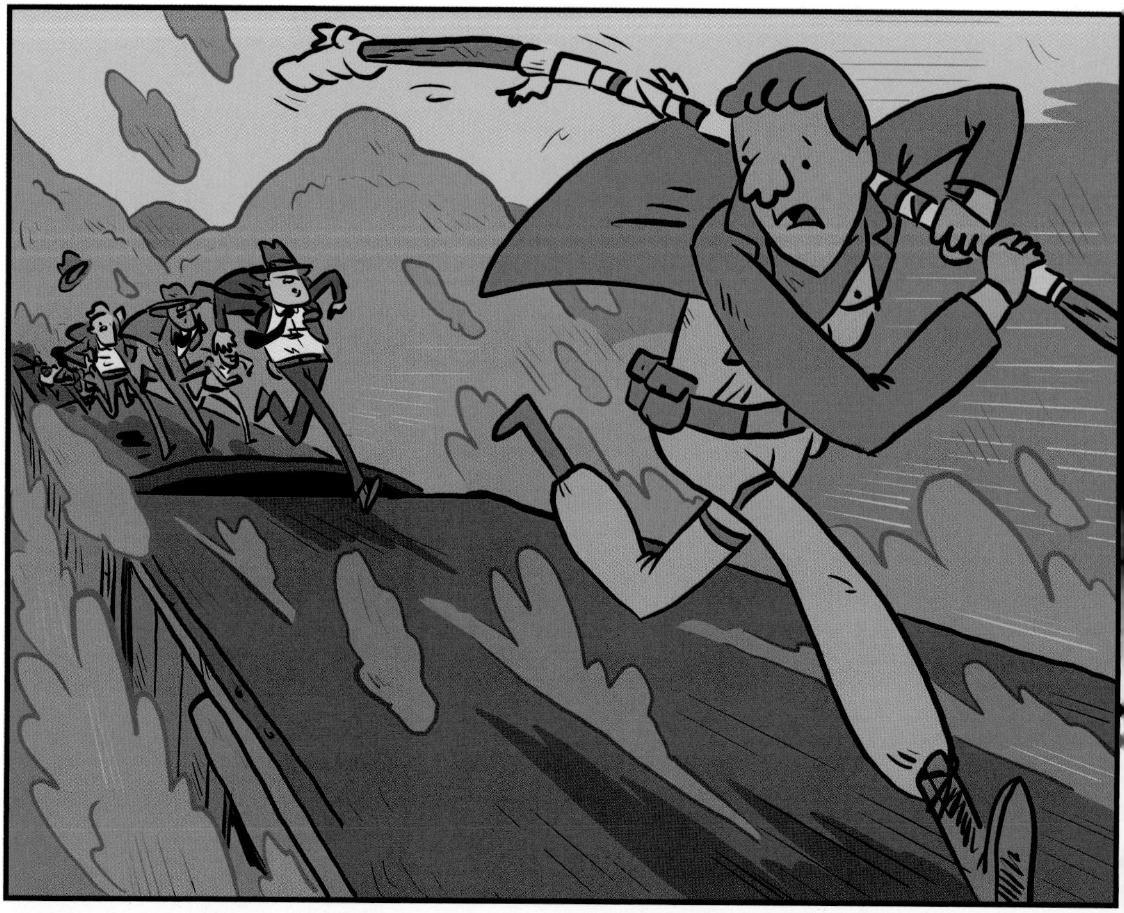

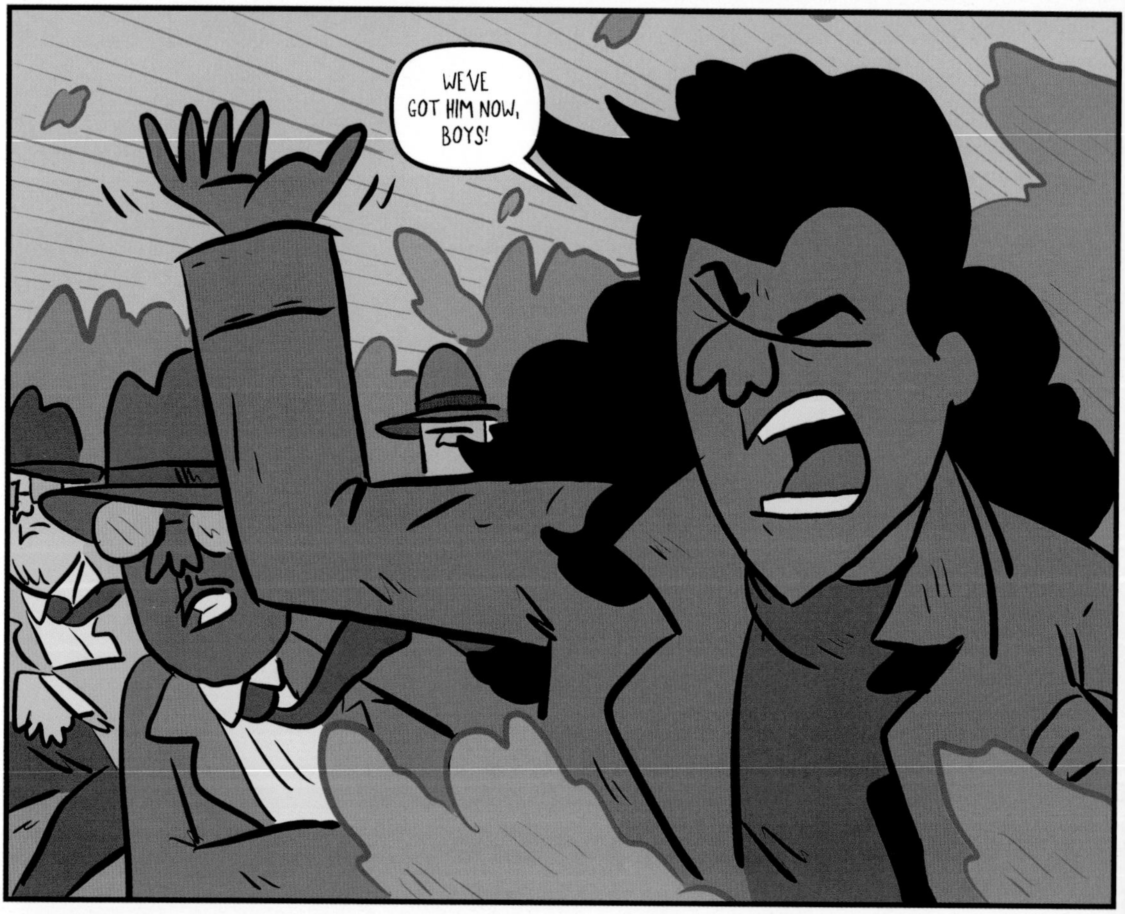
WE'VE GOT HIM NOW, BOYS!

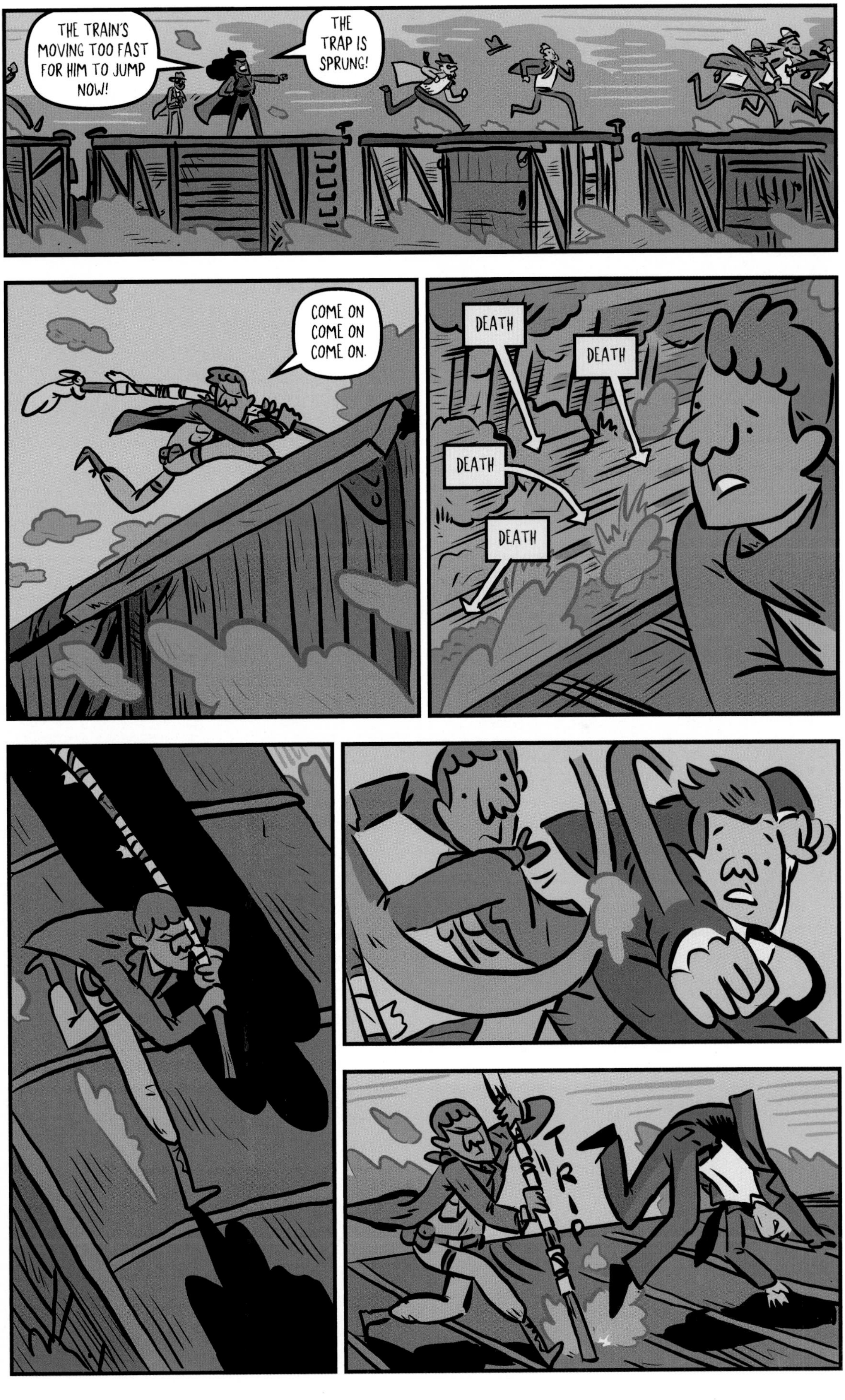
THE TRAIN'S MOVING TOO FAST FOR HIM TO JUMP NOW!
THE TRAP IS SPRUNG!
COME ON COME ON COME ON.
DEATH
DEATH
DEATH
DEATH
TRIP

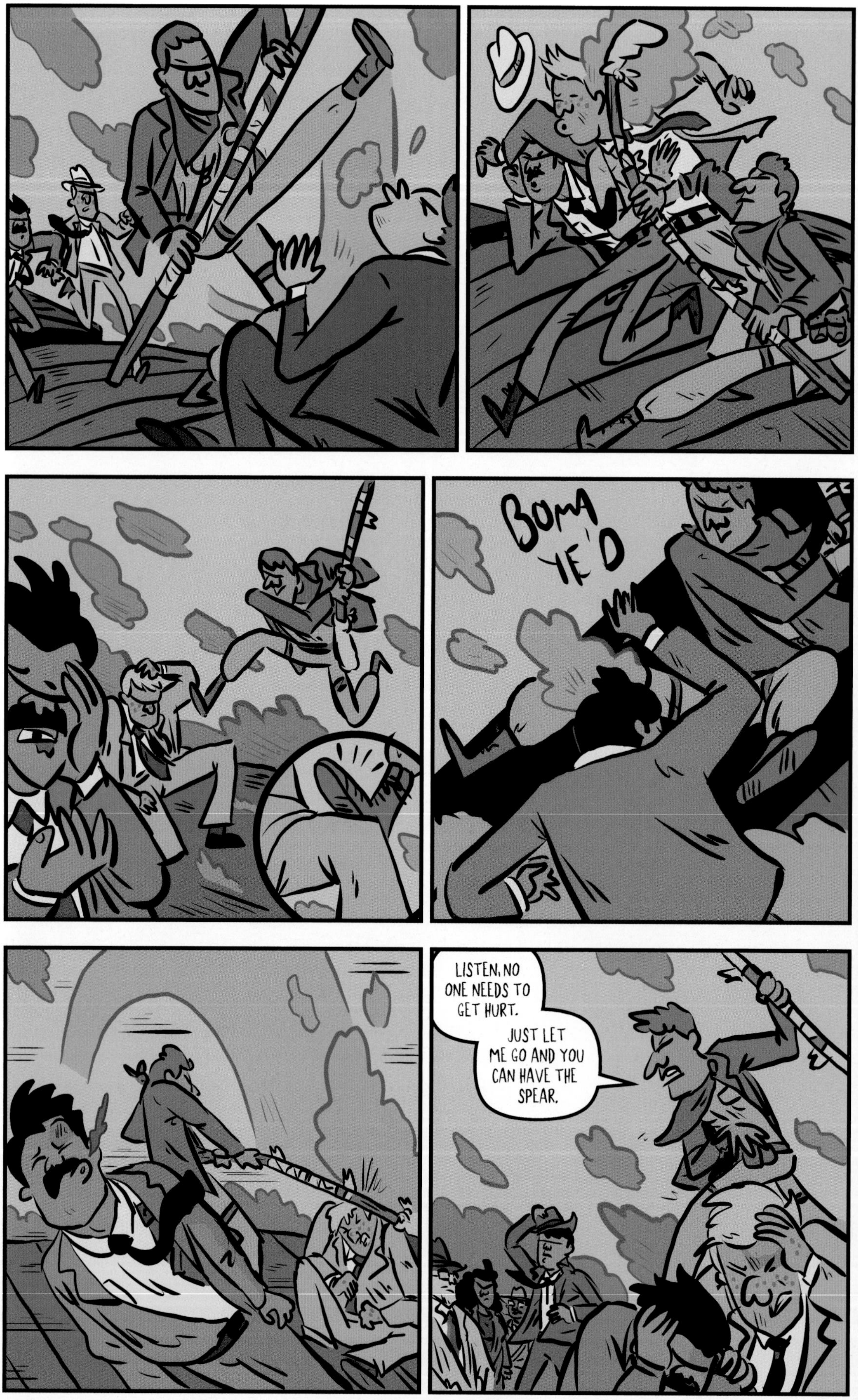
BOMA YE'D
LISTEN, NO ONE NEEDS TO GET HURT.
JUST LET ME GO AND YOU CAN HAVE THE SPEAR.

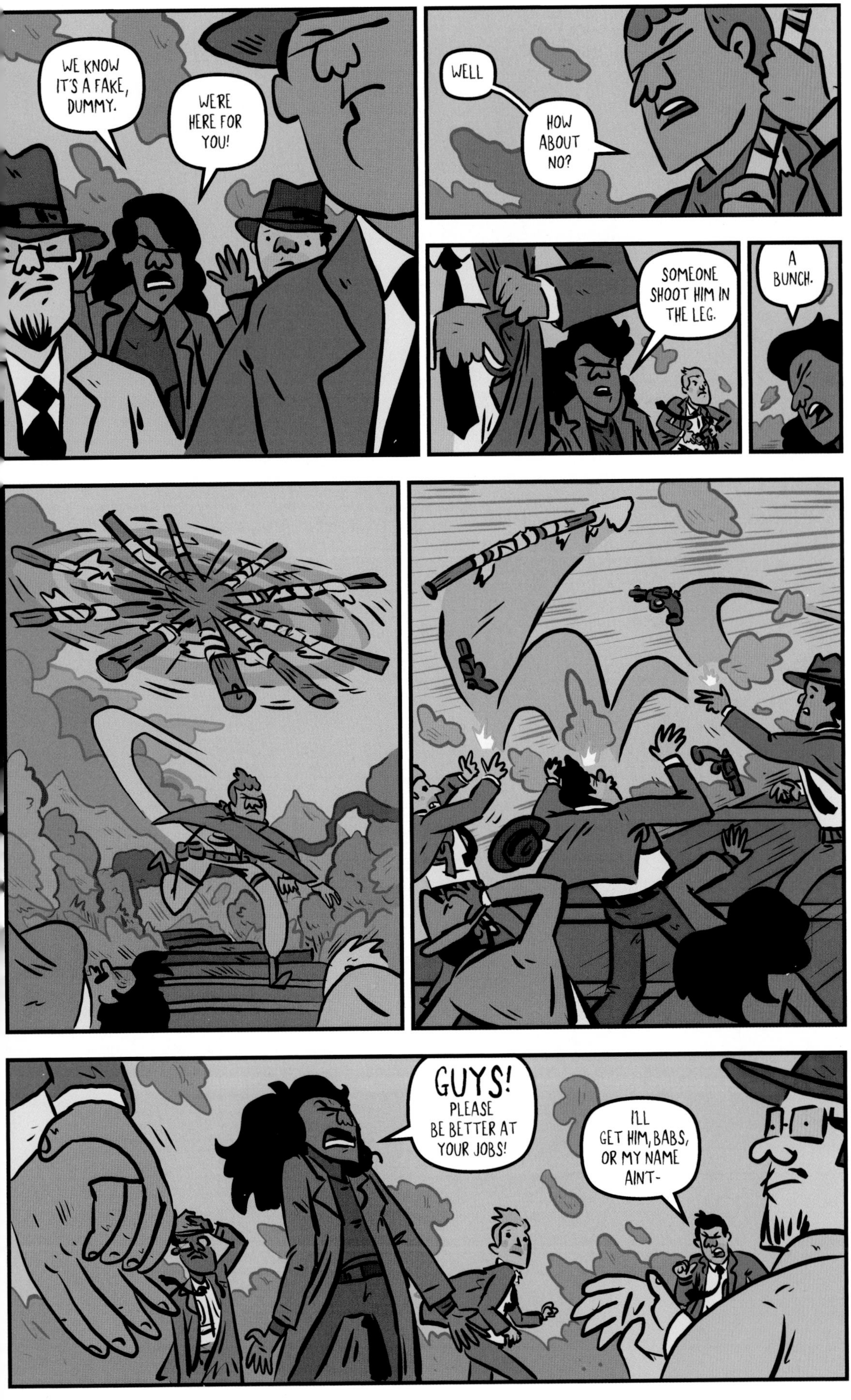
WE KNOW IT'S A FAKE, DUMMY.
WE'RE HERE FOR YOU!
WELL
HOW ABOUT NO?
SOMEONE SHOOT HIM IN THE LEG.
A BUNCH.
GUYS! PLEASE BE BETTER AT YOUR JOBS!
I'LL GET HIM, BABS, OR MY NAME AIN'T-

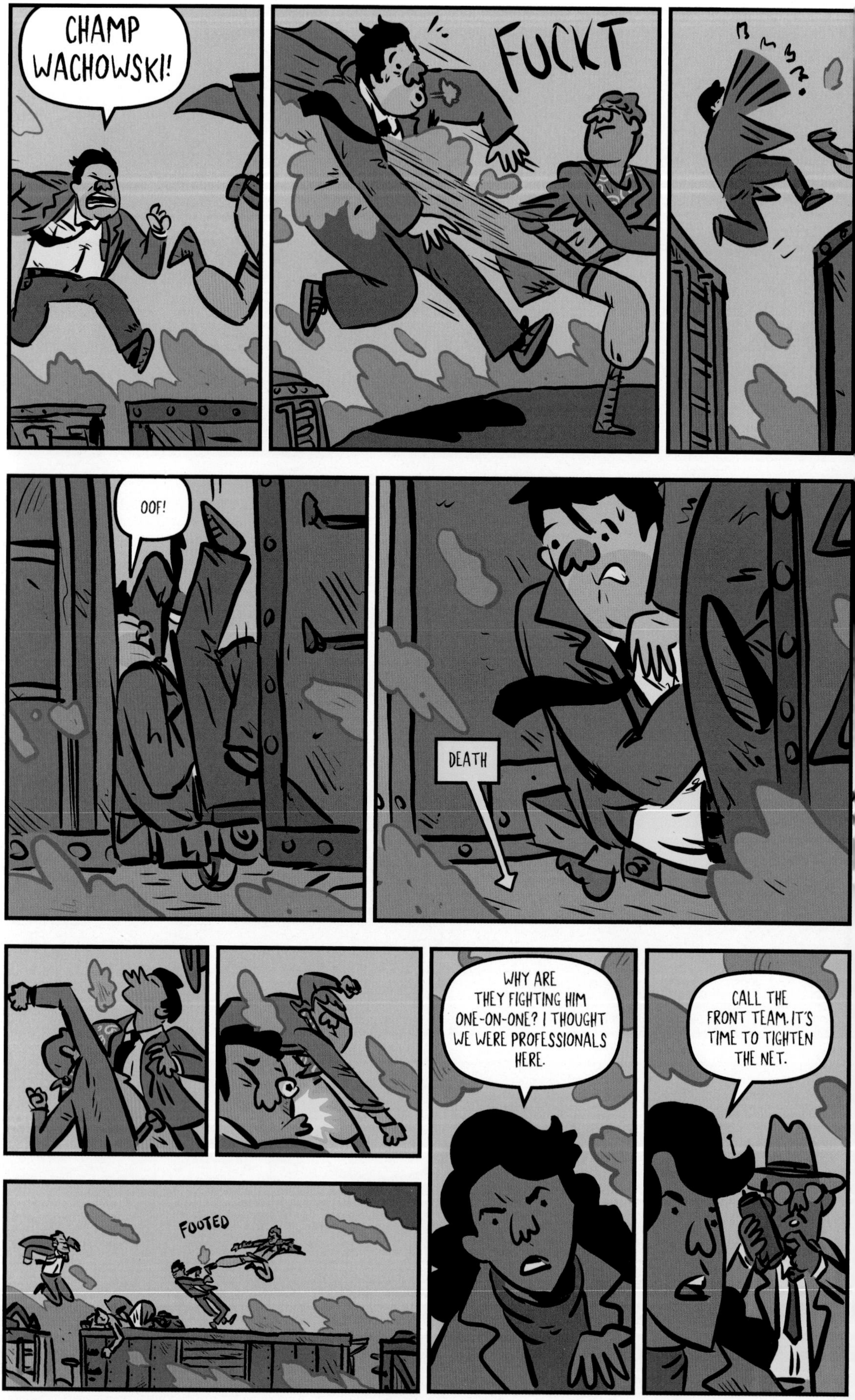
CHAMP WACHOWSKI!
FUCKT
OOF!
DEATH
WHY ARE THEY FIGHTING HIM ONE-ON-ONE? I THOUGHT WE WERE PROFESSIONALS HERE.
CALL THE FRONT TEAM. IT'S TIME TO TIGHTEN THE NET.
FOOTED

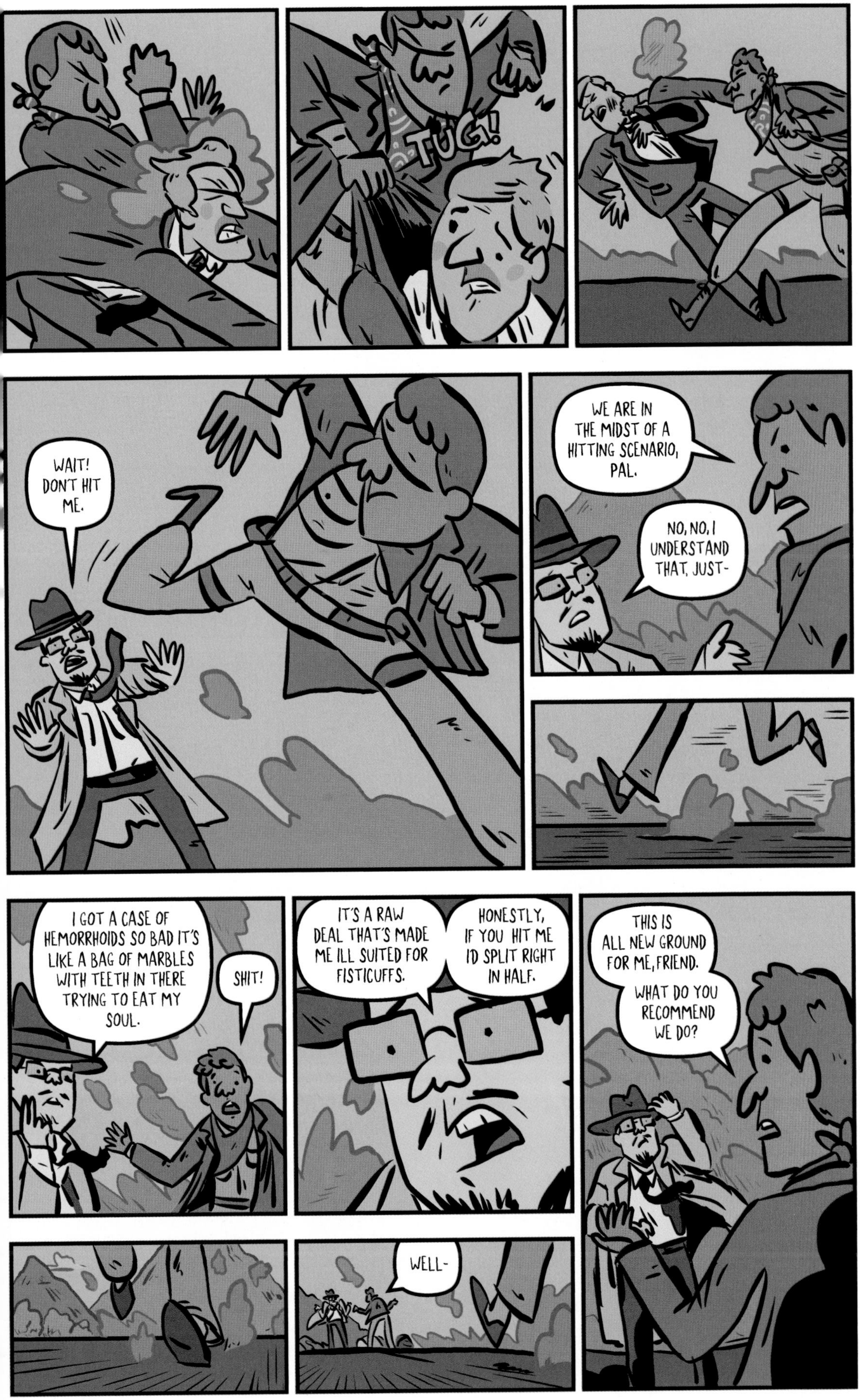
TUG!
WAIT! DON'T HIT ME.
WE ARE IN THE MIDST OF A HITTING SCENARIO, PAL.
NO, NO, I UNDERSTAND THAT, JUST-
I GOT A CASE OF HEMORRHOIDS SO BAD IT'S LIKE A BAG OF MARBLES WITH TEETH IN THERE TRYING TO EAT MY SOUL.
SHIT!
IT'S A RAW DEAL THAT'S MADE ME ILL SUITED FOR FISTICUFFS.
HONESTLY, IF YOU HIT ME I'D SPLIT RIGHT IN HALF.
THIS IS ALL NEW GROUND FOR ME, FRIEND.
WHAT DO YOU RECOMMEND WE DO?
WELL-

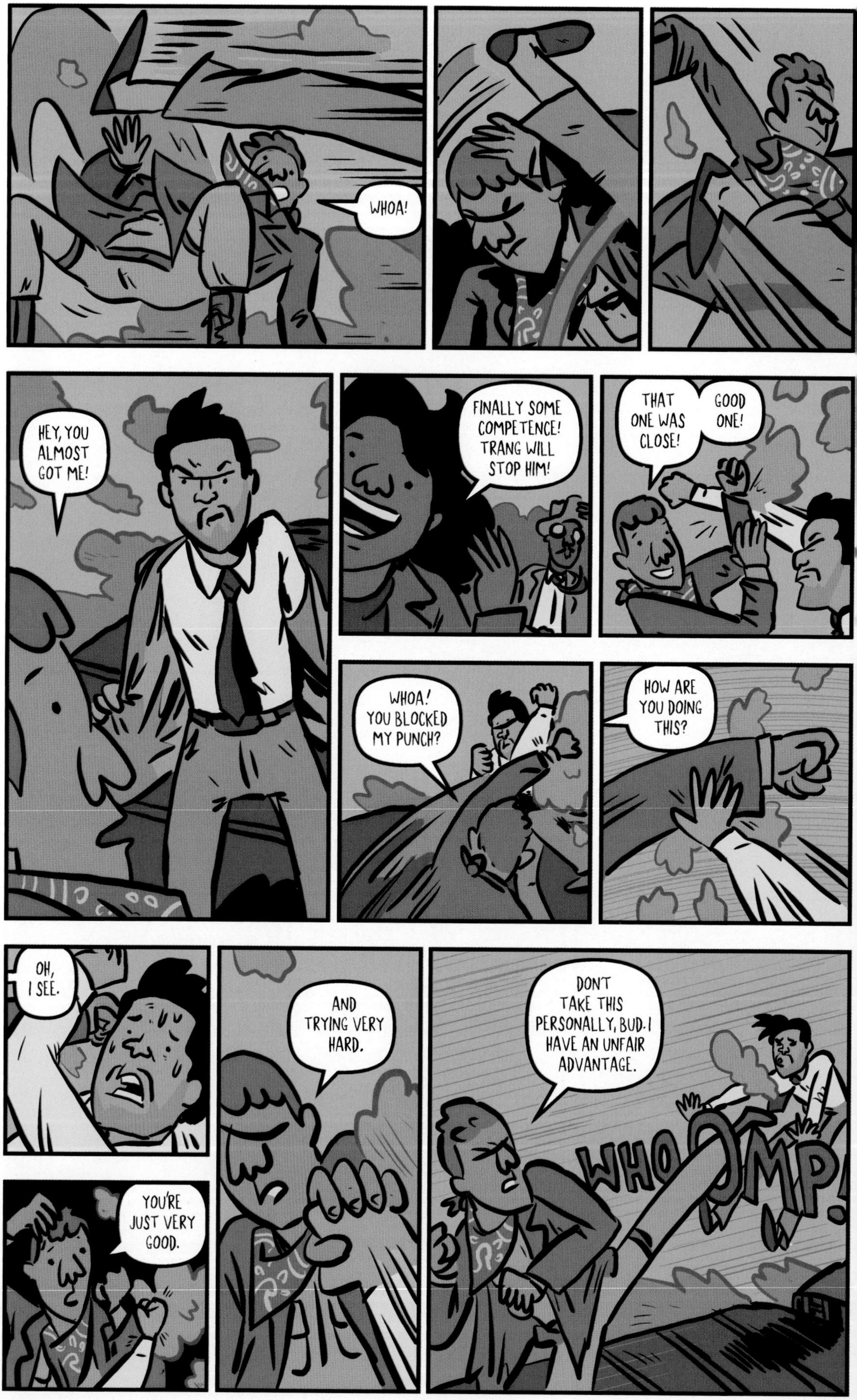
WHOA!
HEY, YOU ALMOST GOT ME!
FINALLY SOME COMPETENCE! TRANG WILL STOP HIM!
THAT ONE WAS CLOSE!
GOOD ONE!
WHOA! YOU BLOCKED MY PUNCH?
HOW ARE YOU DOING THIS?
OH, I SEE.
YOU'RE JUST VERY GOOD.
AND TRYING VERY HARD.
DON'T TAKE THIS PERSONALLY, BUD. I HAVE AN UNFAIR ADVANTAGE.
WHOOMP!

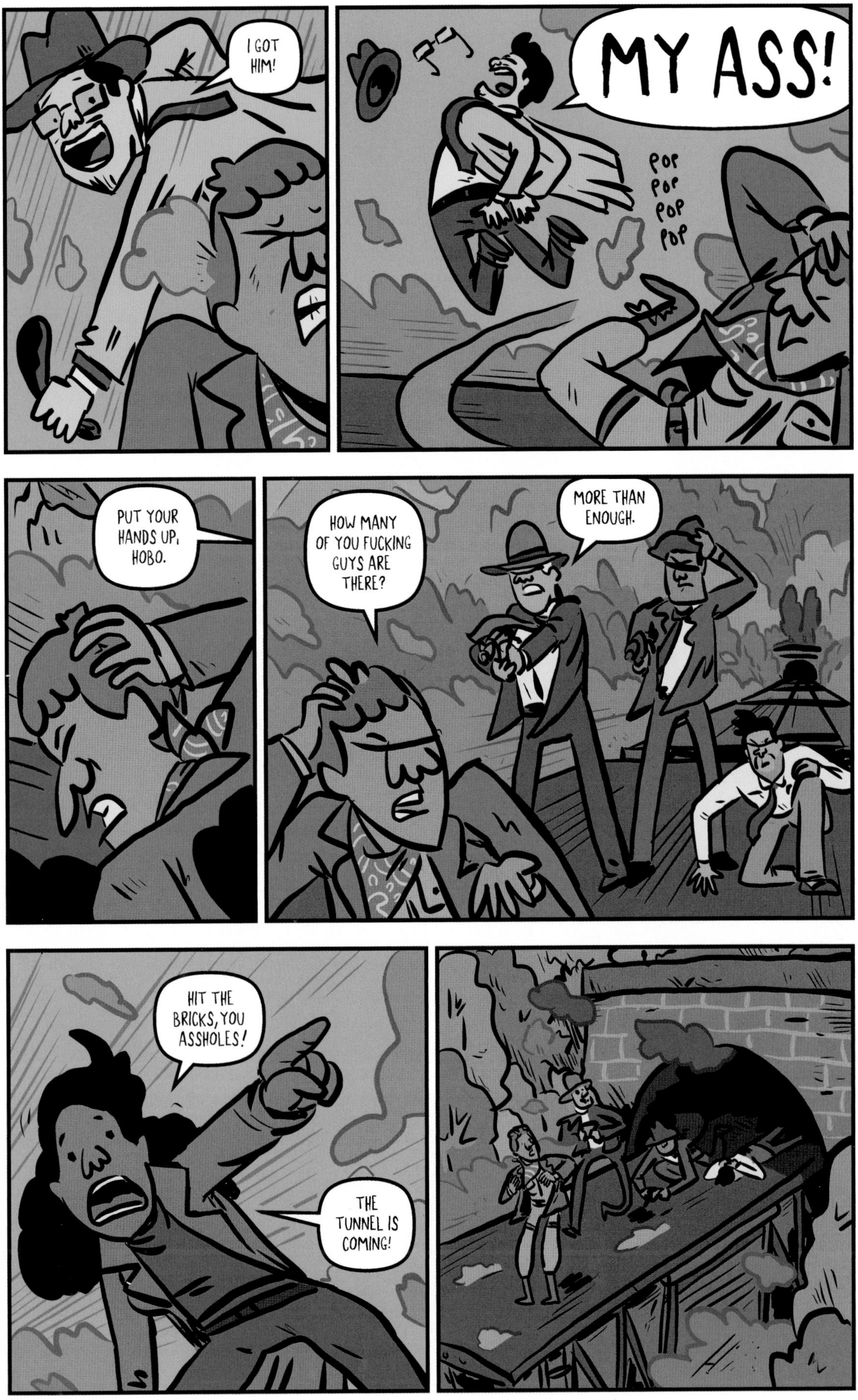
I GOT HIM!
MY ASS!
POP POP POP POP
PUT YOUR HANDS UP, HOBO.
HOW MANY OF YOU FUCKING GUYS ARE THERE?
MORE THAN ENOUGH.
HIT THE BRICKS, YOU ASSHOLES!
THE TUNNEL IS COMING!

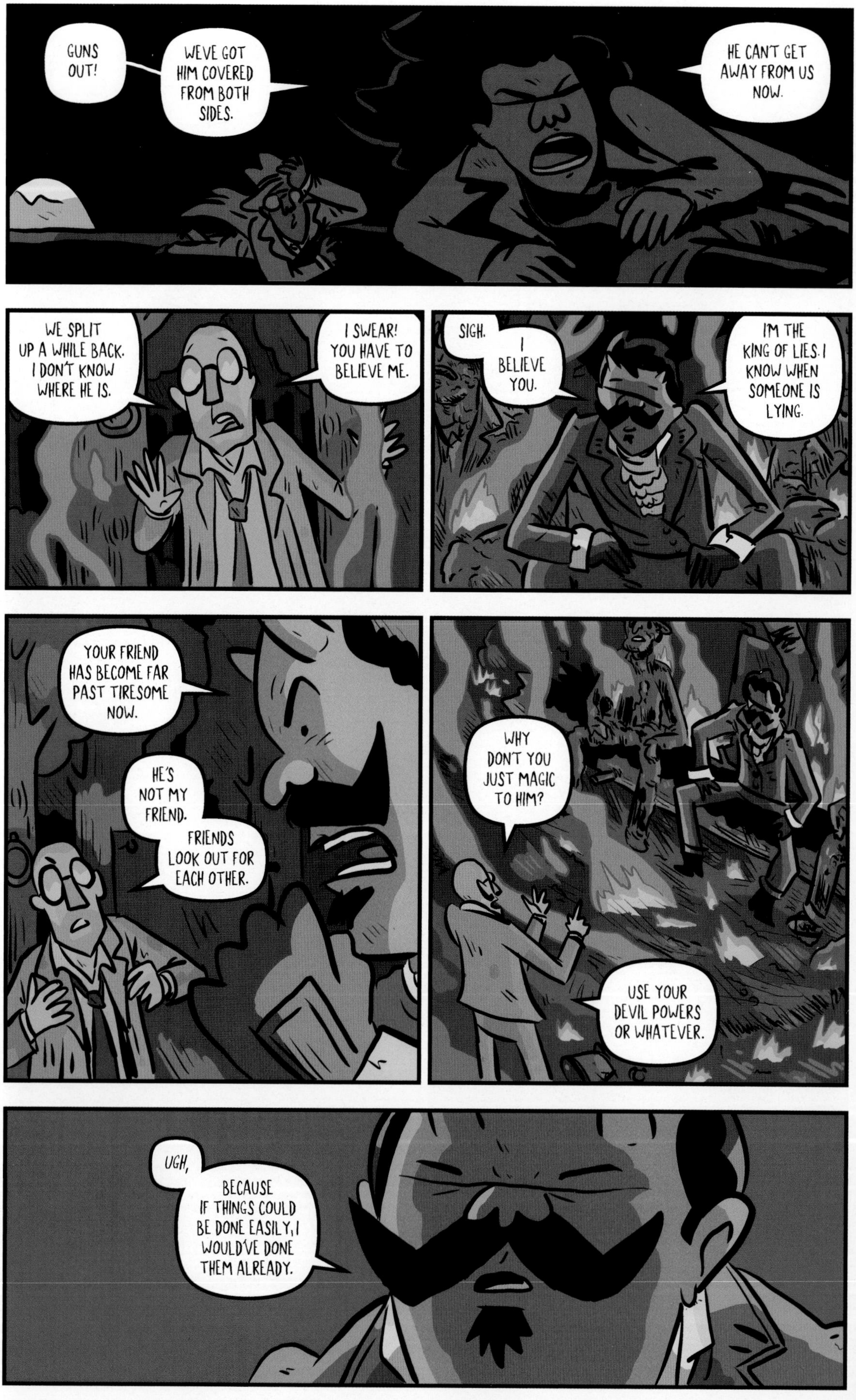
GUNS OUT!
WE'VE GOT HIM COVERED FROM BOTH SIDES.
HE CAN'T GET AWAY FROM US NOW.
WE SPLIT UP A WHILE BACK. I DON'T KNOW WHERE HE IS.
I SWEAR! YOU HAVE TO BELIEVE ME.
SIGH.
I BELIEVE YOU.
I'M THE KING OF LIES. I KNOW WHEN SOMEONE IS LYING.
YOUR FRIEND HAS BECOME FAR PAST TIRESOME NOW.
HE'S NOT MY FRIEND.
FRIENDS LOOK OUT FOR EACH OTHER.
WHY DON'T YOU JUST MAGIC TO HIM?
USE YOUR DEVIL POWERS OR WHATEVER.
UGH,
BECAUSE IF THINGS COULD BE DONE EASILY, I WOULD'VE DONE THEM ALREADY.

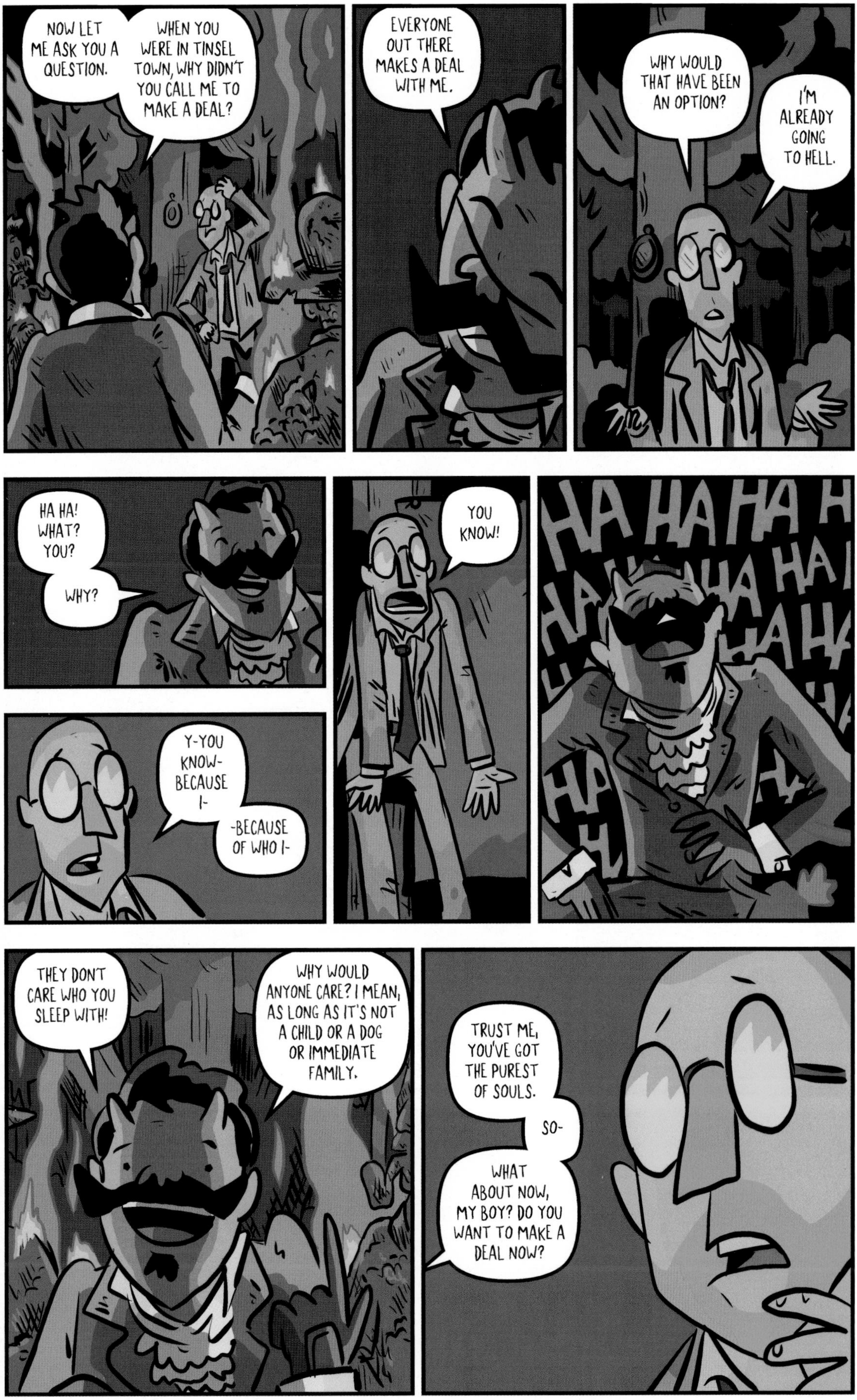
NOW LET ME ASK YOU A QUESTION.
WHEN YOU WERE IN TINSEL TOWN, WHY DIDN'T YOU CALL ME TO MAKE A DEAL?
EVERYONE OUT THERE MAKES A DEAL WITH ME.
WHY WOULD THAT HAVE BEEN AN OPTION?
I'M ALREADY GOING TO HELL.
HA HA! WHAT? YOU?
WHY?
Y-YOU KNOW- BECAUSE I-
-BECAUSE OF WHO I-
YOU KNOW!
HA HA HA HA HA HA HA HA HA HA HA
THEY DON'T CARE WHO YOU SLEEP WITH!
WHY WOULD ANYONE CARE? I MEAN, AS LONG AS IT'S NOT A CHILD OR A DOG OR IMMEDIATE FAMILY.
TRUST ME, YOU'VE GOT THE PUREST OF SOULS.
SO-
WHAT ABOUT NOW, MY BOY? DO YOU WANT TO MAKE A DEAL NOW?

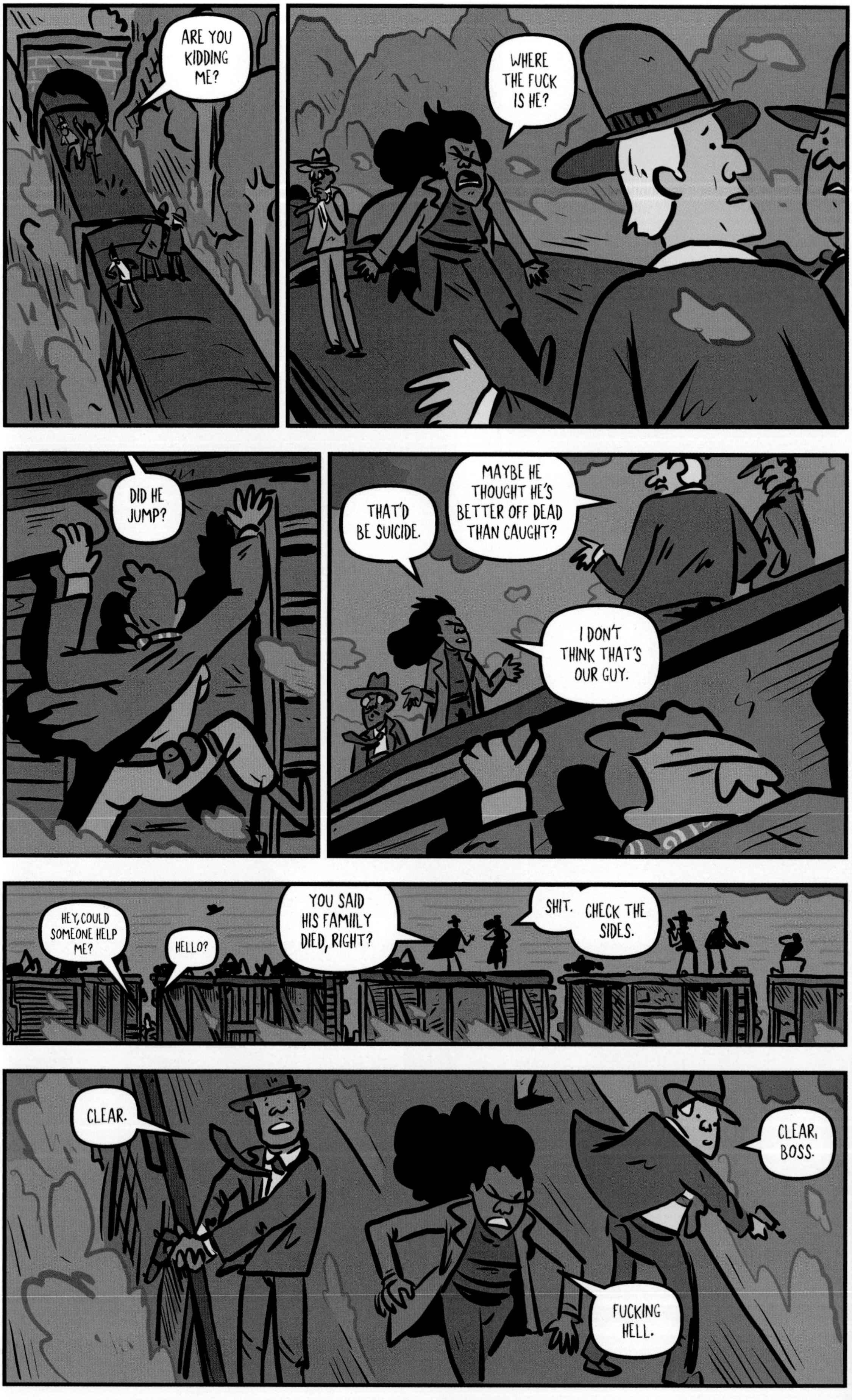
ARE YOU KIDDING ME?
WHERE THE FUCK IS HE?
DID HE JUMP?
MAYBE HE THOUGHT HE'S BETTER OFF DEAD THAN CAUGHT?
THAT'D BE SUICIDE.
I DON'T THINK THAT'S OUR GUY.
HEY, COULD SOMEONE HELP ME?
HELLO?
YOU SAID HIS FAMILY DIED, RIGHT?
SHIT.
CHECK THE SIDES.
CLEAR.
CLEAR, BOSS.
FUCKING HELL.

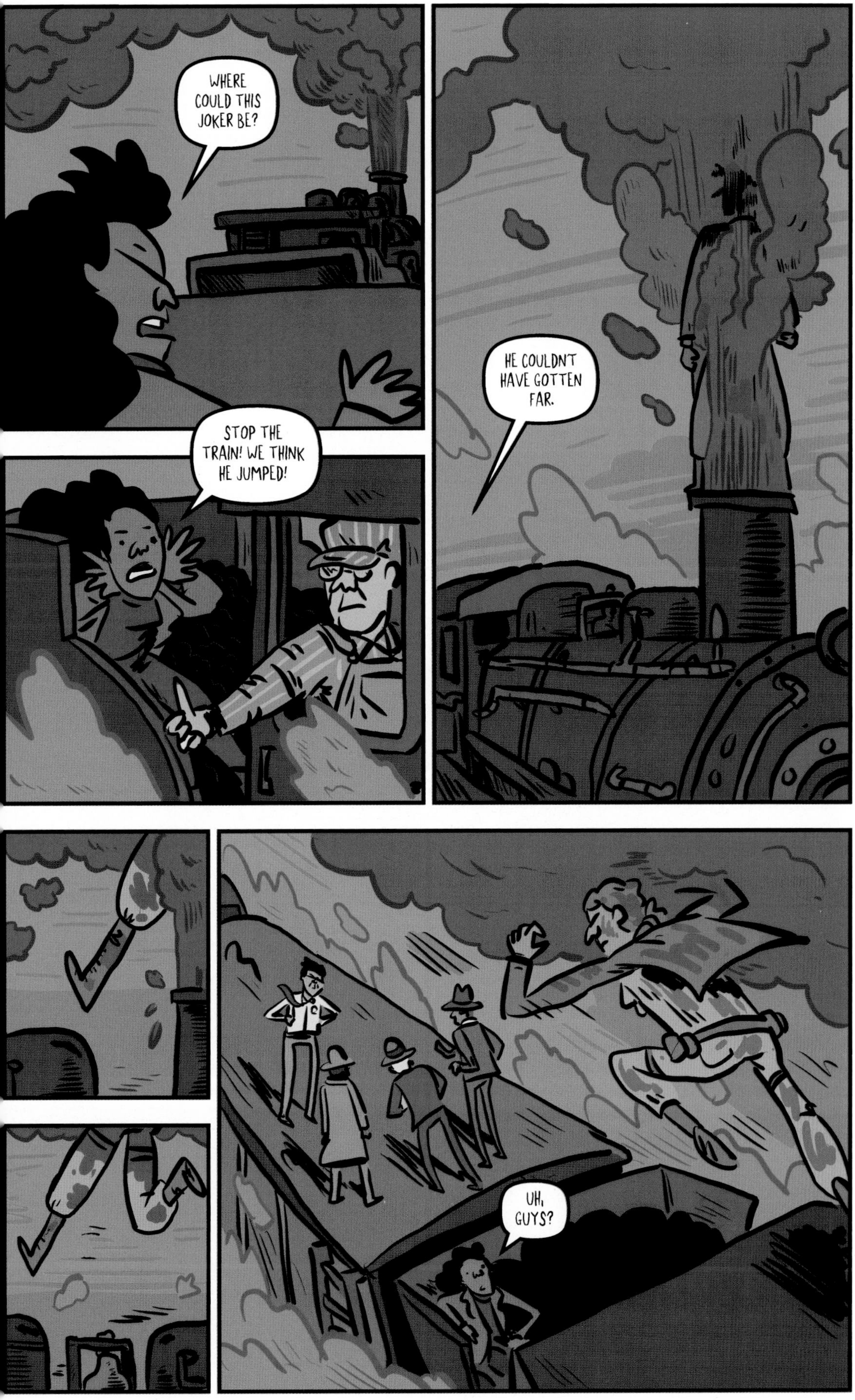
WHERE COULD THIS JOKER BE?
STOP THE TRAIN! WE THINK HE JUMPED!
HE COULDN'T HAVE GOTTEN FAR.
UH, GUYS?

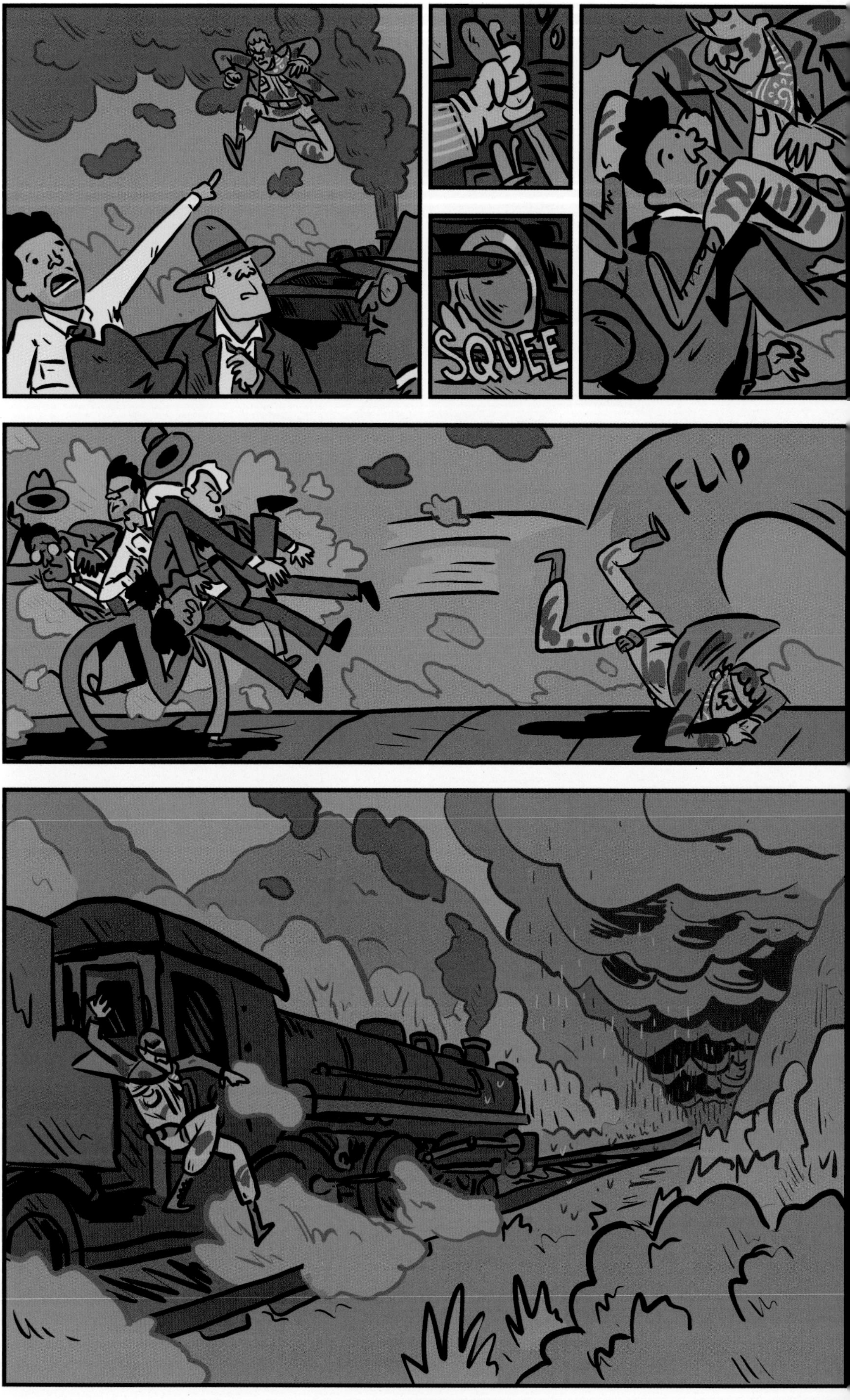
SQUEE
FLIP

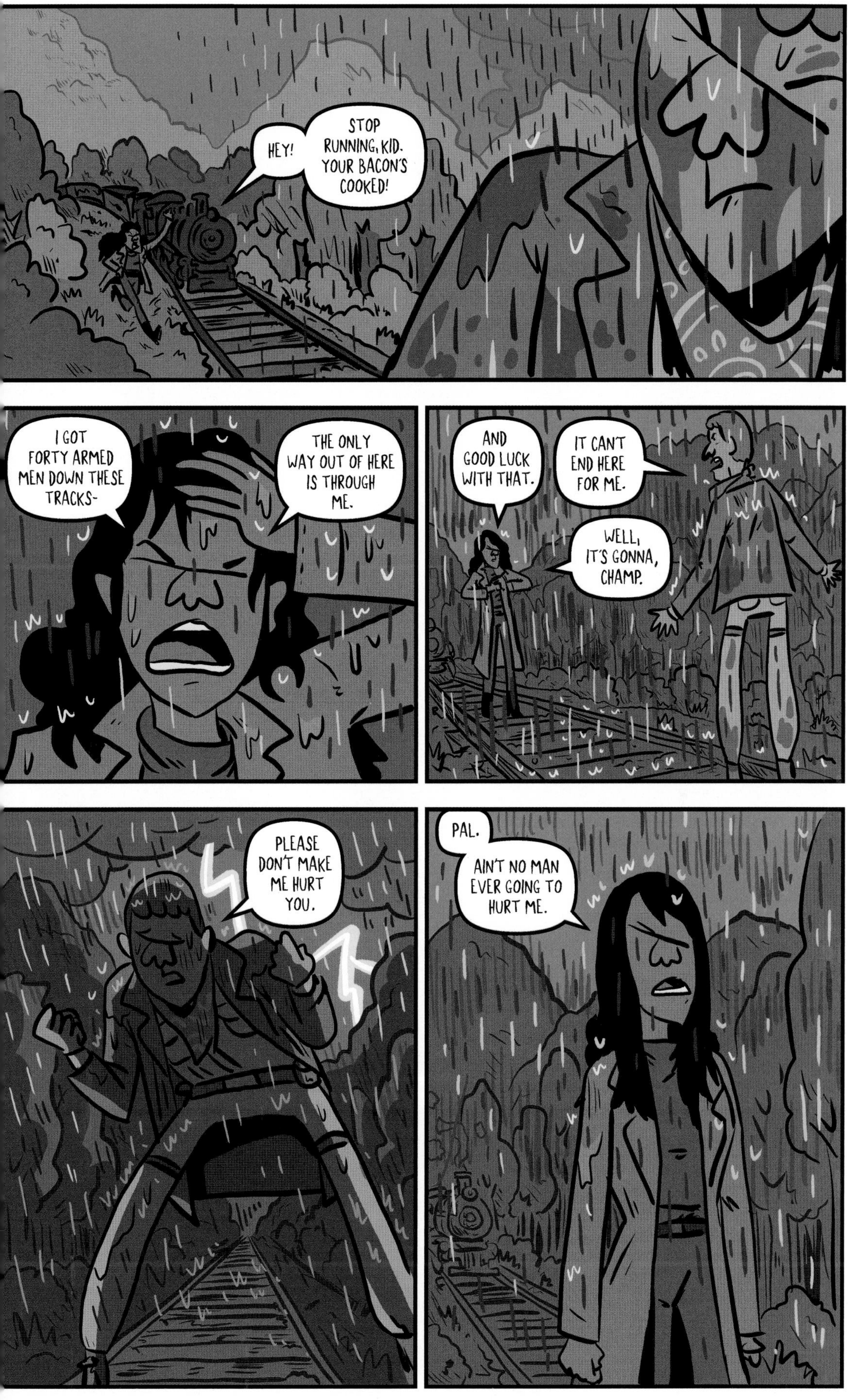
HEY!
STOP RUNNING, KID. YOUR BACON'S COOKED!
I GOT FORTY ARMED MEN DOWN THESE TRACKS-
THE ONLY WAY OUT OF HERE IS THROUGH ME.
AND GOOD LUCK WITH THAT.
IT CAN'T END HERE FOR ME.
WELL, IT'S GONNA, CHAMP.
PLEASE DON'T MAKE ME HURT YOU.
PAL.
AIN'T NO MAN EVER GOING TO HURT ME.

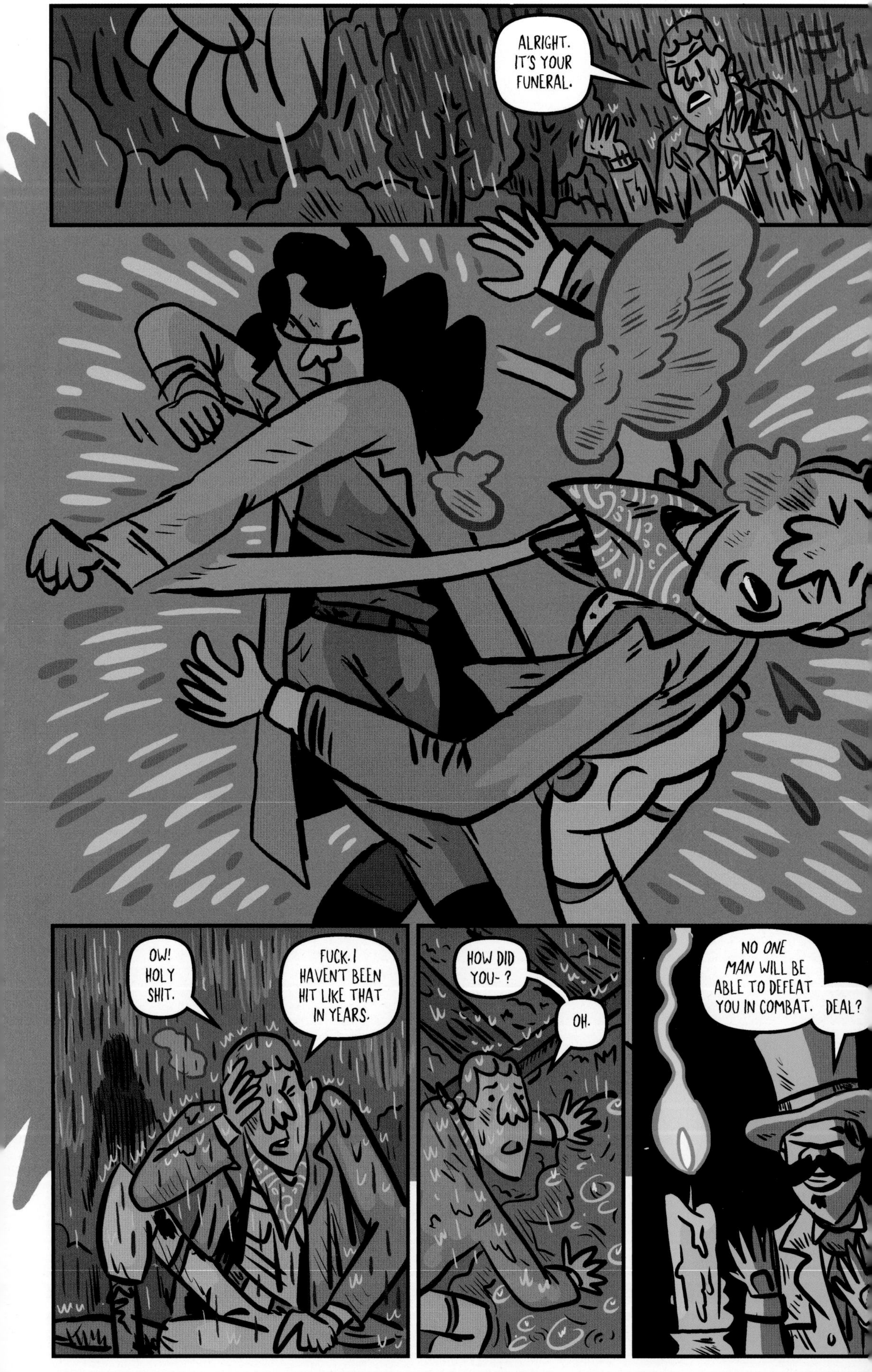
ALRIGHT. IT'S YOUR FUNERAL.
OW! HOLY SHIT.
FUCK. I HAVEN'T BEEN HIT LIKE THAT IN YEARS.
HOW DID YOU- ?
OH.
NO *ONE MAN* WILL BE ABLE TO DEFEAT YOU IN COMBAT.
DEAL?

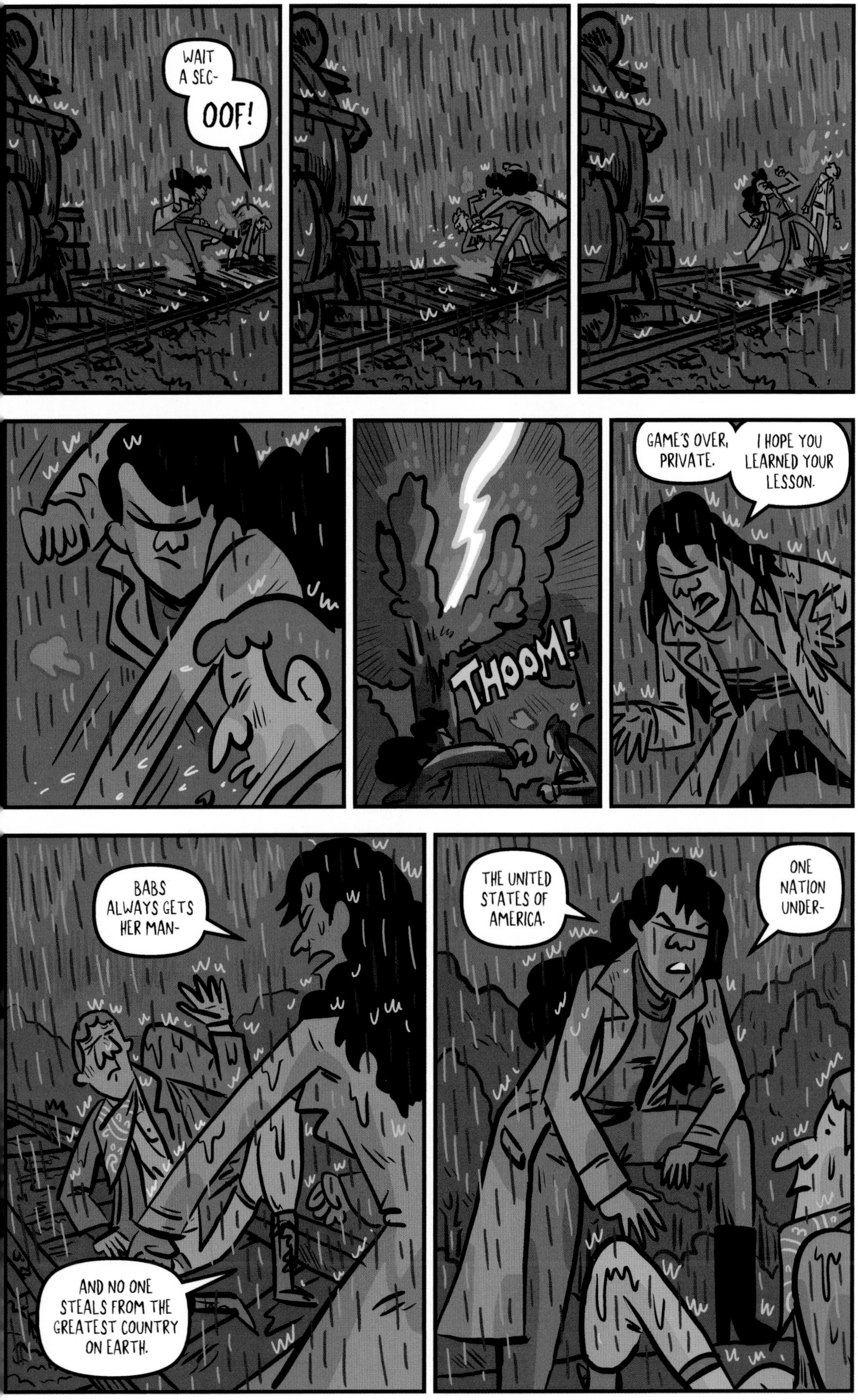
WAIT A SEC-
OOF!
GAME'S OVER, PRIVATE.
I HOPE YOU LEARNED YOUR LESSON.
THOOM!
BABS ALWAYS GETS HER MAN-
AND NO ONE STEALS FROM THE GREATEST COUNTRY ON EARTH.
THE UNITED STATES OF AMERICA.
ONE NATION UNDER-

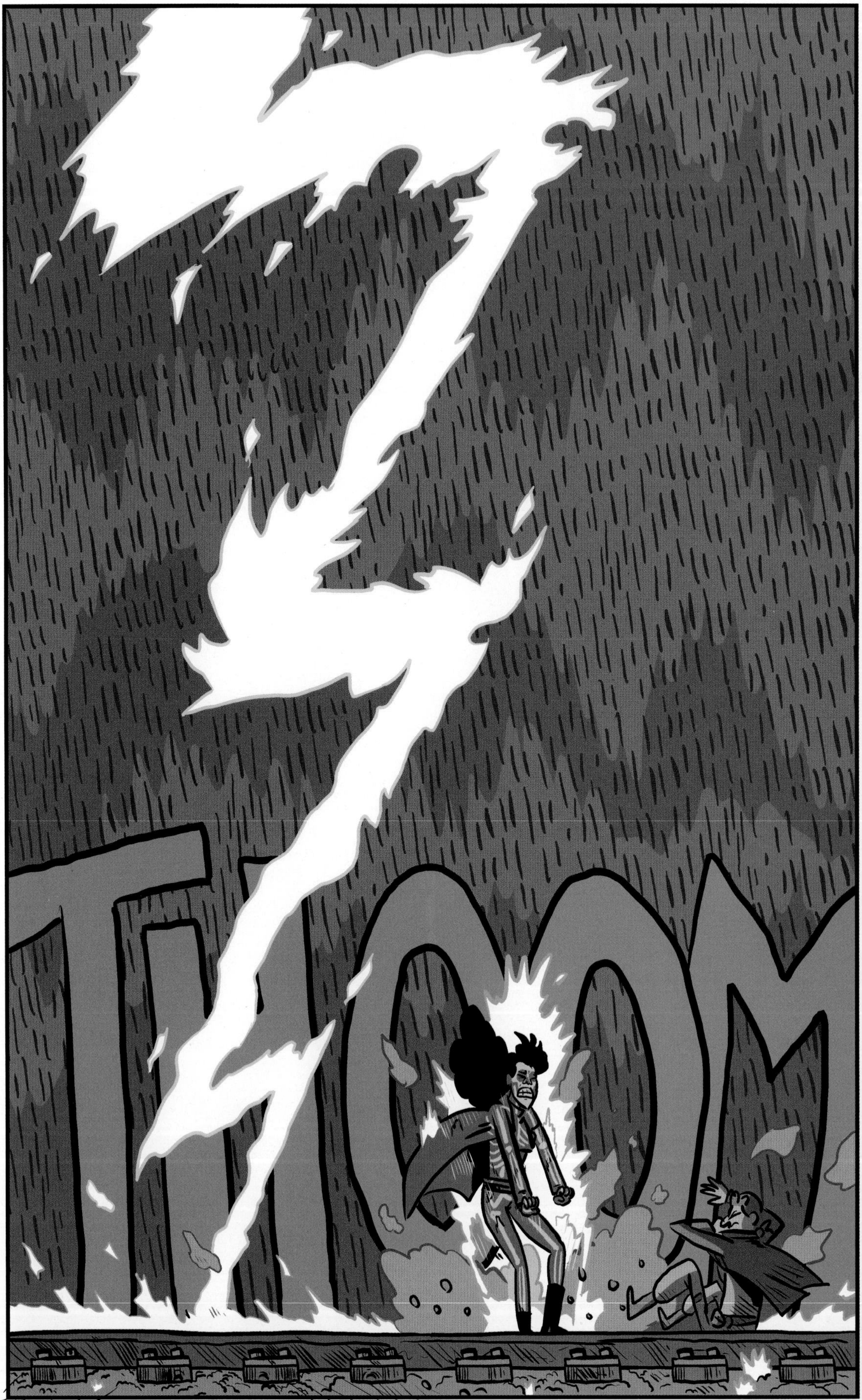
THOOM

SHIT!

BOSS, ARE YOU ALRIGHT?

BOSS, DON'T MOVE.

GOD?

SOMEONE CALL HEAD-QUARTERS!

NO. I DON'T THINK SO.

I MEAN, I WAS *REALLY* TERRIBLE AT ACTING AND EVERYONE WAS SORT OF INSINCERE.

I SORT OF HATED IT.

BUT YOU *DO* WANT TO BE FAMOUS, RIGHT?

GIMME THAT PERFECT SOUL AND EVERYONE WILL KNOW YOUR NAME.

I DON'T THINK I EVER WANTED TO BE FAMOUS, I—

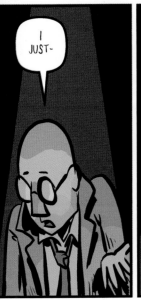
I JUST—

MY PARENTS DIED WHEN I WAS LITTLE, AND NO ONE'S EVER REALLY BEEN—

SIGH.

I JUST WANTED PEOPLE TO FINALLY LIKE ME.

I JUST DIDN'T WANT TO BE ALONE ANYMORE.

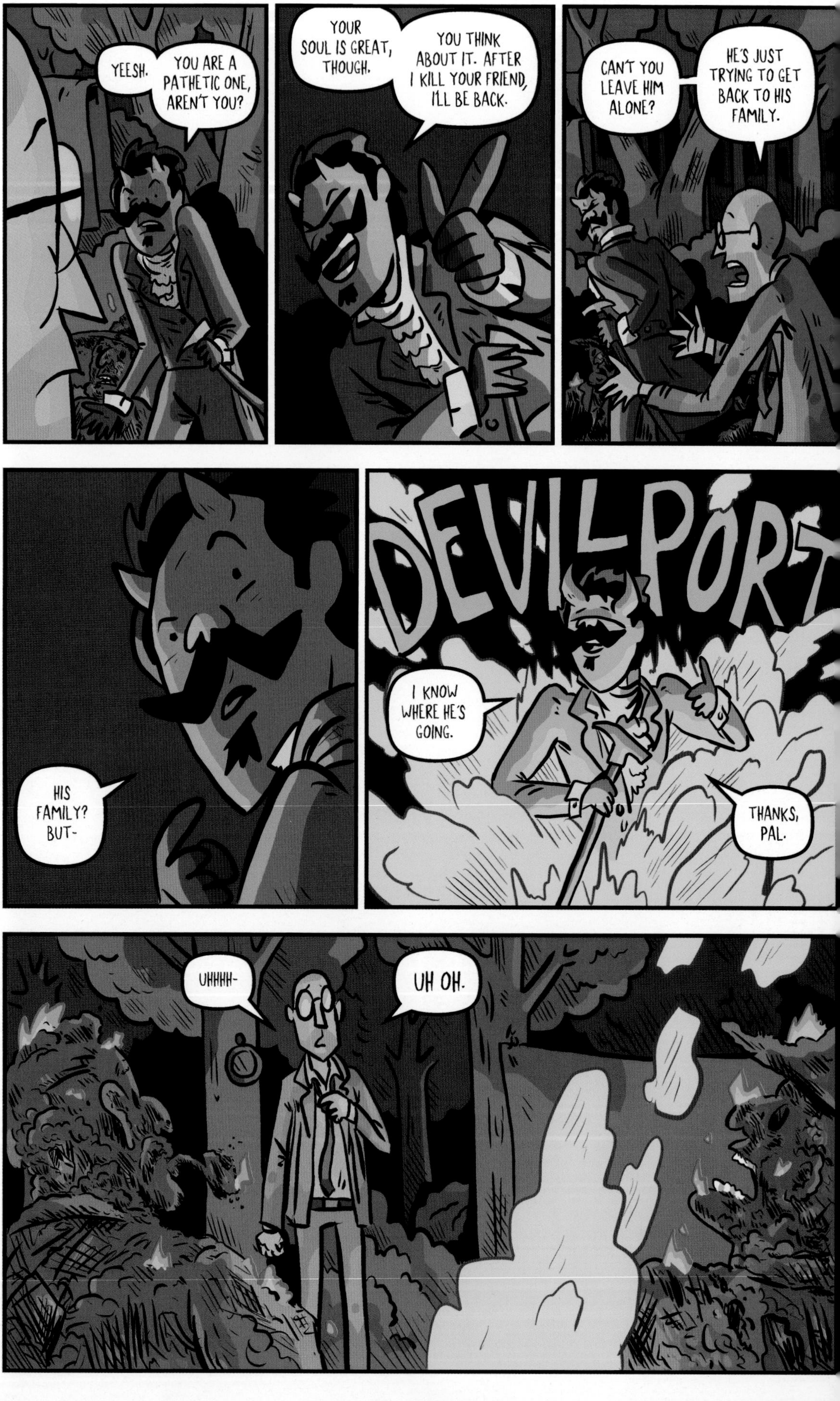
YEESH.
YOU ARE A PATHETIC ONE, AREN'T YOU?
YOUR SOUL IS GREAT, THOUGH.
YOU THINK ABOUT IT. AFTER I KILL YOUR FRIEND, I'LL BE BACK.
CAN'T YOU LEAVE HIM ALONE?
HE'S JUST TRYING TO GET BACK TO HIS FAMILY.
HIS FAMILY? BUT-
DEVILPORT
I KNOW WHERE HE'S GOING.
THANKS, PAL.
UHHHH-
UH OH.

# *CHAPTER SEVEN*

## "The jungle fires were burning."

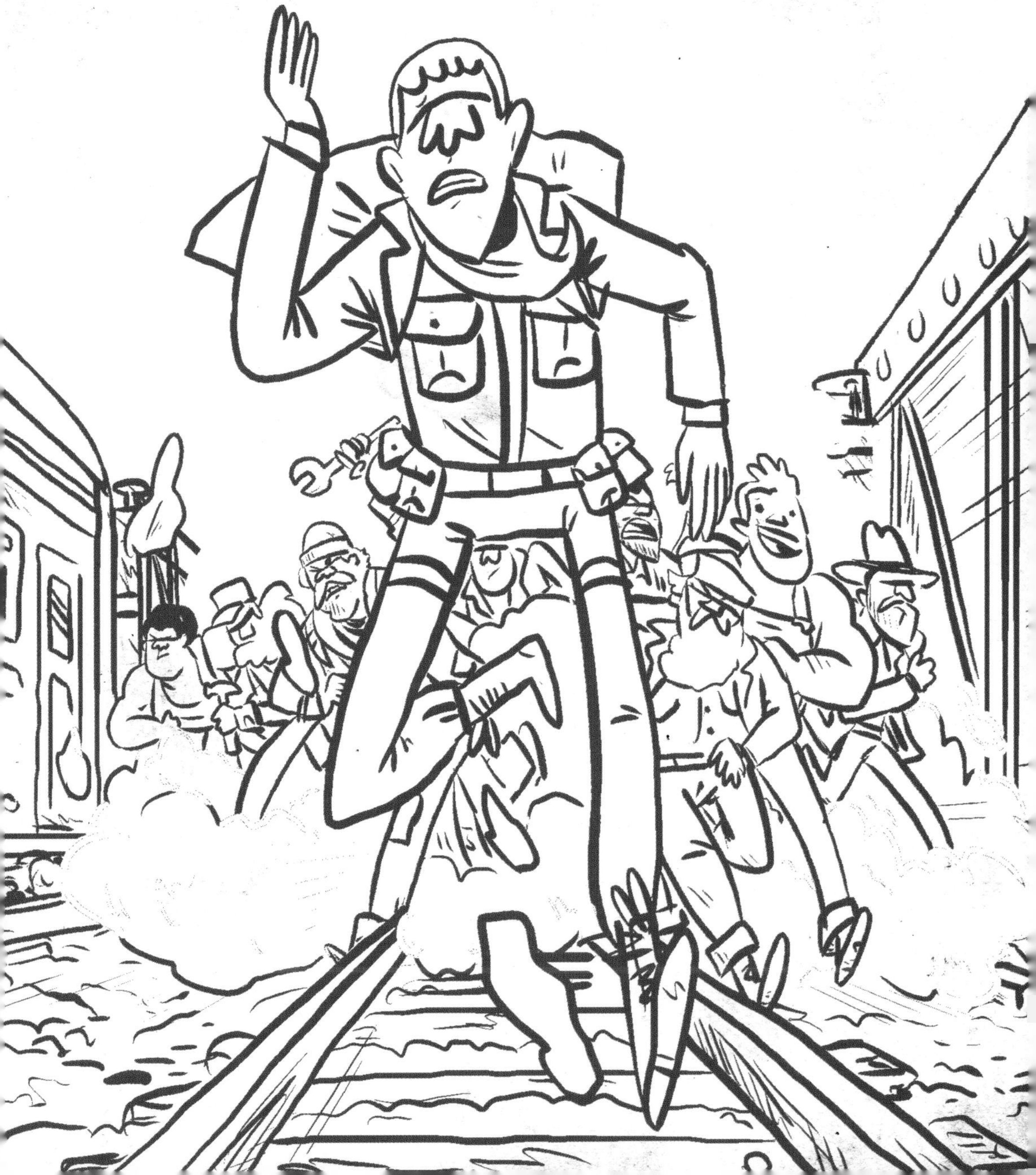

# III

*"this is not*
*a safe place."*

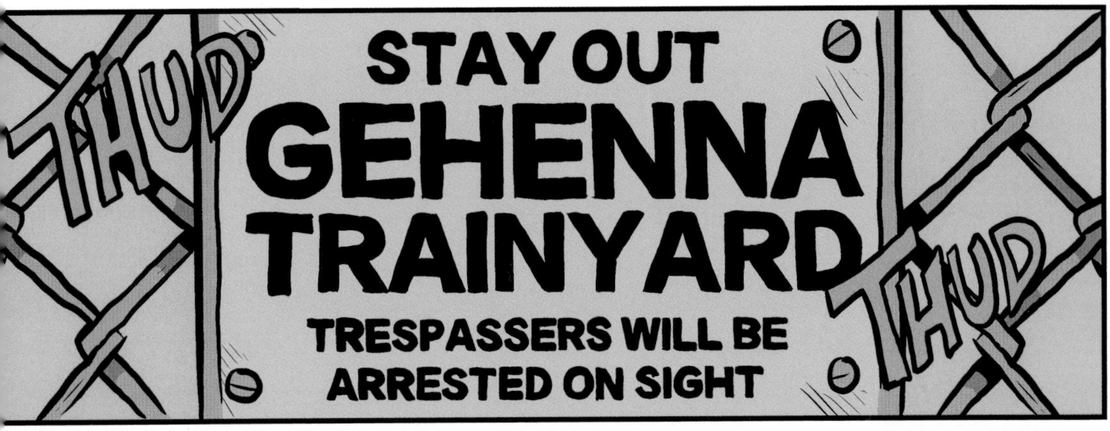
THUD
STAY OUT
GEHENNA
TRAINYARD
TRESPASSERS WILL BE
ARRESTED ON SIGHT
THUD

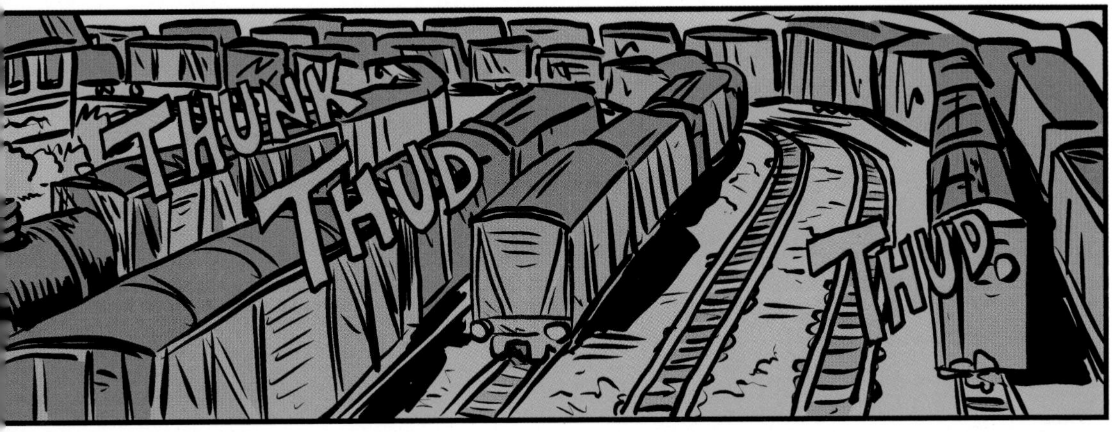
THUNK
THUD
THUD

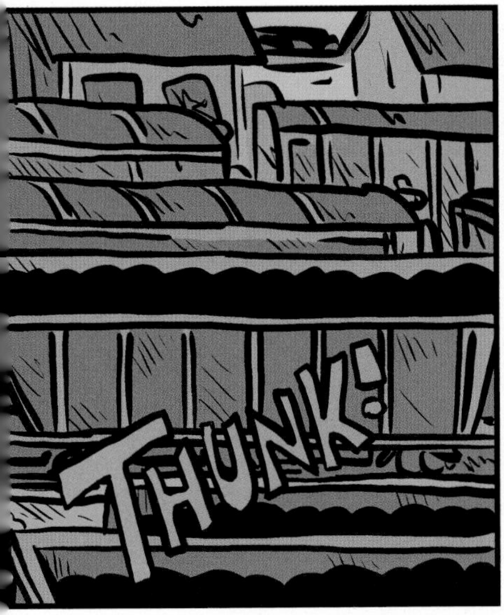
THUNK!

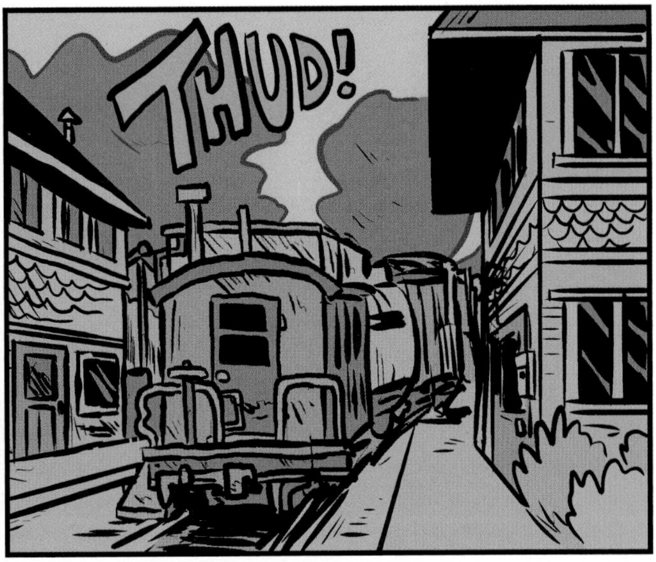
THUD!

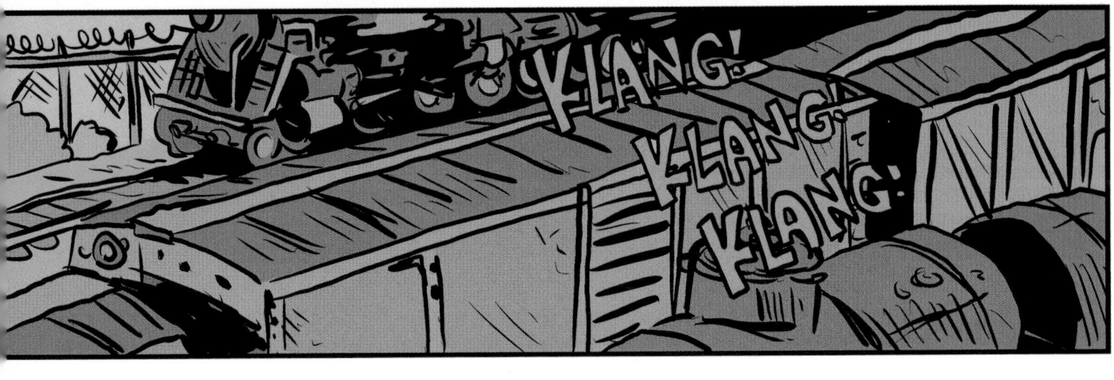
KLANG!
KLANG!
KLANG!
KLANG!

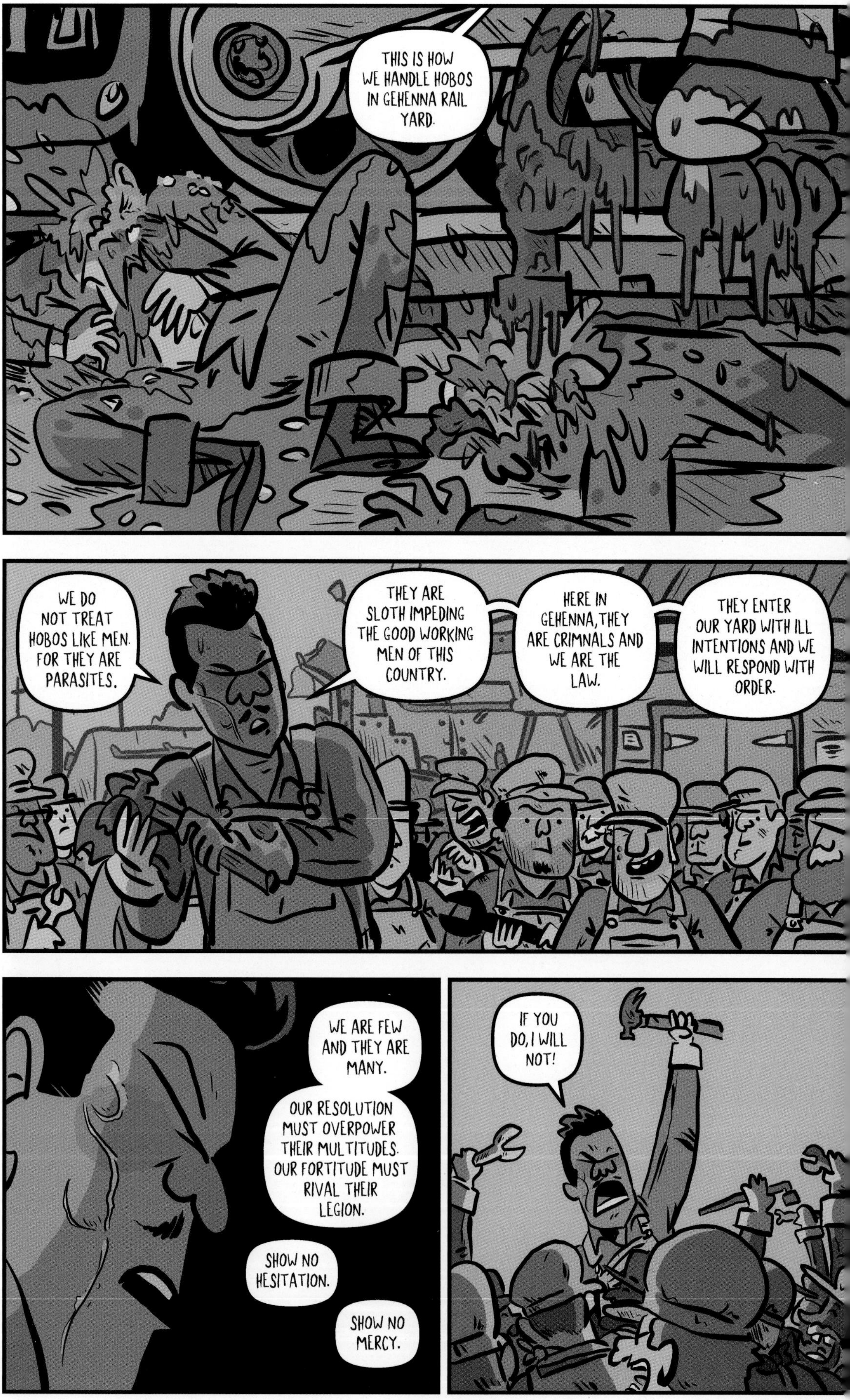
THIS IS HOW WE HANDLE HOBOS IN GEHENNA RAIL YARD.
WE DO NOT TREAT HOBOS LIKE MEN. FOR THEY ARE PARASITES.
THEY ARE SLOTH IMPEDING THE GOOD WORKING MEN OF THIS COUNTRY.
HERE IN GEHENNA, THEY ARE CRIMNALS AND WE ARE THE LAW.
THEY ENTER OUR YARD WITH ILL INTENTIONS AND WE WILL RESPOND WITH ORDER.
WE ARE FEW AND THEY ARE MANY.
OUR RESOLUTION MUST OVERPOWER THEIR MULTITUDES. OUR FORTITUDE MUST RIVAL THEIR LEGION.
SHOW NO HESITATION.
SHOW NO MERCY.
IF YOU DO, I WILL NOT!

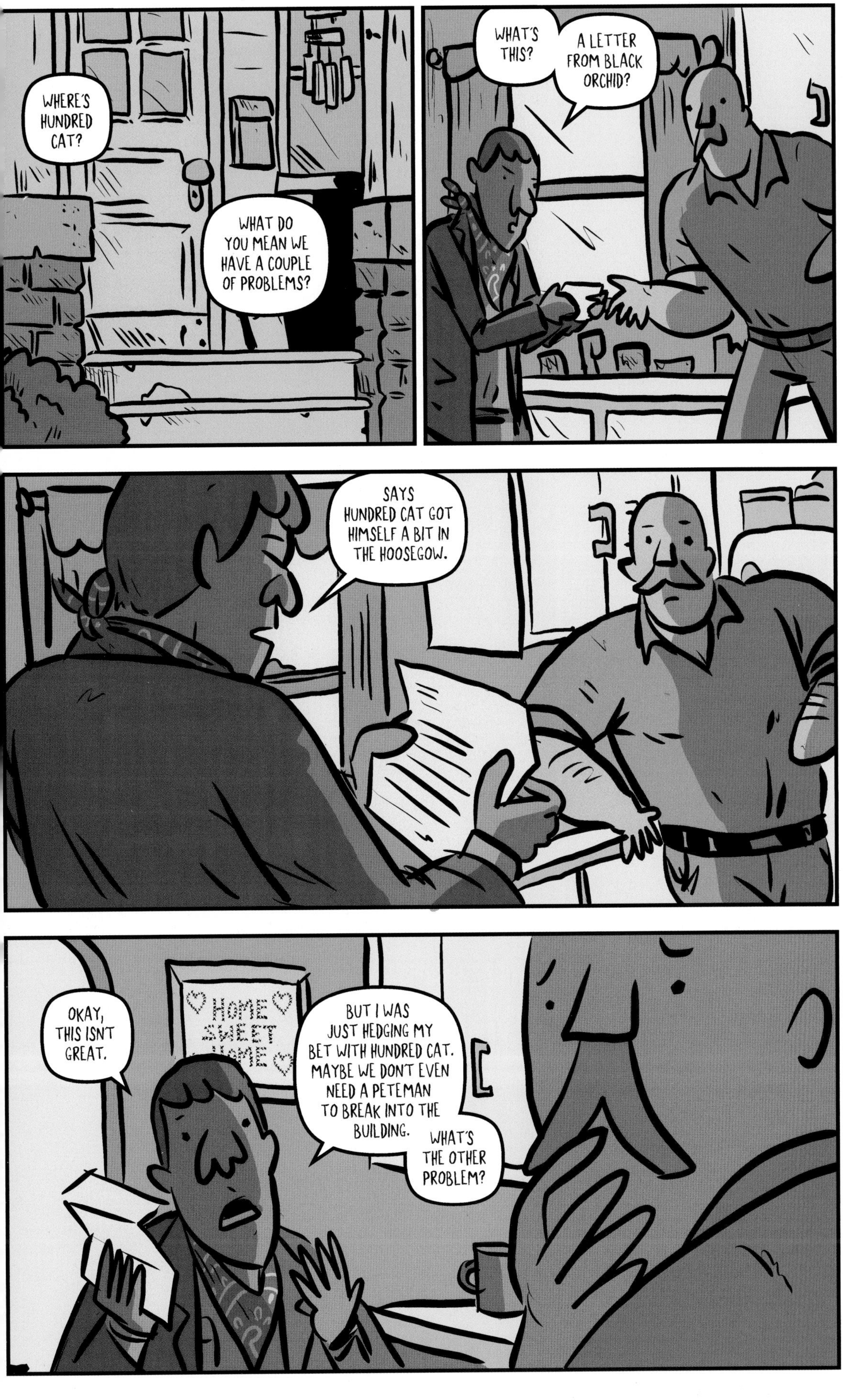
WHERE'S HUNDRED CAT?
WHAT DO YOU MEAN WE HAVE A COUPLE OF PROBLEMS?
WHAT'S THIS?
A LETTER FROM BLACK ORCHID?
SAYS HUNDRED CAT GOT HIMSELF A BIT IN THE HOOSEGOW.
OKAY, THIS ISN'T GREAT.
HOME SWEET HOME
BUT I WAS JUST HEDGING MY BET WITH HUNDRED CAT. MAYBE WE DON'T EVEN NEED A PETEMAN TO BREAK INTO THE BUILDING.
WHAT'S THE OTHER PROBLEM?

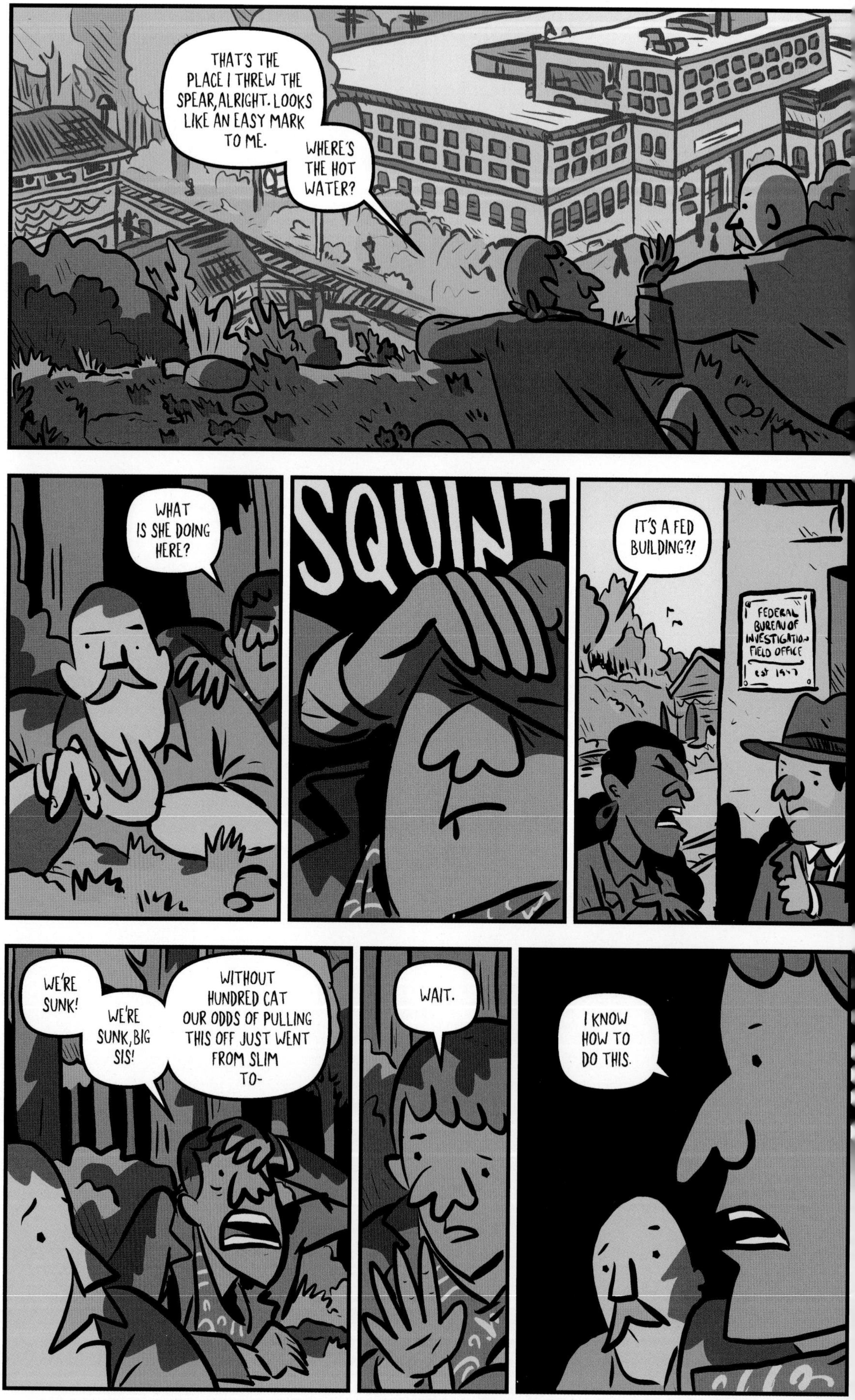
THAT'S THE PLACE I THREW THE SPEAR, ALRIGHT. LOOKS LIKE AN EASY MARK TO ME.
WHERE'S THE HOT WATER?
WHAT IS SHE DOING HERE?
SQUINT
IT'S A FED BUILDING?!
FEDERAL BUREAU OF INVESTIGATION FIELD OFFICE
WE'RE SUNK!
WE'RE SUNK, BIG SIS!
WITHOUT HUNDRED CAT OUR ODDS OF PULLING THIS OFF JUST WENT FROM SLIM TO-
WAIT.
I KNOW HOW TO DO THIS.

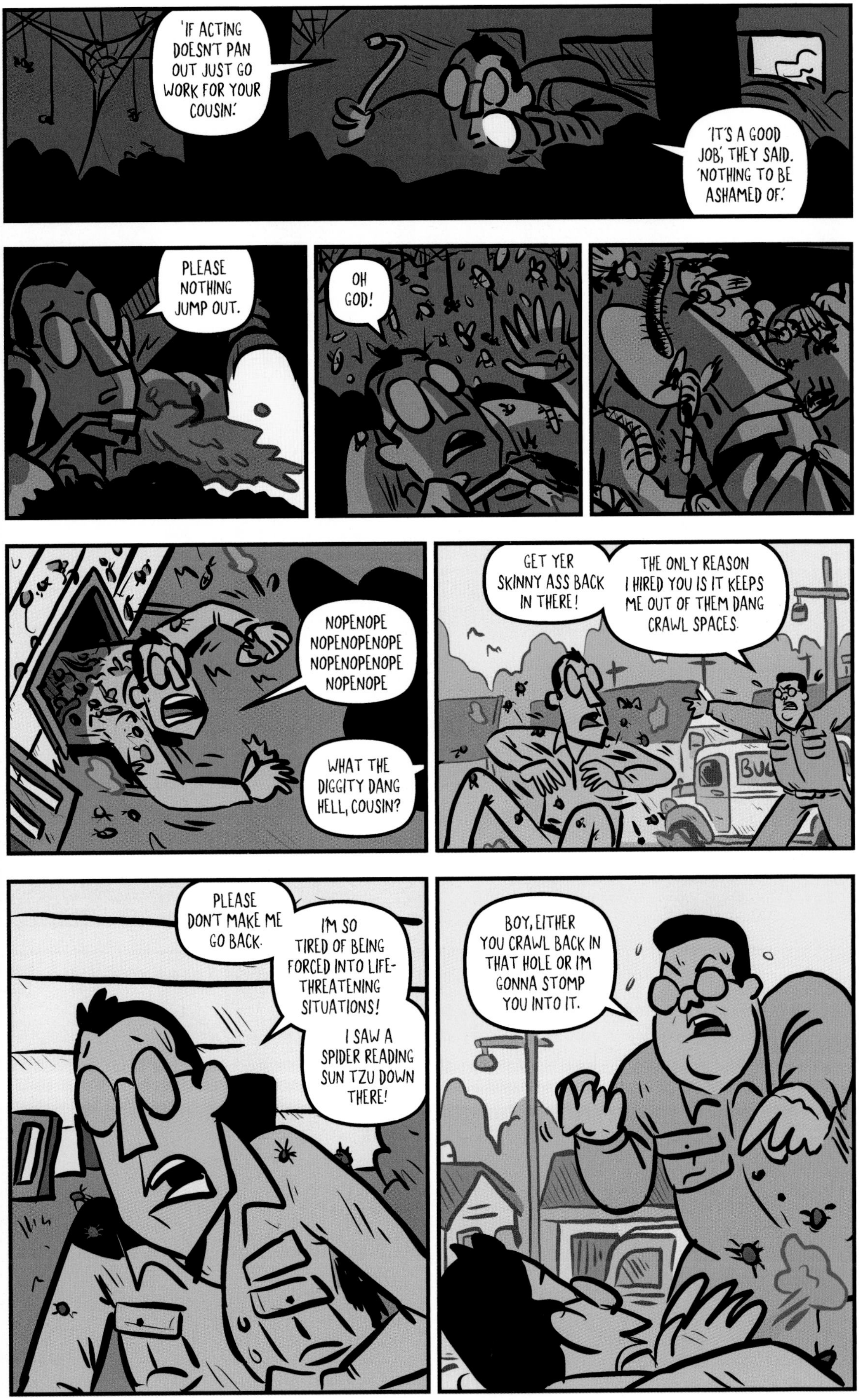
'IF ACTING DOESN'T PAN OUT JUST GO WORK FOR YOUR COUSIN.'
'IT'S A GOOD JOB,' THEY SAID. 'NOTHING TO BE ASHAMED OF.'
PLEASE NOTHING JUMP OUT.
OH GOD!
NOPENOPE NOPENOPENOPE NOPENOPENOPE NOPENOPE
WHAT THE DIGGITY DANG HELL, COUSIN?
GET YER SKINNY ASS BACK IN THERE!
THE ONLY REASON I HIRED YOU IS IT KEEPS ME OUT OF THEM DANG CRAWL SPACES.
BUG
PLEASE DON'T MAKE ME GO BACK.
I'M SO TIRED OF BEING FORCED INTO LIFE-THREATENING SITUATIONS!
I SAW A SPIDER READING SUN TZU DOWN THERE!
BOY, EITHER YOU CRAWL BACK IN THAT HOLE OR I'M GONNA STOMP YOU INTO IT.

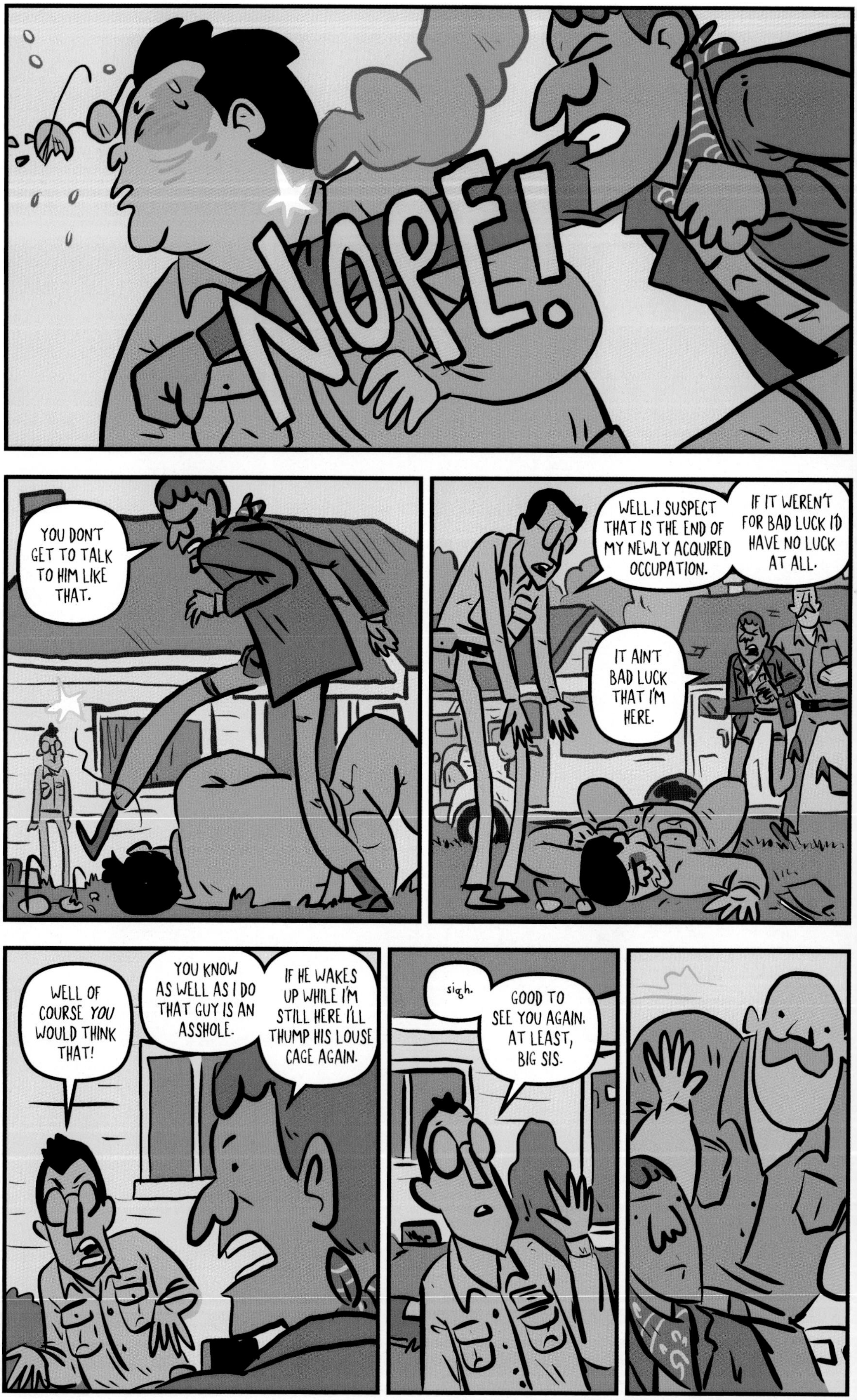
NOPE!
YOU DON'T GET TO TALK TO HIM LIKE THAT.
WELL, I SUSPECT THAT IS THE END OF MY NEWLY ACQUIRED OCCUPATION.
IF IT WEREN'T FOR BAD LUCK I'D HAVE NO LUCK AT ALL.
IT AIN'T BAD LUCK THAT I'M HERE.
WELL OF COURSE YOU WOULD THINK THAT!
YOU KNOW AS WELL AS I DO THAT GUY IS AN ASSHOLE.
IF HE WAKES UP WHILE I'M STILL HERE I'LL THUMP HIS LOUSE CAGE AGAIN.
sigh.
GOOD TO SEE YOU AGAIN, AT LEAST, BIG SIS.

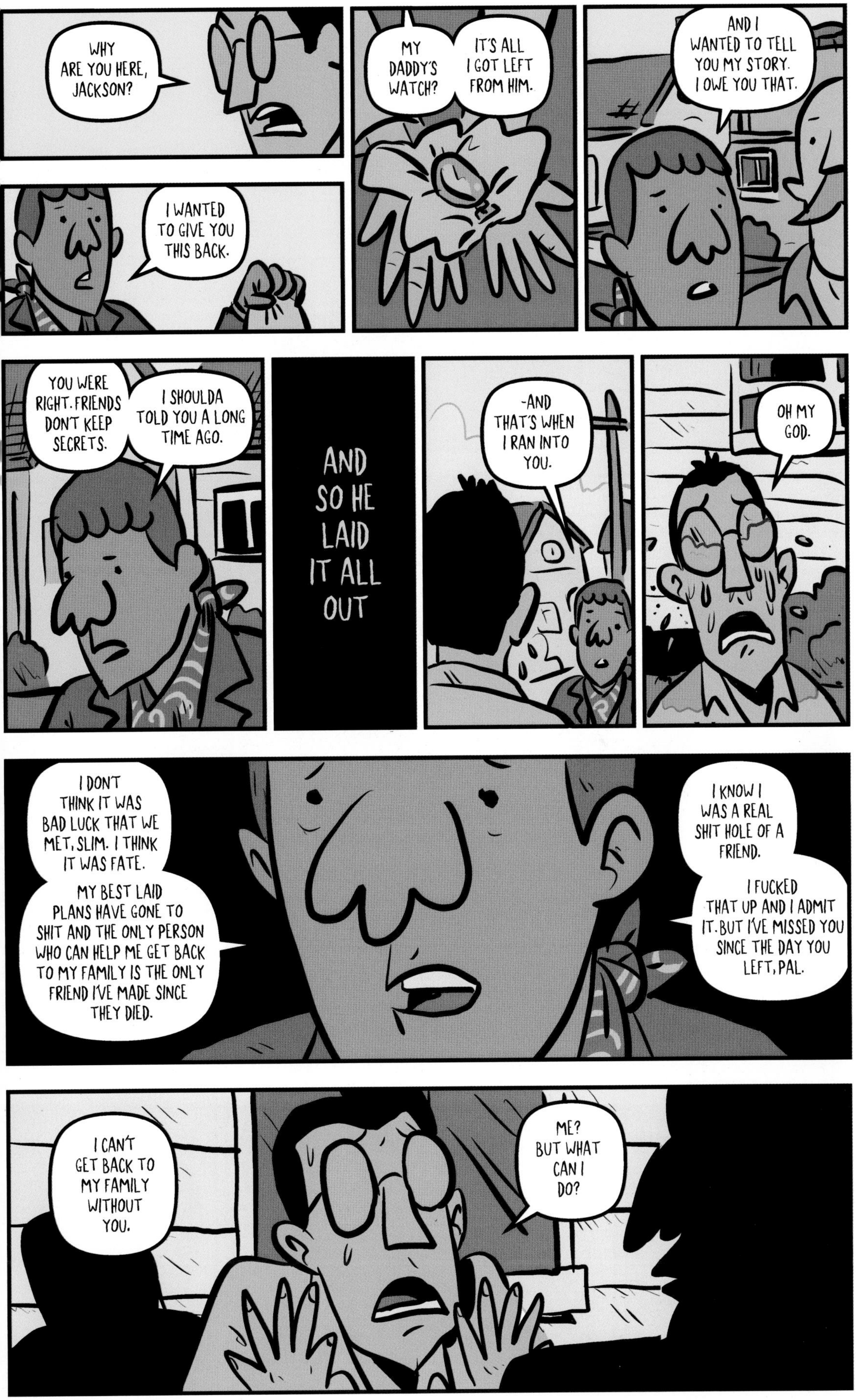
WHY ARE YOU HERE, JACKSON?
I WANTED TO GIVE YOU THIS BACK.
MY DADDY'S WATCH?
IT'S ALL I GOT LEFT FROM HIM.
AND I WANTED TO TELL YOU MY STORY. I OWE YOU THAT.
YOU WERE RIGHT. FRIENDS DON'T KEEP SECRETS.
I SHOULDA TOLD YOU A LONG TIME AGO.
AND SO HE LAID IT ALL OUT
-AND THAT'S WHEN I RAN INTO YOU.
OH MY GOD.
I DON'T THINK IT WAS BAD LUCK THAT WE MET, SLIM. I THINK IT WAS FATE.
MY BEST LAID PLANS HAVE GONE TO SHIT AND THE ONLY PERSON WHO CAN HELP ME GET BACK TO MY FAMILY IS THE ONLY FRIEND I'VE MADE SINCE THEY DIED.
I KNOW I WAS A REAL SHIT HOLE OF A FRIEND.
I FUCKED THAT UP AND I ADMIT IT. BUT I'VE MISSED YOU SINCE THE DAY YOU LEFT, PAL.
I CAN'T GET BACK TO MY FAMILY WITHOUT YOU.
ME? BUT WHAT CAN I DO?

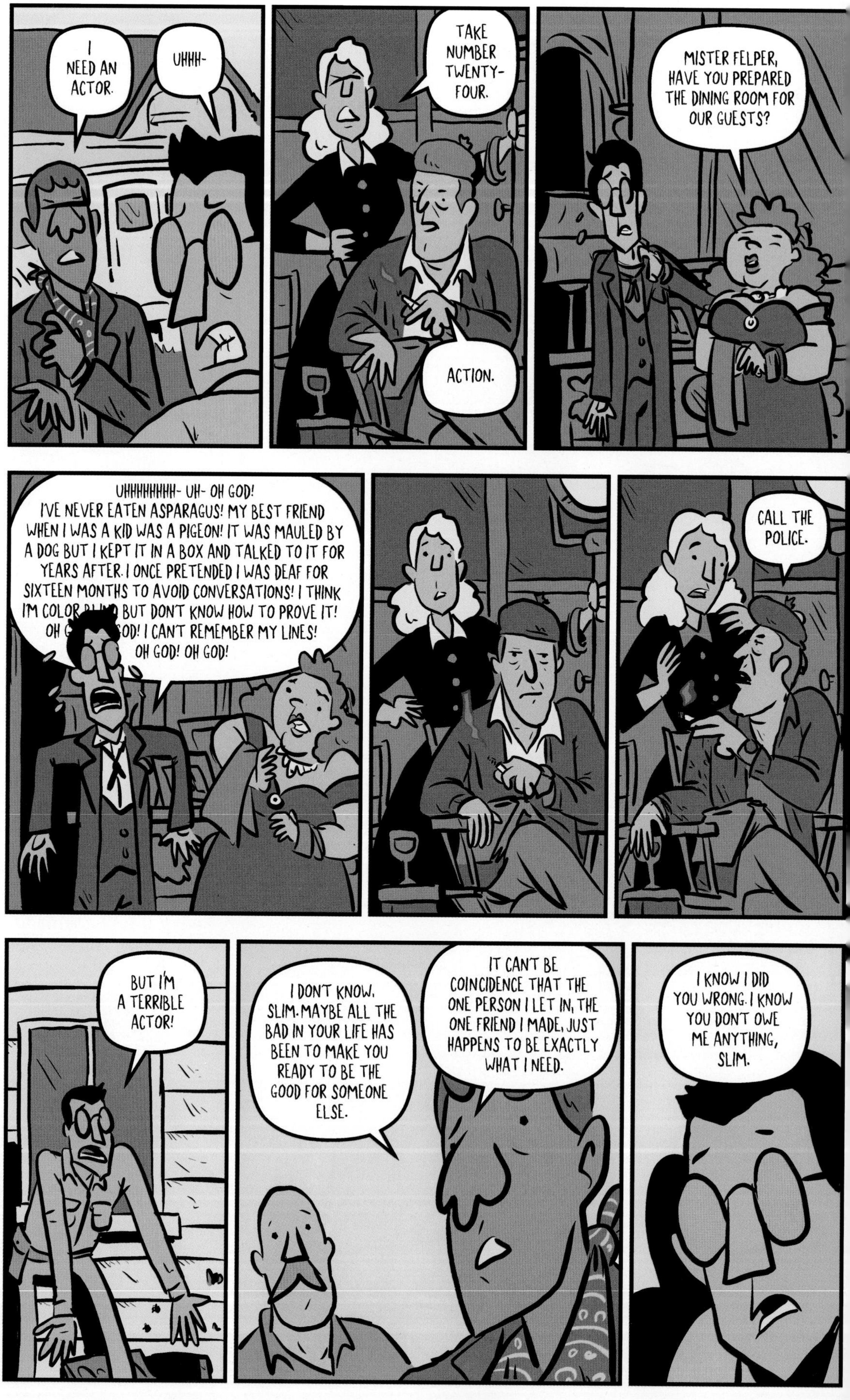
I NEED AN ACTOR.
UHHH-
TAKE NUMBER TWENTY-FOUR.
ACTION.
MISTER FELPER, HAVE YOU PREPARED THE DINING ROOM FOR OUR GUESTS?
UHHHHHHHH- UH- OH GOD! I'VE NEVER EATEN ASPARAGUS! MY BEST FRIEND WHEN I WAS A KID WAS A PIGEON! IT WAS MAULED BY A DOG BUT I KEPT IT IN A BOX AND TALKED TO IT FOR YEARS AFTER. I ONCE PRETENDED I WAS DEAF FOR SIXTEEN MONTHS TO AVOID CONVERSATIONS! I THINK I'M COLOR BUT DON'T KNOW HOW TO PROVE IT! OH GOD! I CAN'T REMEMBER MY LINES! OH GOD! OH GOD!
CALL THE POLICE.
BUT I'M A TERRIBLE ACTOR!
I DON'T KNOW, SLIM. MAYBE ALL THE BAD IN YOUR LIFE HAS BEEN TO MAKE YOU READY TO BE THE GOOD FOR SOMEONE ELSE.
IT CAN'T BE COINCIDENCE THAT THE ONE PERSON I LET IN, THE ONE FRIEND I MADE, JUST HAPPENS TO BE EXACTLY WHAT I NEED.
I KNOW I DID YOU WRONG. I KNOW YOU DON'T OWE ME ANYTHING, SLIM.

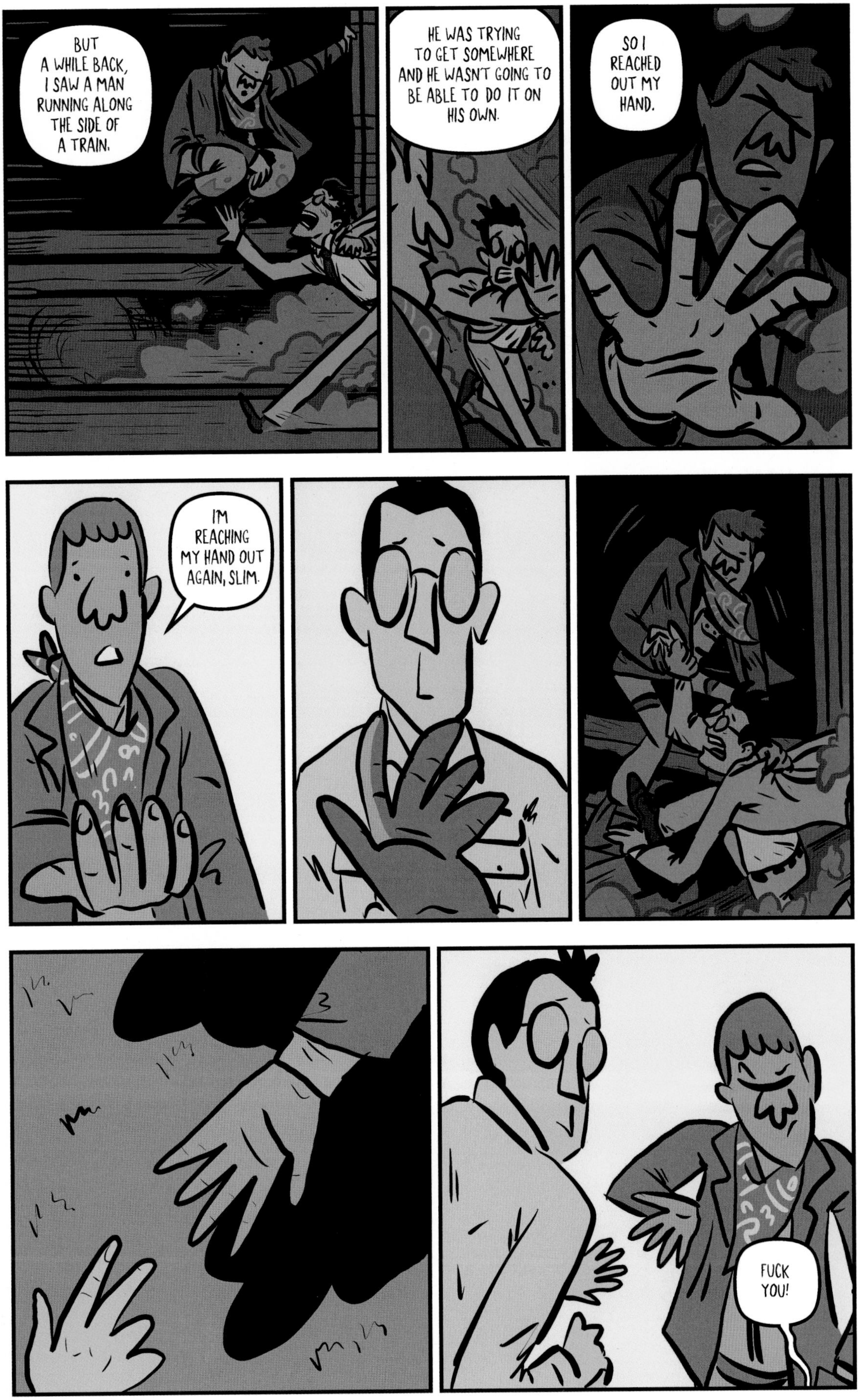
BUT A WHILE BACK, I SAW A MAN RUNNING ALONG THE SIDE OF A TRAIN.
HE WAS TRYING TO GET SOMEWHERE AND HE WASN'T GOING TO BE ABLE TO DO IT ON HIS OWN.
SO I REACHED OUT MY HAND.
I'M REACHING MY HAND OUT AGAIN, SLIM.
FUCK YOU!

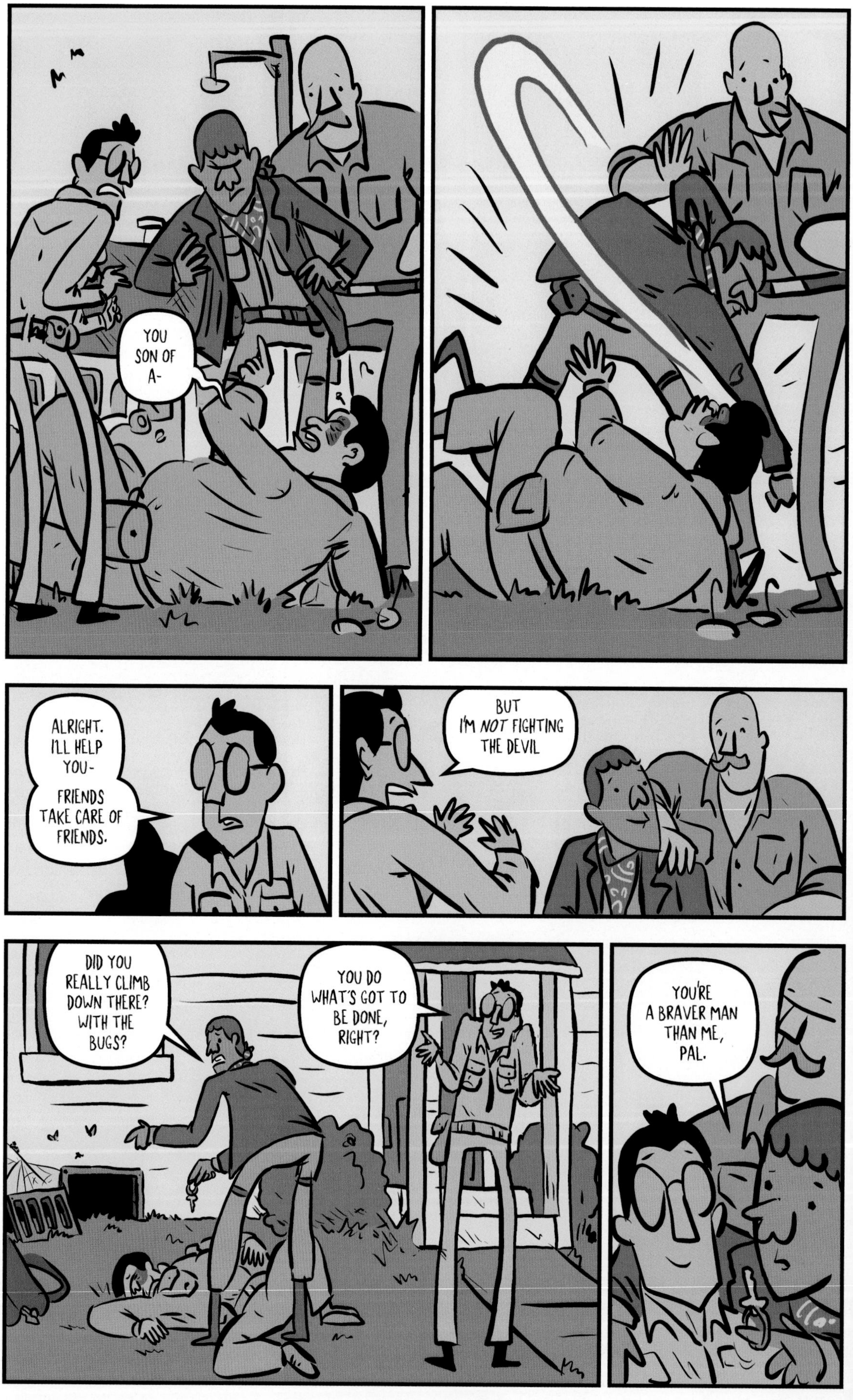
YOU SON OF A-
ALRIGHT. I'LL HELP YOU-
FRIENDS TAKE CARE OF FRIENDS.
BUT I'M *NOT* FIGHTING THE DEVIL
DID YOU REALLY CLIMB DOWN THERE? WITH THE BUGS?
YOU DO WHAT'S GOT TO BE DONE, RIGHT?
YOU'RE A BRAVER MAN THAN ME, PAL.

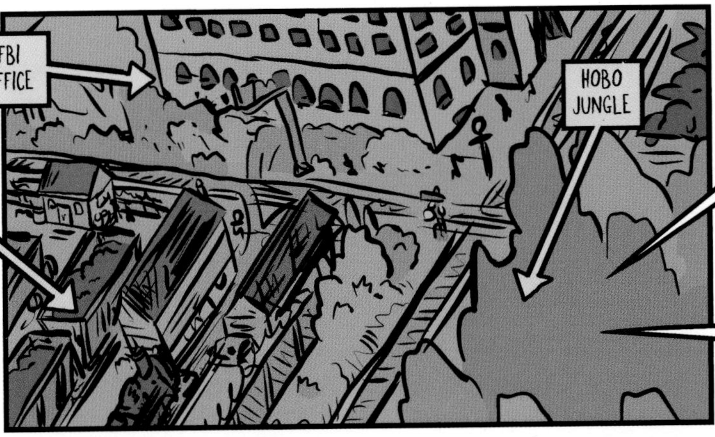
FBI OFFICE
GEHENNA STATION
HOBO JUNGLE
ALRIGHT, LIVEN UP YOU CRUM BUMS. THIS AIN'T NO CONVENTION.
WHY'RE WE CONGREGATIN' HERE, FLIMBO?

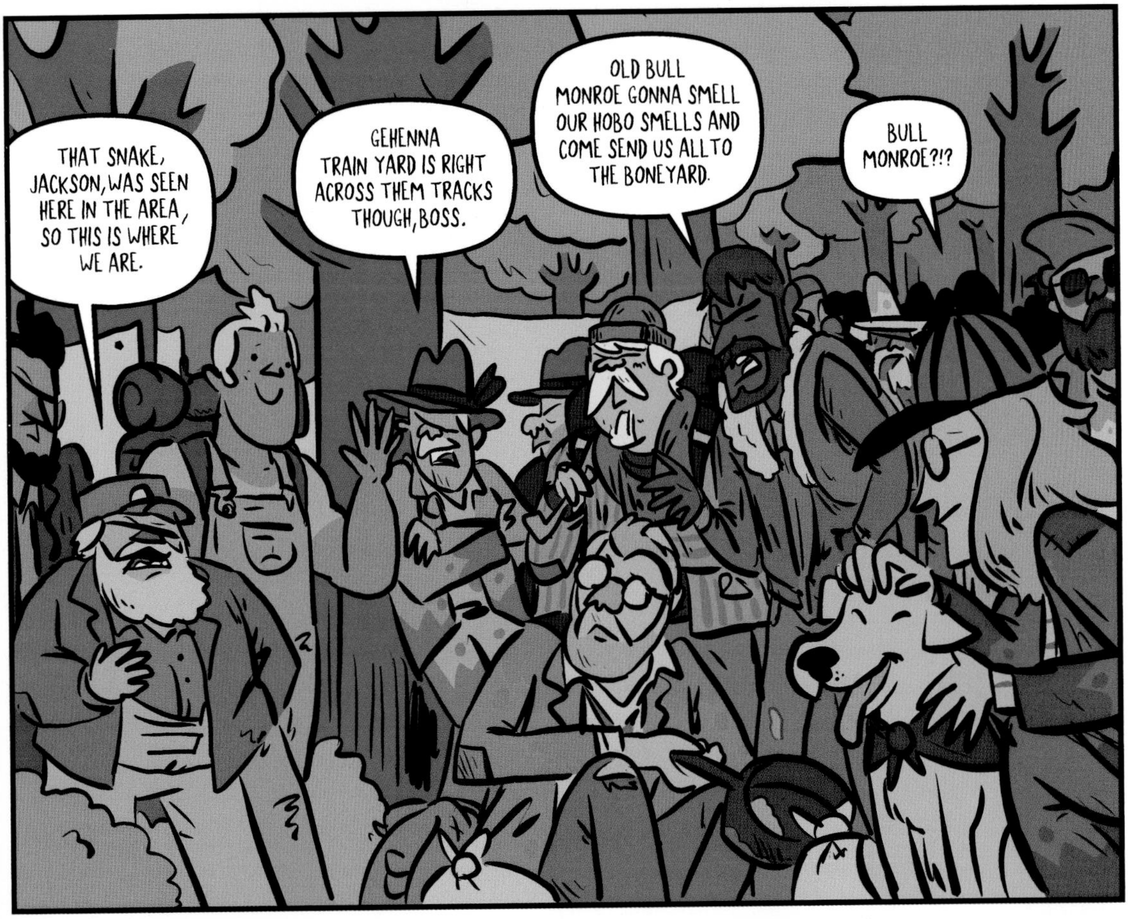
THAT SNAKE, JACKSON, WAS SEEN HERE IN THE AREA, SO THIS IS WHERE WE ARE.
GEHENNA TRAIN YARD IS RIGHT ACROSS THEM TRACKS THOUGH, BOSS.
OLD BULL MONROE GONNA SMELL OUR HOBO SMELLS AND COME SEND US ALL TO THE BONEYARD.
BULL MONROE?!?

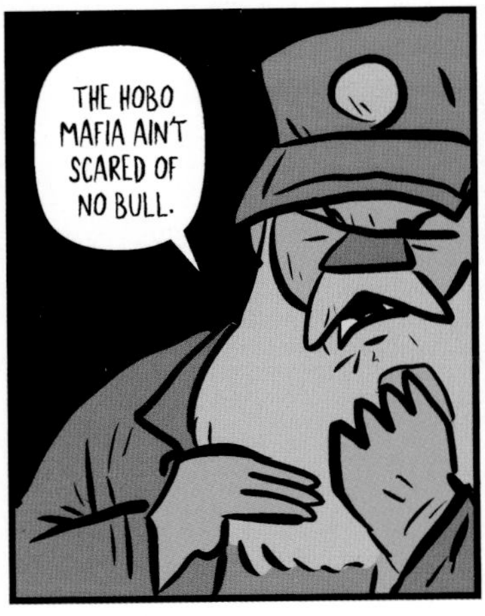
THE HOBO MAFIA AIN'T SCARED OF NO BULL.

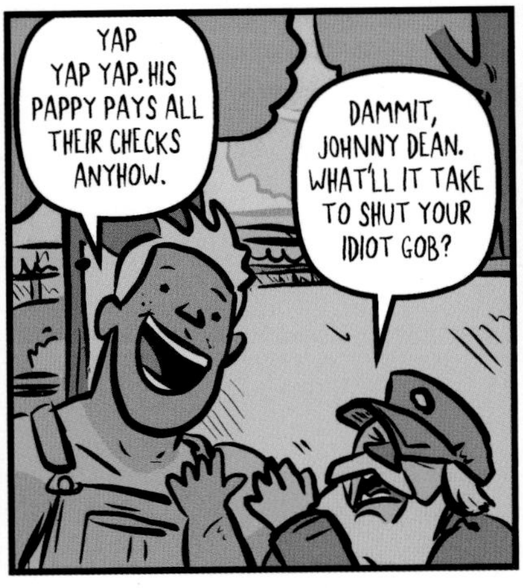
YAP YAP YAP. HIS PAPPY PAYS ALL THEIR CHECKS ANYHOW.
DAMMIT, JOHNNY DEAN. WHAT'LL IT TAKE TO SHUT YOUR IDIOT GOB?

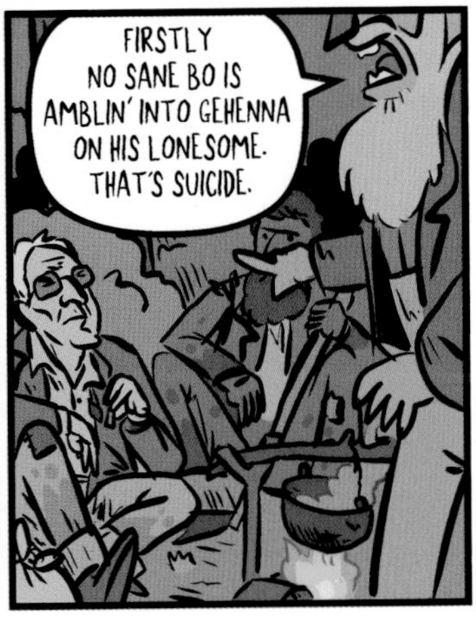
FIRSTLY NO SANE BO IS AMBLIN' INTO GEHENNA ON HIS LONESOME. THAT'S SUICIDE.

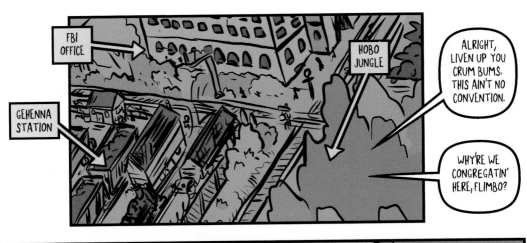

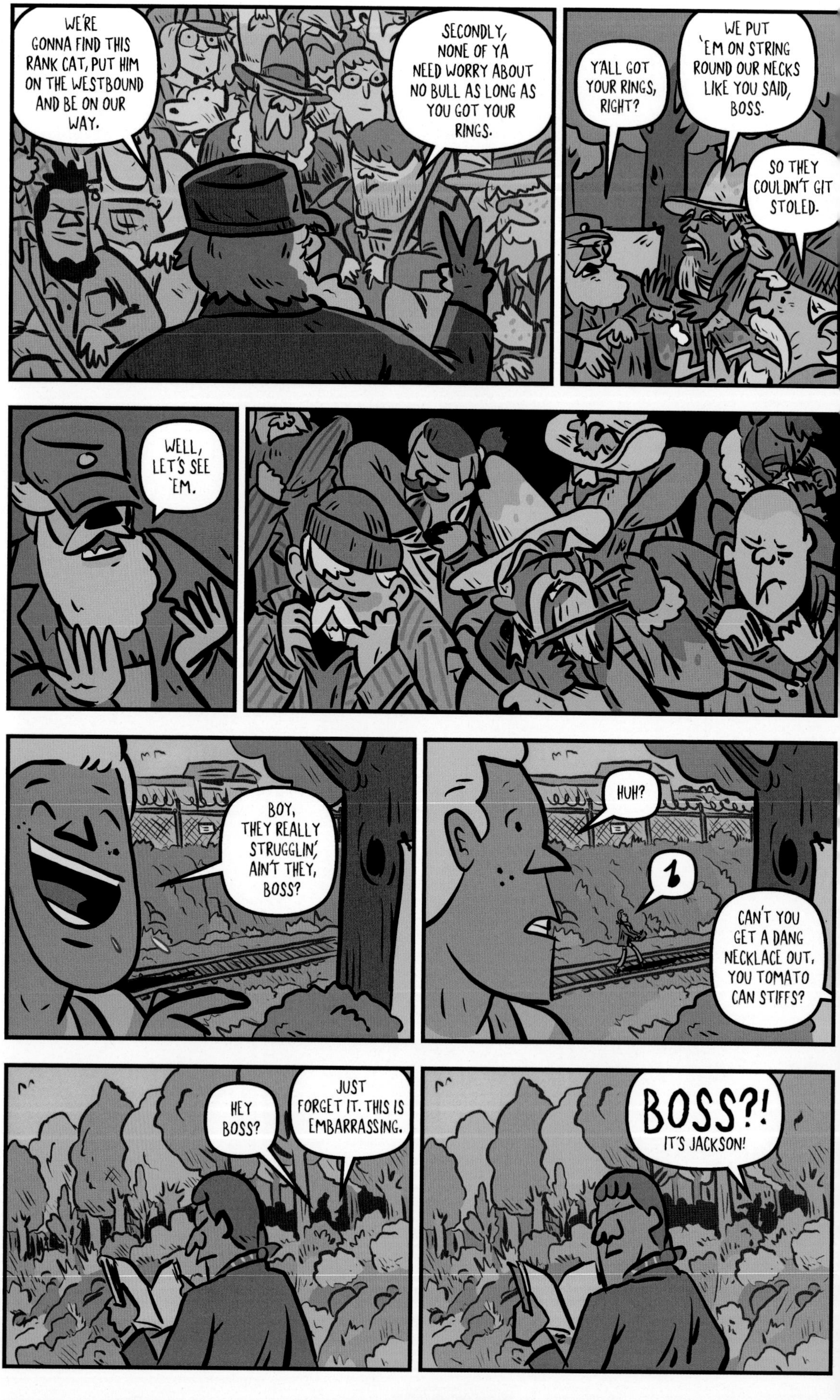
WE'RE GONNA FIND THIS RANK CAT, PUT HIM ON THE WESTBOUND AND BE ON OUR WAY.
SECONDLY, NONE OF YA NEED WORRY ABOUT NO BULL AS LONG AS YOU GOT YOUR RINGS.
Y'ALL GOT YOUR RINGS, RIGHT?
WE PUT 'EM ON STRING ROUND OUR NECKS LIKE YOU SAID, BOSS.
SO THEY COULDN'T GIT STOLED.
WELL, LET'S SEE 'EM.
BOY, THEY REALLY STRUGGLIN', AIN'T THEY, BOSS?
HUH?
CAN'T YOU GET A DANG NECKLACE OUT, YOU TOMATO CAN STIFFS?
HEY BOSS?
JUST FORGET IT. THIS IS EMBARRASSING.
BOSS?!
IT'S JACKSON!

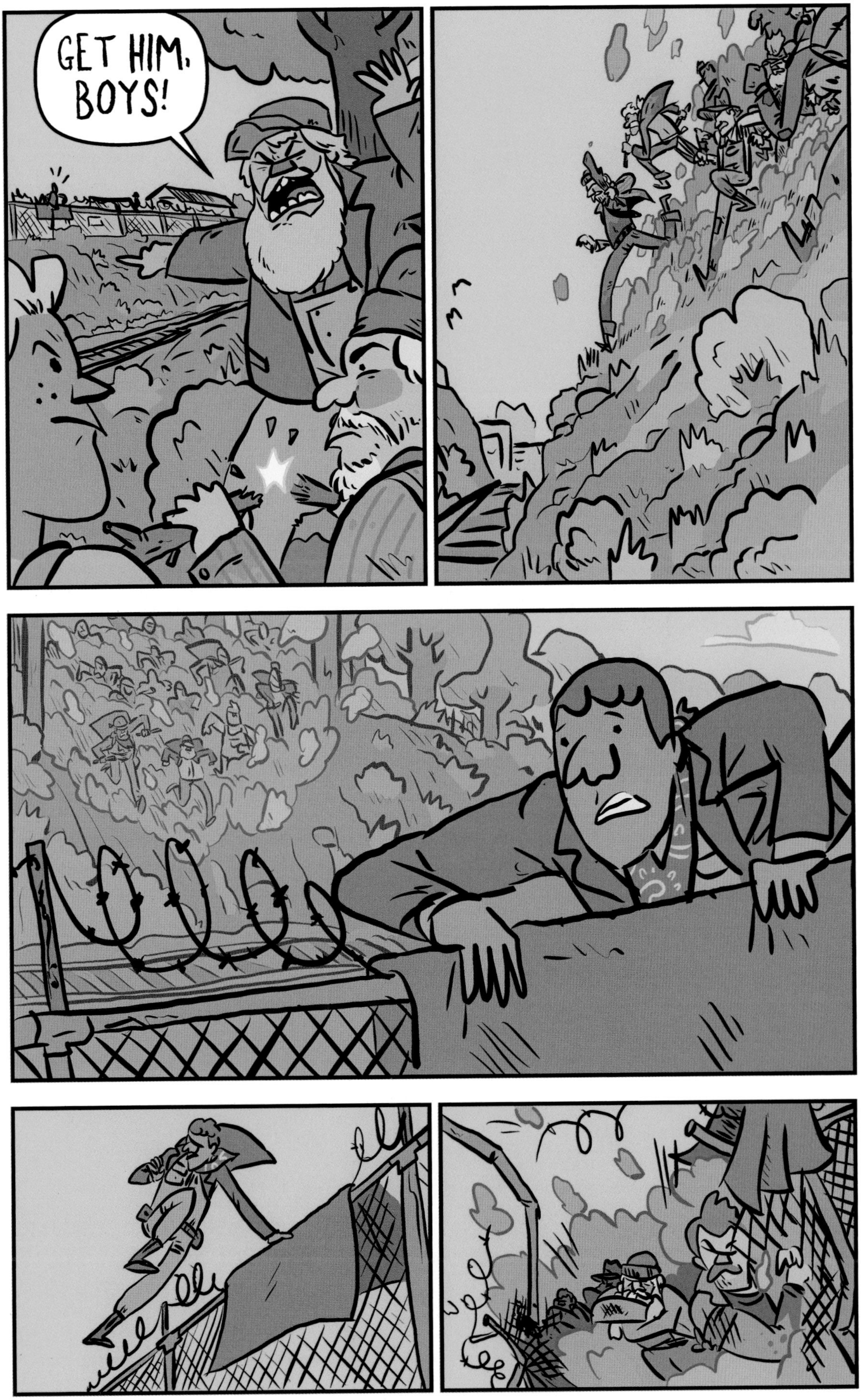
GET HIM, BOYS!

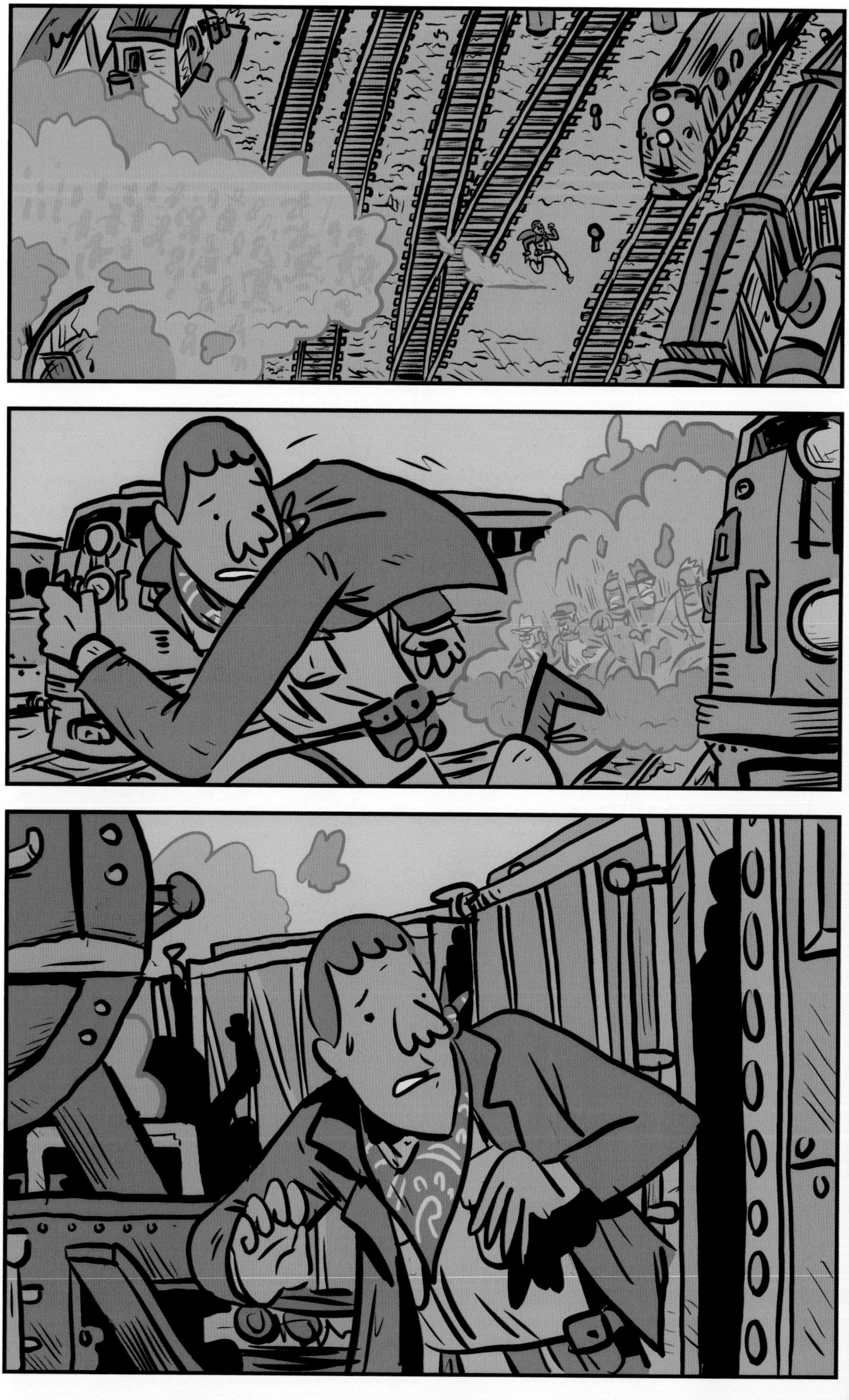

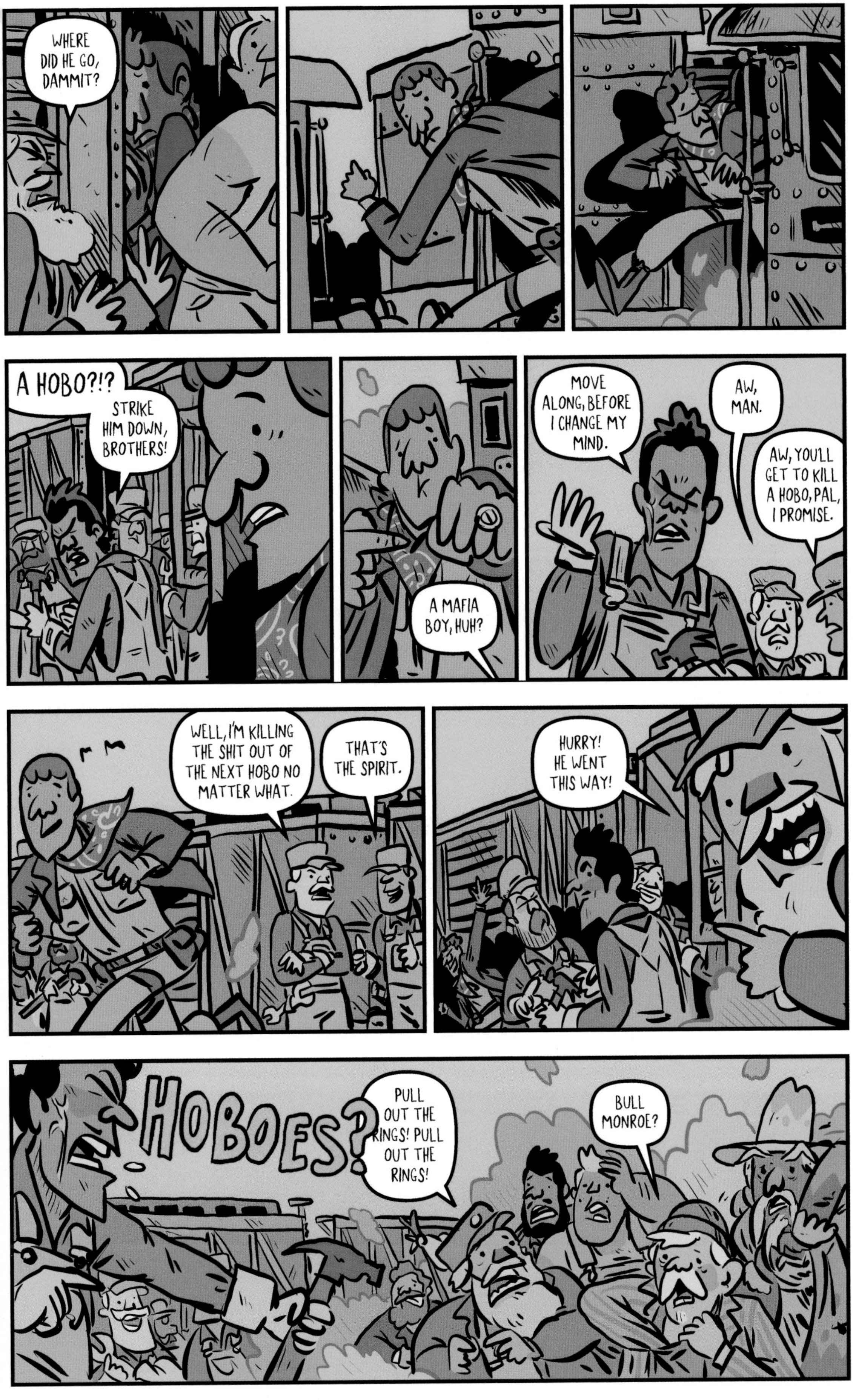
WHERE DID HE GO, DAMMIT?
A HOBO?!?
STRIKE HIM DOWN, BROTHERS!
A MAFIA BOY, HUH?
MOVE ALONG, BEFORE I CHANGE MY MIND.
AW, MAN.
AW, YOU'LL GET TO KILL A HOBO, PAL, I PROMISE.
WELL, I'M KILLING THE SHIT OUT OF THE NEXT HOBO NO MATTER WHAT.
THAT'S THE SPIRIT.
HURRY! HE WENT THIS WAY!
HOBOES?
PULL OUT THE RINGS! PULL OUT THE RINGS!
BULL MONROE?

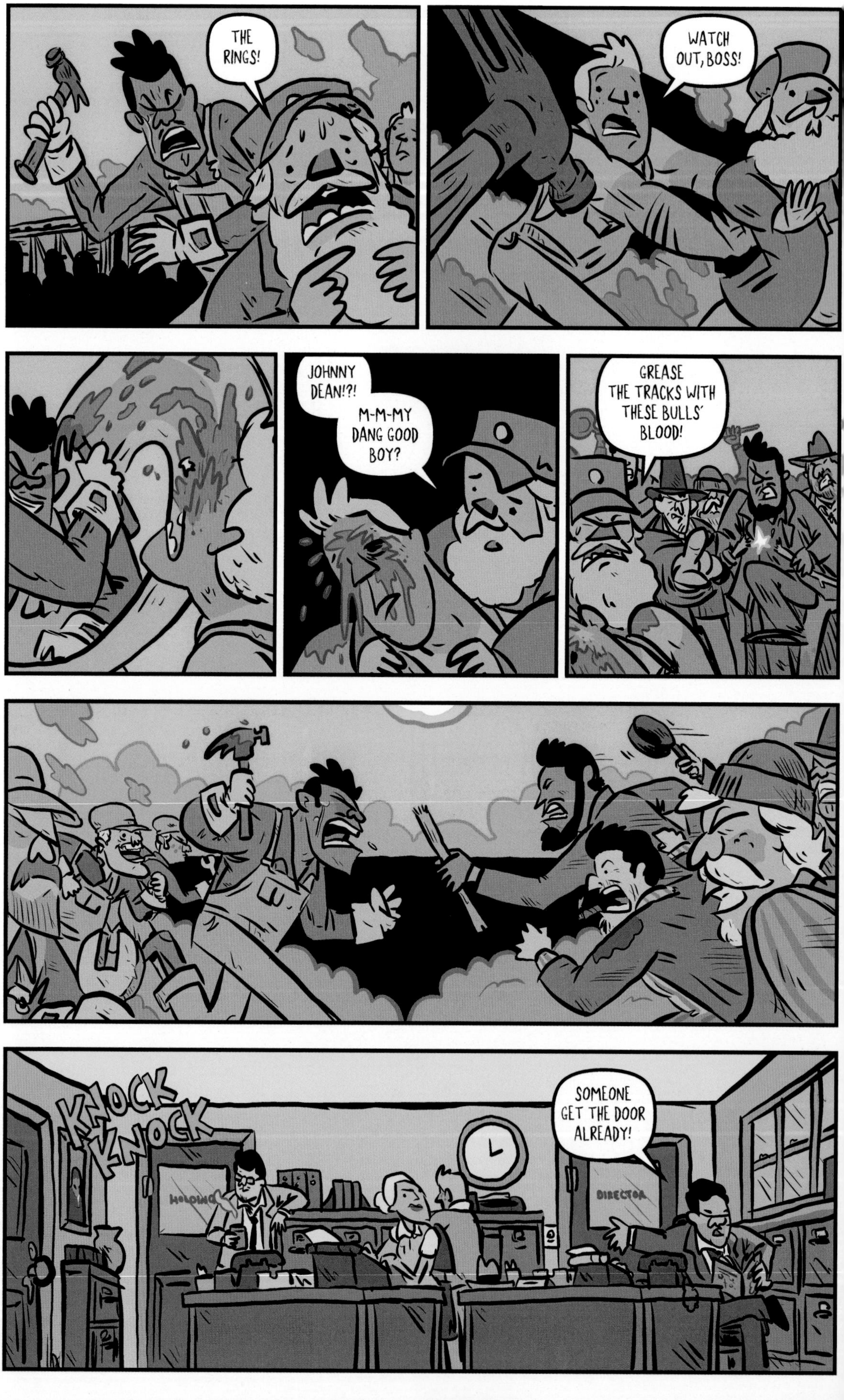
THE RINGS!
WATCH OUT, BOSS!
JOHNNY DEAN!?!
M-M-MY DANG GOOD BOY?
GREASE THE TRACKS WITH THESE BULLS' BLOOD!
KNOCK KNOCK
HOLDING
DIRECTOR
SOMEONE GET THE DOOR ALREADY!

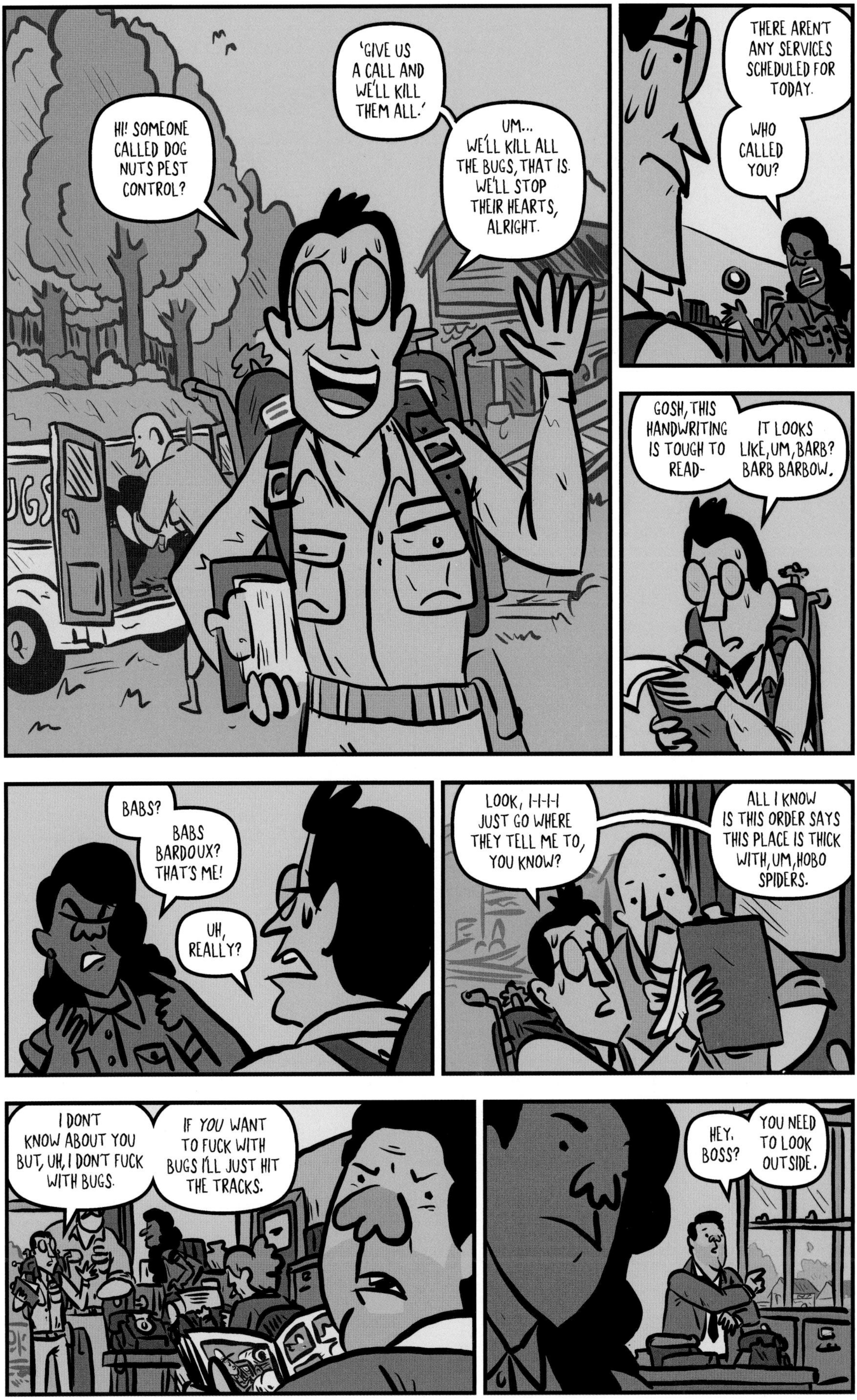
HI! SOMEONE CALLED DOG NUTS PEST CONTROL?
'GIVE US A CALL AND WE'LL KILL THEM ALL.'
UM... WE'LL KILL ALL THE BUGS, THAT IS. WE'LL STOP THEIR HEARTS, ALRIGHT.
UGS
THERE AREN'T ANY SERVICES SCHEDULED FOR TODAY.
WHO CALLED YOU?
GOSH, THIS HANDWRITING IS TOUGH TO READ-
IT LOOKS LIKE, UM, BARB? BARB BARBOW.
BABS?
BABS BARDOUX? THAT'S ME!
UH, REALLY?
LOOK, I-I-I-I JUST GO WHERE THEY TELL ME TO, YOU KNOW?
ALL I KNOW IS THIS ORDER SAYS THIS PLACE IS THICK WITH, UM, HOBO SPIDERS.
I DONT KNOW ABOUT YOU BUT, UH, I DON'T FUCK WITH BUGS.
IF *YOU* WANT TO FUCK WITH BUGS I'LL JUST HIT THE TRACKS.
HEY, BOSS?
YOU NEED TO LOOK OUTSIDE.

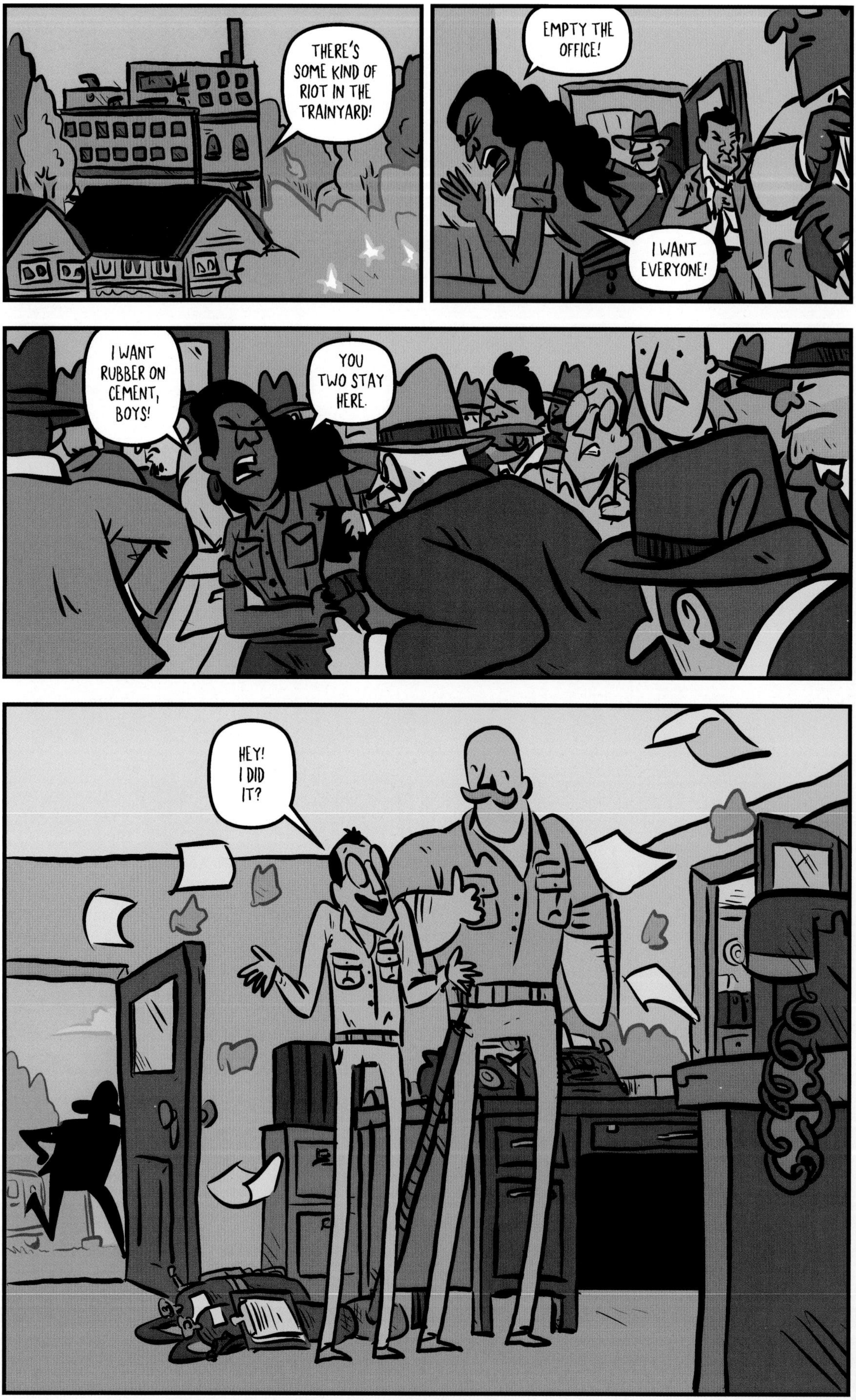
THERE'S SOME KIND OF RIOT IN THE TRAINYARD!
EMPTY THE OFFICE!
I WANT EVERYONE!
I WANT RUBBER ON CEMENT, BOYS!
YOU TWO STAY HERE.
HEY! I DID IT?

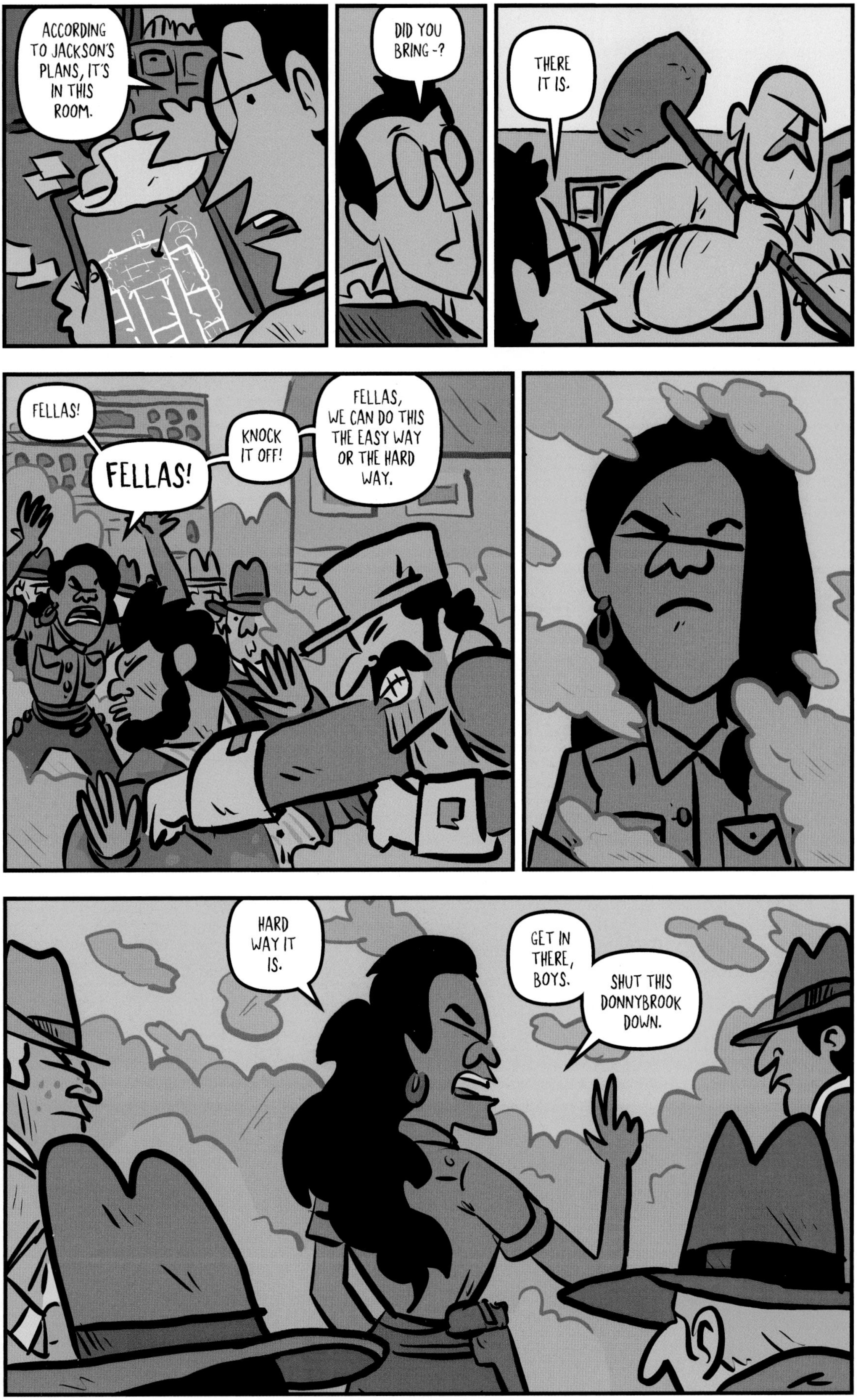
ACCORDING TO JACKSON'S PLANS, IT'S IN THIS ROOM.
DID YOU BRING-?
THERE IT IS.
FELLAS!
FELLAS!
KNOCK IT OFF!
FELLAS, WE CAN DO THIS THE EASY WAY OR THE HARD WAY.
HARD WAY IT IS.
GET IN THERE, BOYS.
SHUT THIS DONNYBROOK DOWN.

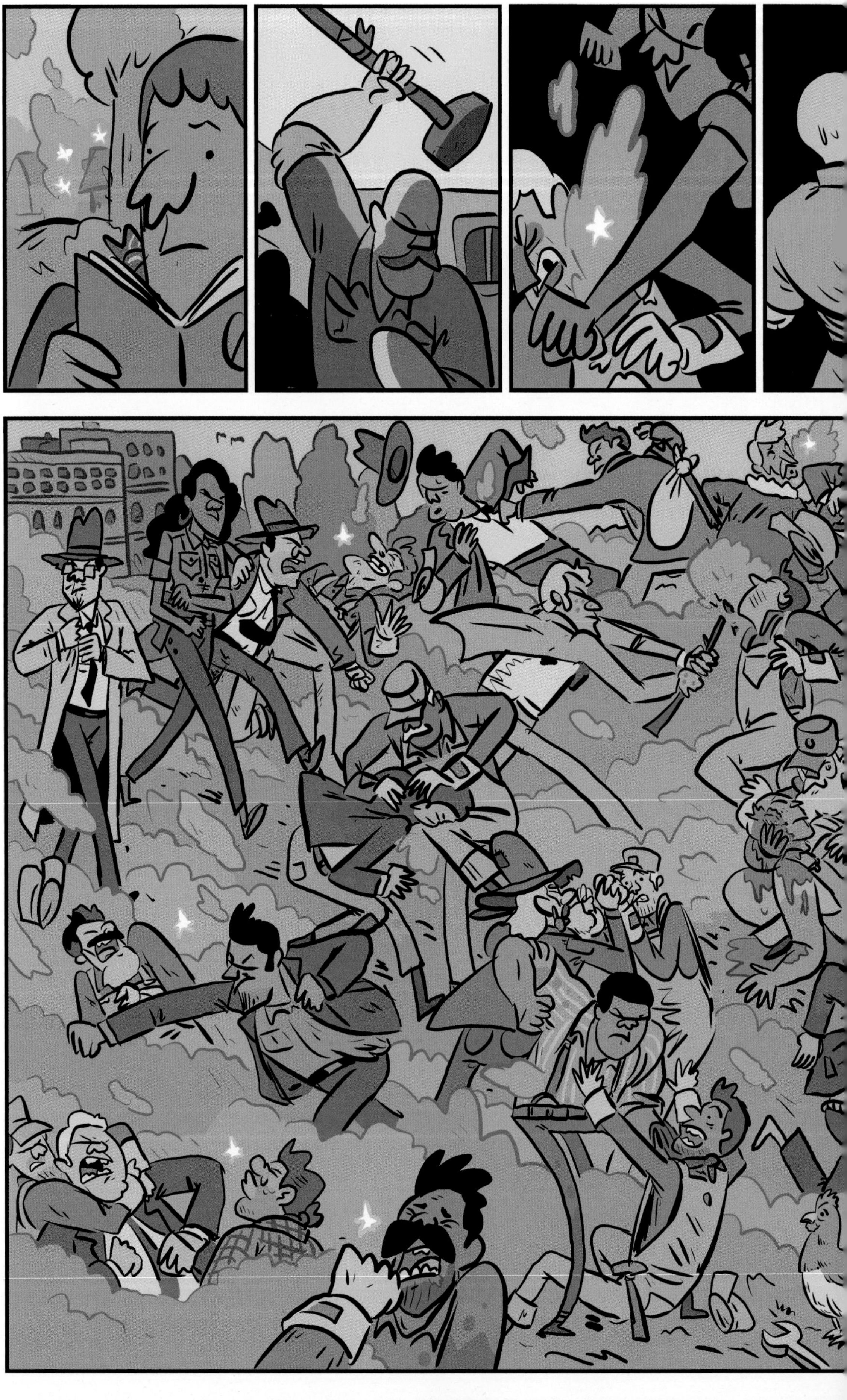

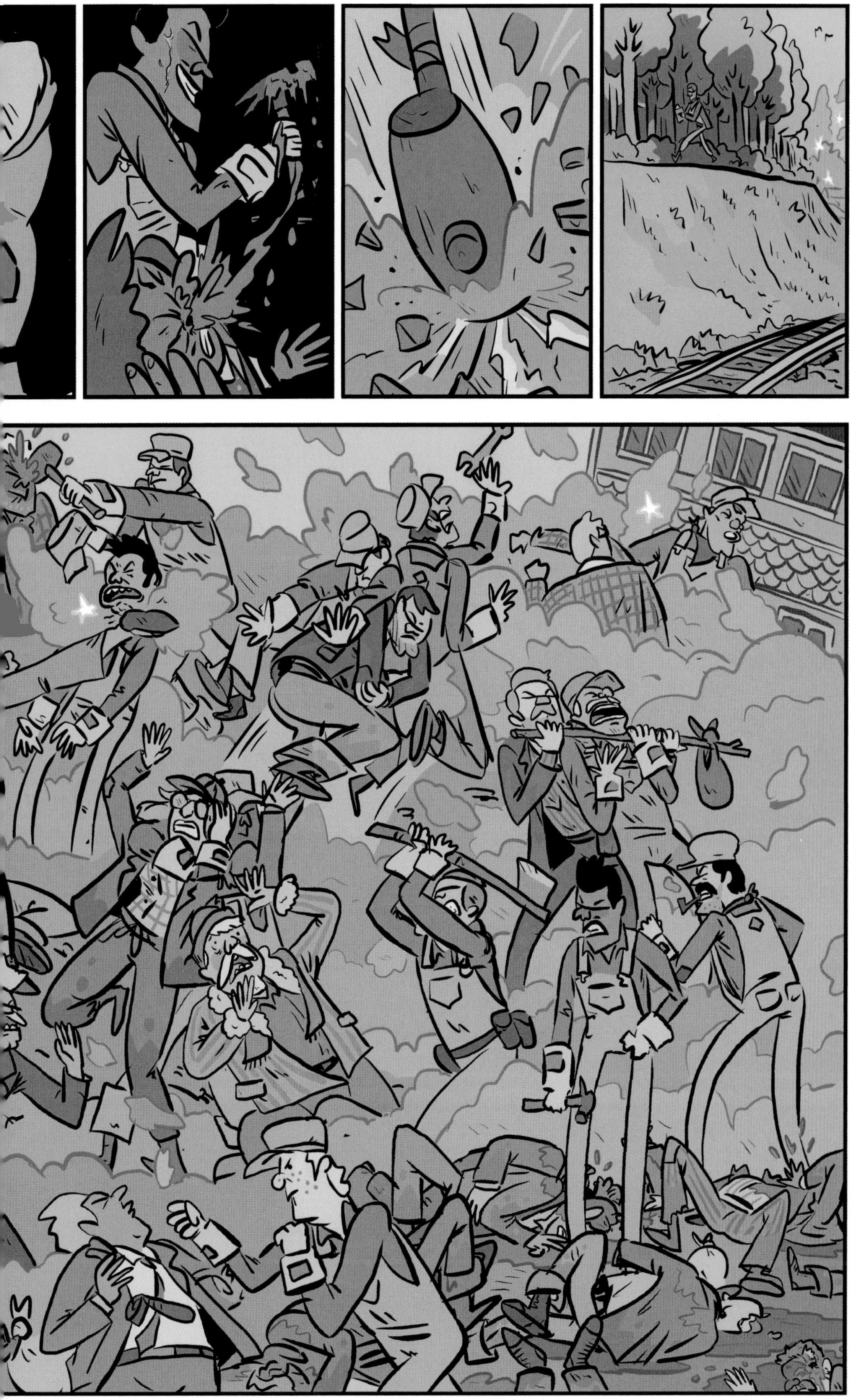

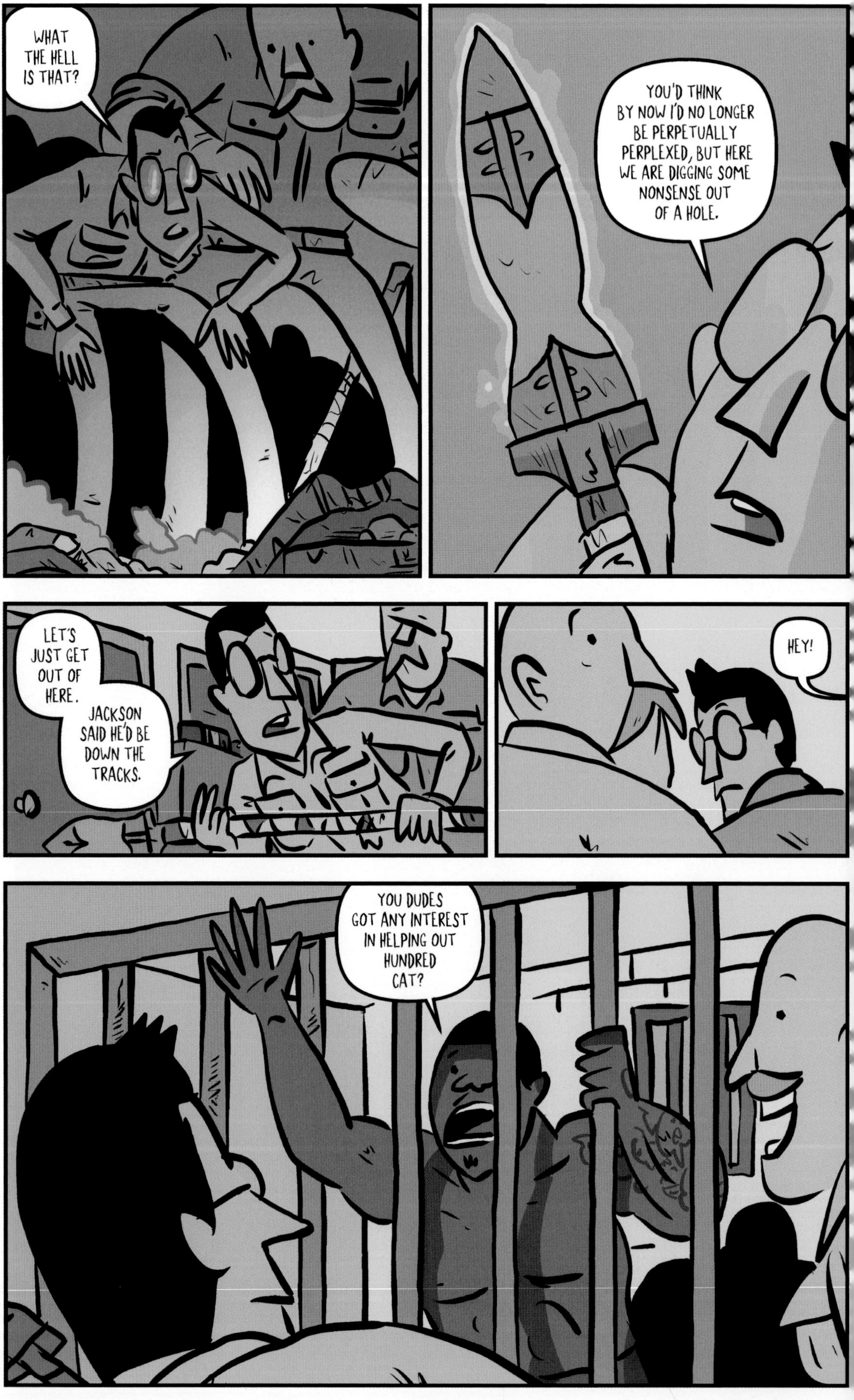
WHAT THE HELL IS THAT?
YOU'D THINK BY NOW I'D NO LONGER BE PERPETUALLY PERPLEXED, BUT HERE WE ARE DIGGING SOME NONSENSE OUT OF A HOLE.
LET'S JUST GET OUT OF HERE.
JACKSON SAID HE'D BE DOWN THE TRACKS.
HEY!
YOU DUDES GOT ANY INTEREST IN HELPING OUT HUNDRED CAT?

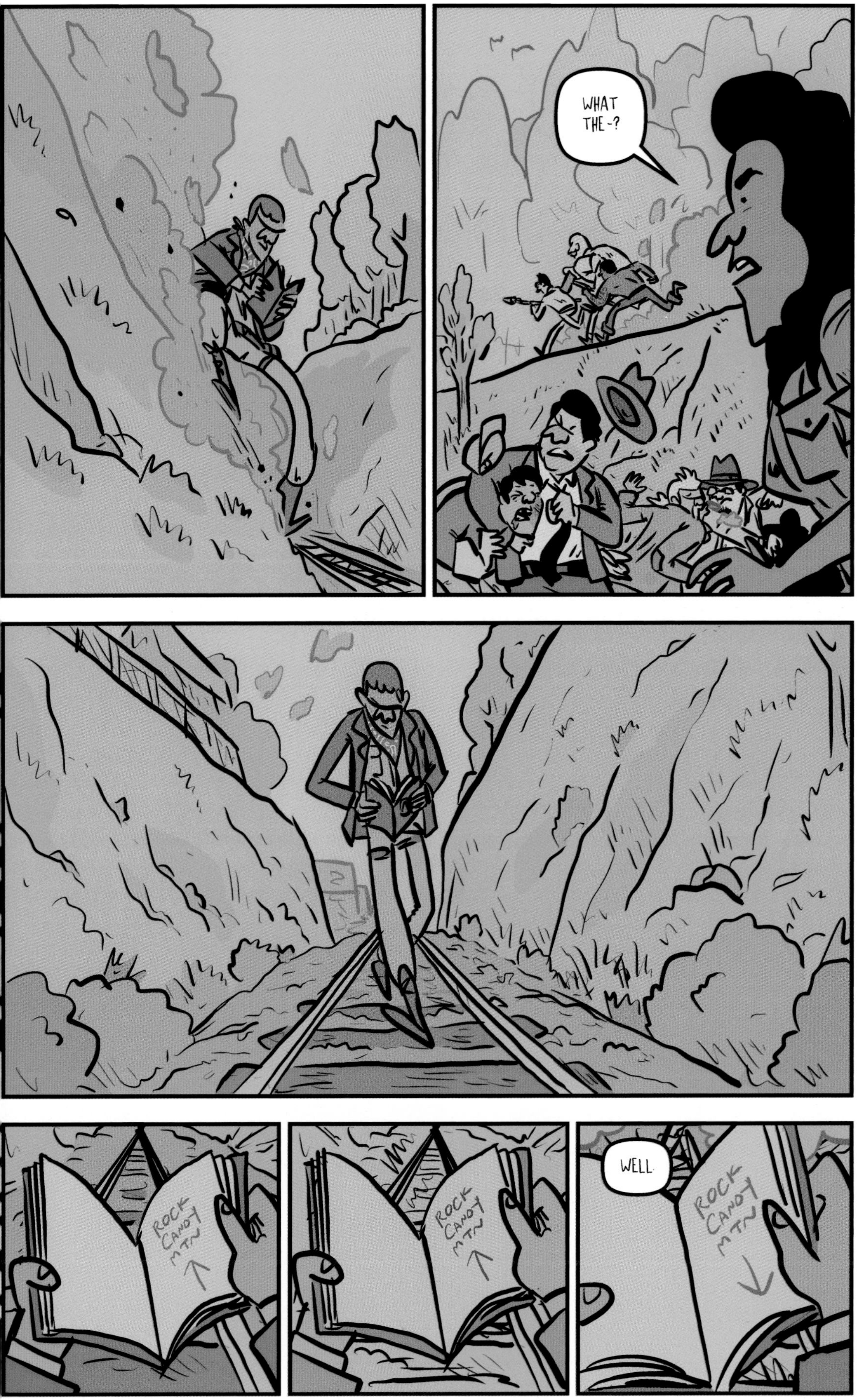
WHAT THE-?
ROCK CANDY MTN
ROCK CANDY MTN
WELL.
ROCK CANDY MTN

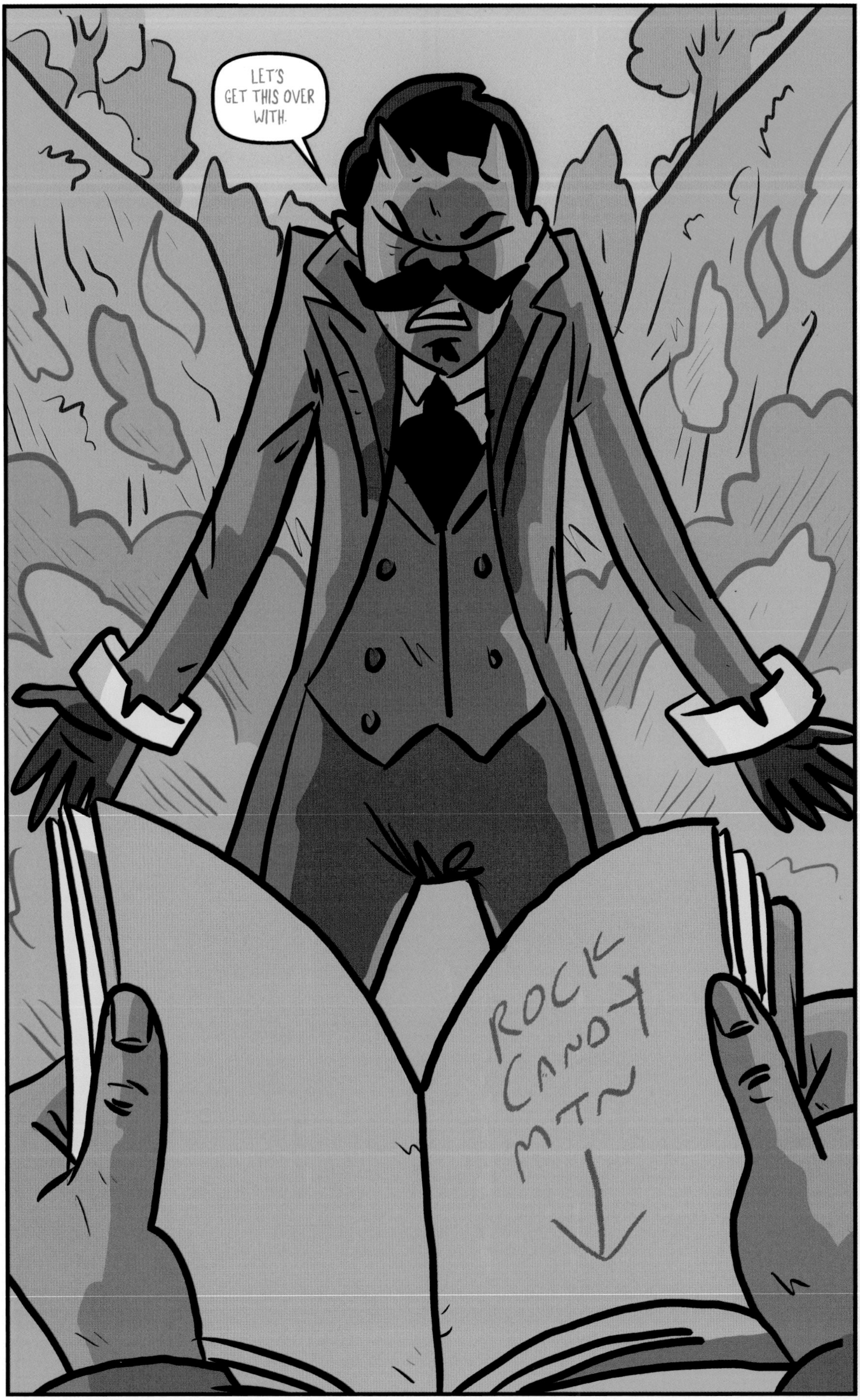
LET'S GET THIS OVER WITH.
ROCK CANDY MTN

## CHAPTER EIGHT

# "I'm bound to go."

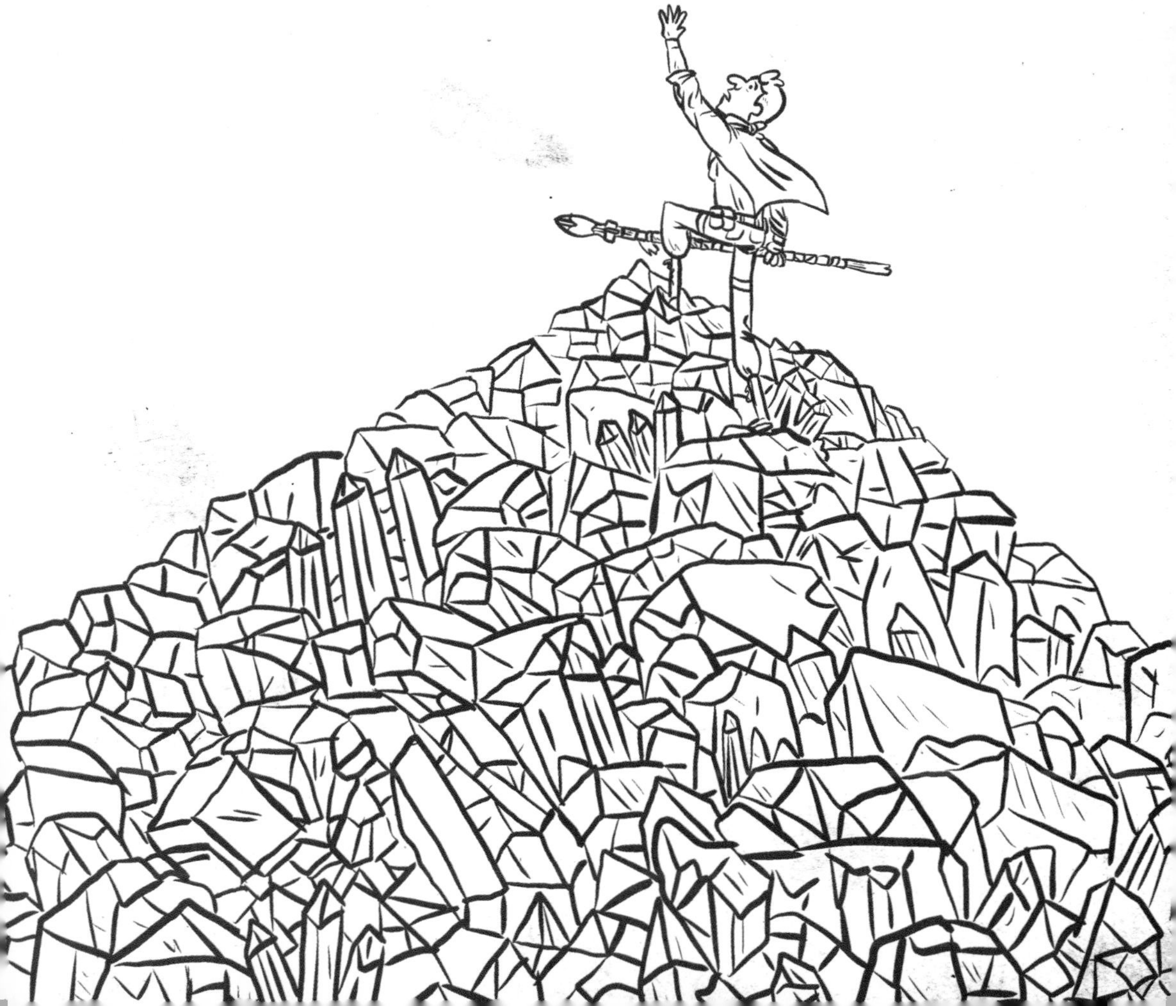

# "sky's the limit."

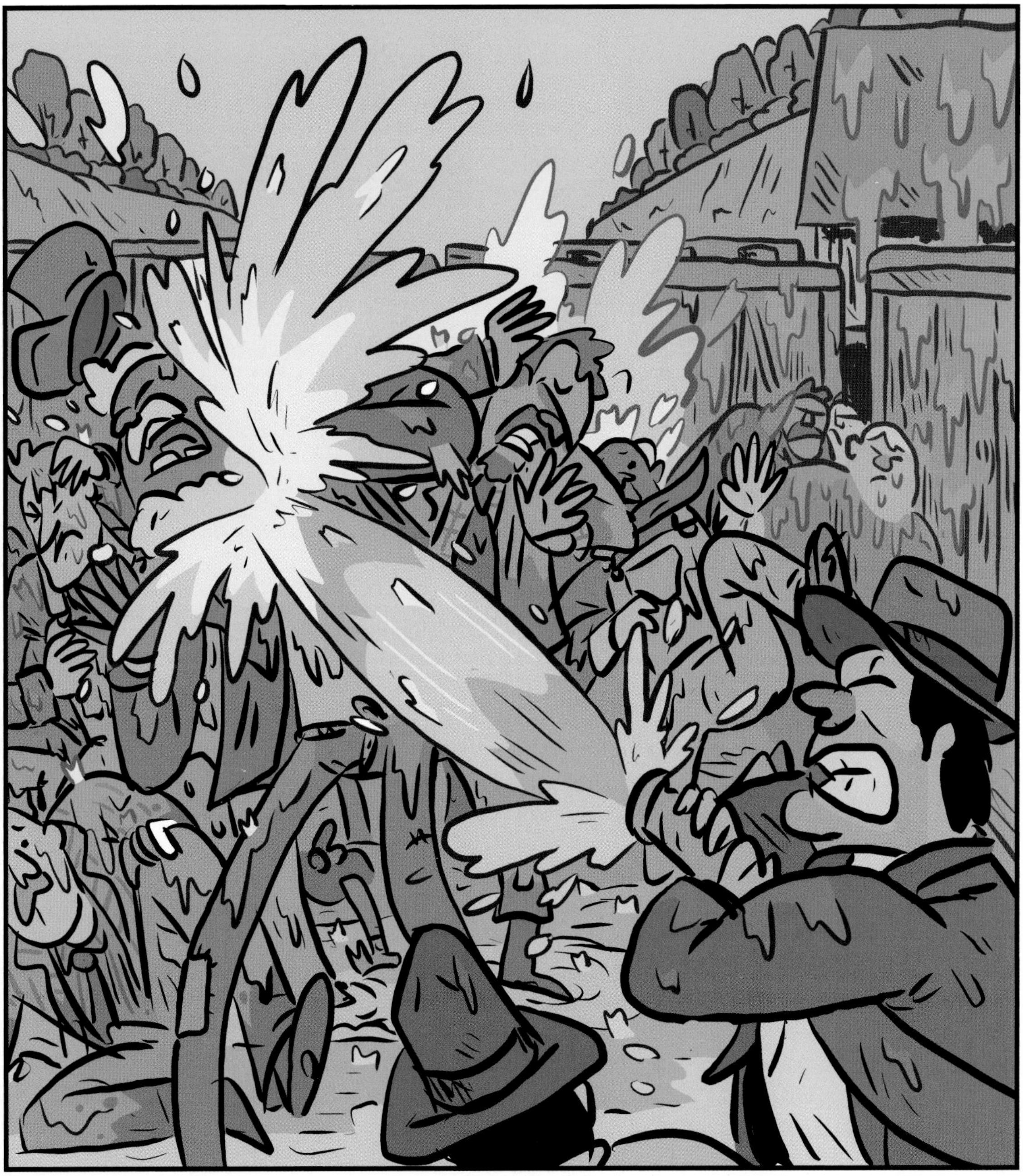

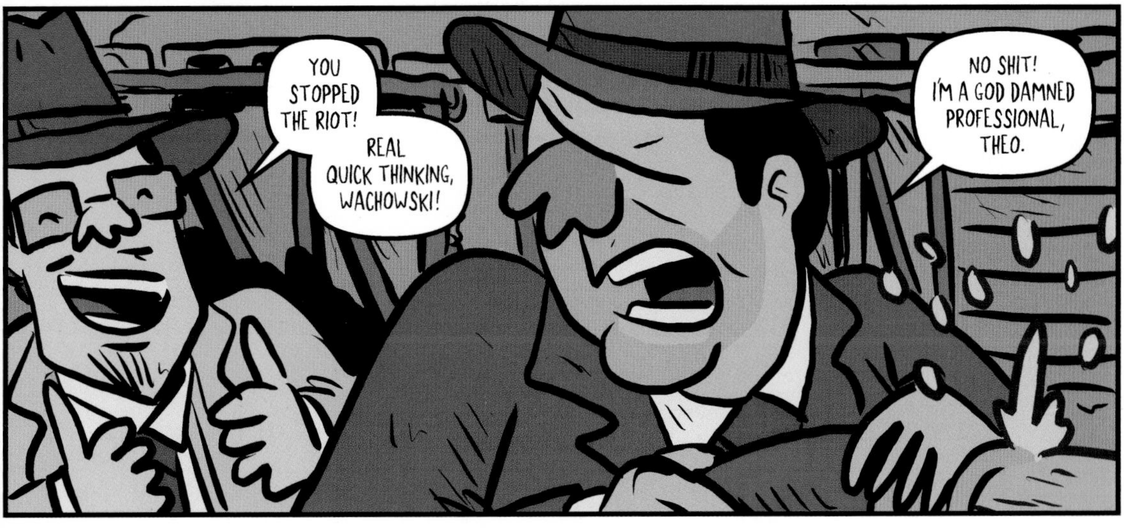
YOU STOPPED THE RIOT!
REAL QUICK THINKING, WACHOWSKI!
NO SHIT! I'M A GOD DAMNED PROFESSIONAL, THEO.

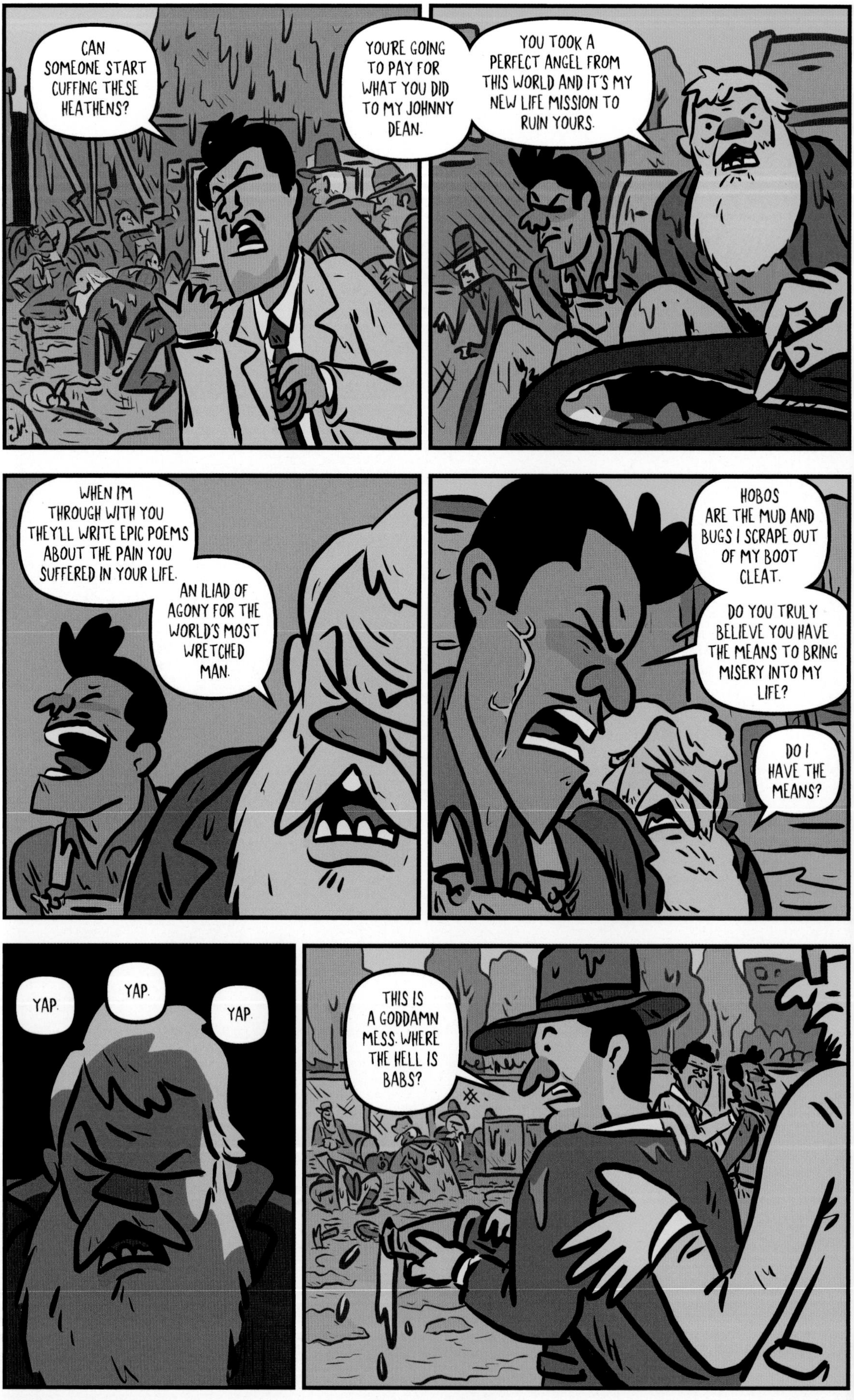
CAN SOMEONE START CUFFING THESE HEATHENS?
YOU'RE GOING TO PAY FOR WHAT YOU DID TO MY JOHNNY DEAN.
YOU TOOK A PERFECT ANGEL FROM THIS WORLD AND IT'S MY NEW LIFE MISSION TO RUIN YOURS.
WHEN I'M THROUGH WITH YOU THEY'LL WRITE EPIC POEMS ABOUT THE PAIN YOU SUFFERED IN YOUR LIFE.
AN ILIAD OF AGONY FOR THE WORLD'S MOST WRETCHED MAN.
HOBOS ARE THE MUD AND BUGS I SCRAPE OUT OF MY BOOT CLEAT.
DO YOU TRULY BELIEVE YOU HAVE THE MEANS TO BRING MISERY INTO MY LIFE?
DO I HAVE THE MEANS?
YAP.
YAP.
YAP.
THIS IS A GODDAMN MESS. WHERE THE HELL IS BABS?

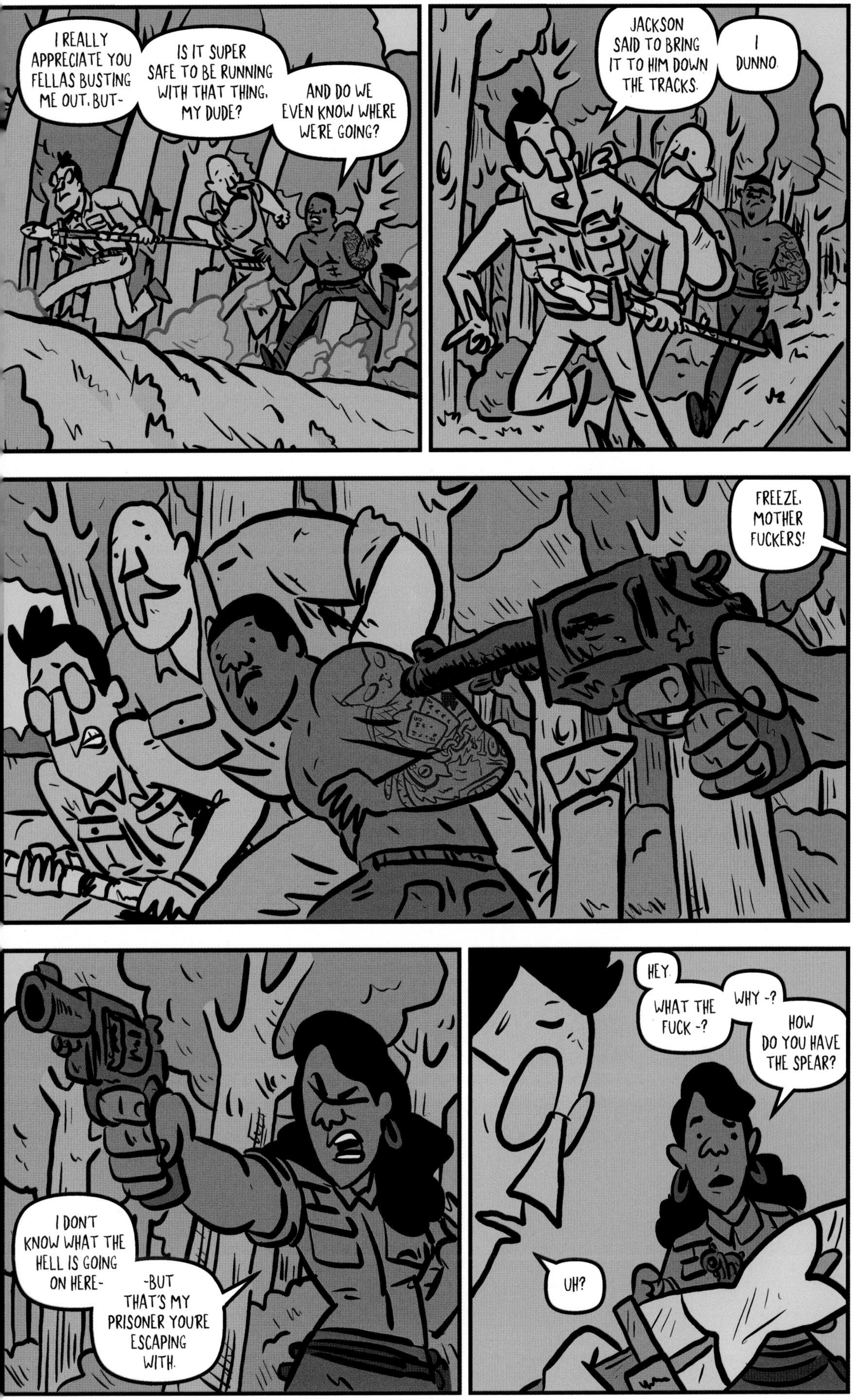
I REALLY APPRECIATE YOU FELLAS BUSTING ME OUT, BUT-
IS IT SUPER SAFE TO BE RUNNING WITH THAT THING, MY DUDE?
AND DO WE EVEN KNOW WHERE WE'RE GOING?
JACKSON SAID TO BRING IT TO HIM DOWN THE TRACKS.
I DUNNO.
FREEZE, MOTHER FUCKERS!
I DON'T KNOW WHAT THE HELL IS GOING ON HERE-
-BUT THAT'S MY PRISONER YOU'RE ESCAPING WITH.
HEY.
WHAT THE FUCK -?
WHY -?
HOW DO YOU HAVE THE SPEAR?
UH?

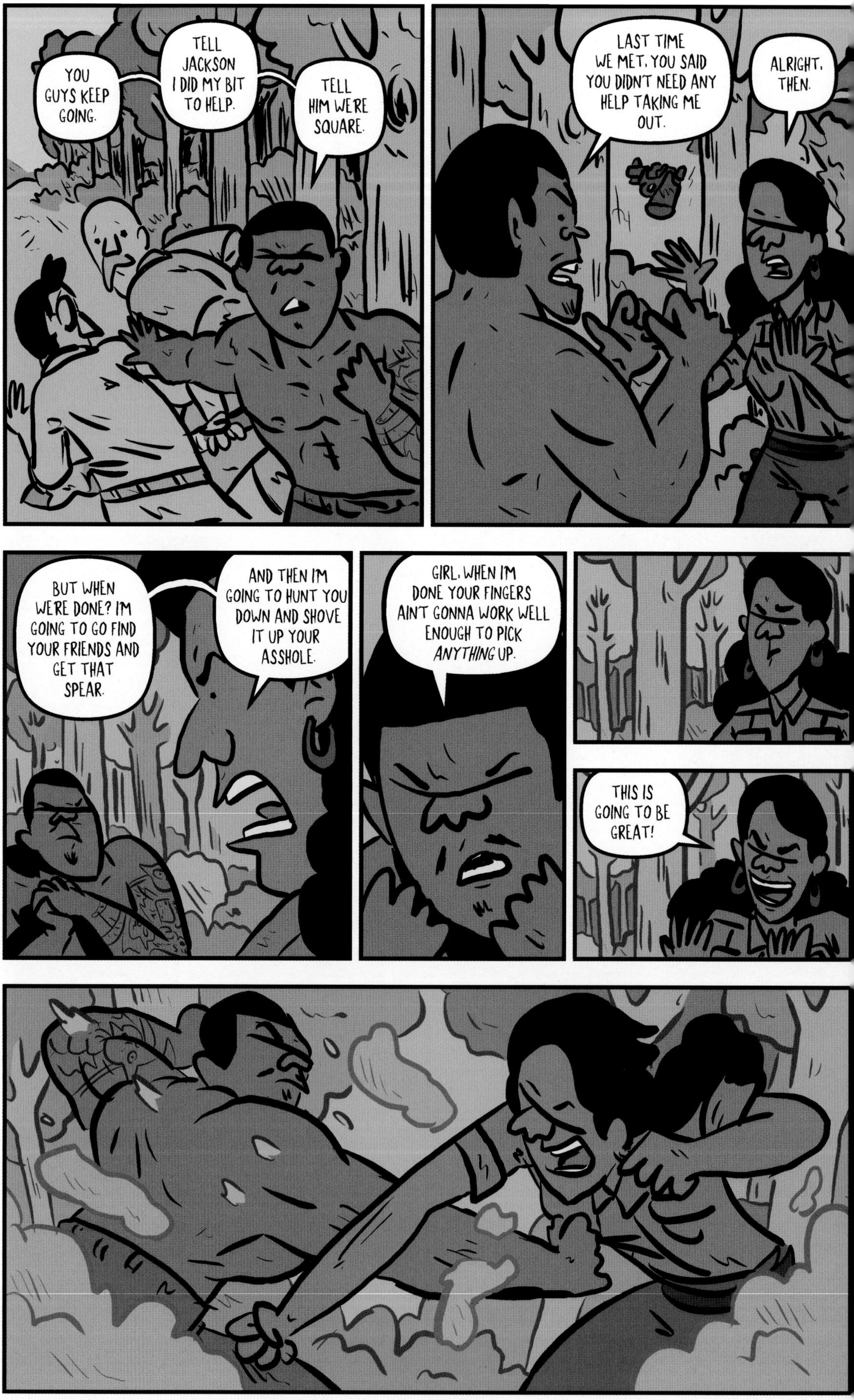

YOU GUYS KEEP GOING.
TELL JACKSON I DID MY BIT TO HELP.
TELL HIM WE'RE SQUARE.
LAST TIME WE MET, YOU SAID YOU DIDN'T NEED ANY HELP TAKING ME OUT.
ALRIGHT, THEN.
BUT WHEN WE'RE DONE? I'M GOING TO GO FIND YOUR FRIENDS AND GET THAT SPEAR.
AND THEN I'M GOING TO HUNT YOU DOWN AND SHOVE IT UP YOUR ASSHOLE.
GIRL, WHEN I'M DONE YOUR FINGERS AIN'T GONNA WORK WELL ENOUGH TO PICK *ANYTHING* UP.
THIS IS GOING TO BE GREAT!

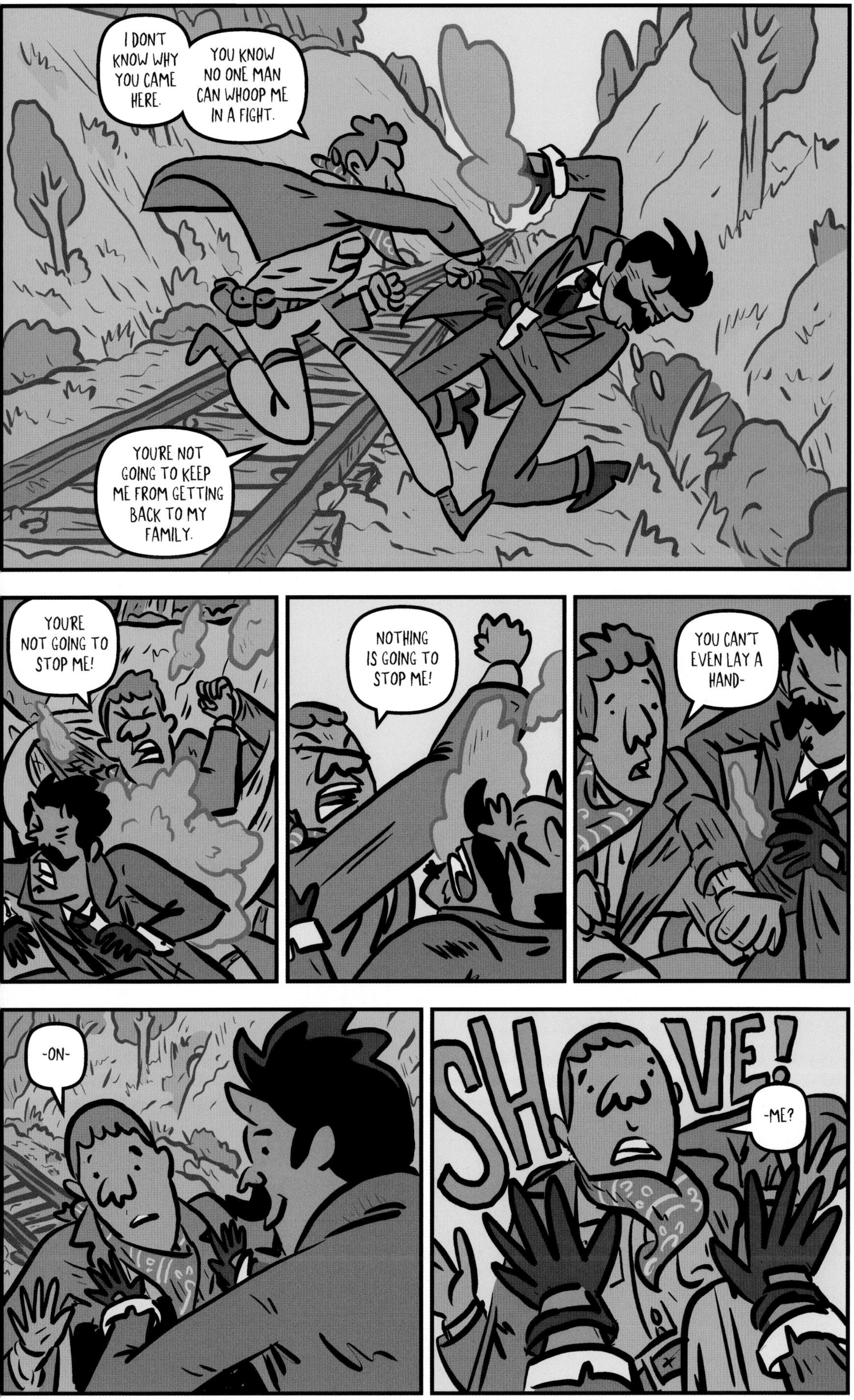
I DON'T KNOW WHY YOU CAME HERE.
YOU KNOW NO ONE MAN CAN WHOOP ME IN A FIGHT.
YOU'RE NOT GOING TO KEEP ME FROM GETTING BACK TO MY FAMILY.
YOU'RE NOT GOING TO STOP ME!
NOTHING IS GOING TO STOP ME!
YOU CAN'T EVEN LAY A HAND-
-ON-
SHOVE!
-ME?

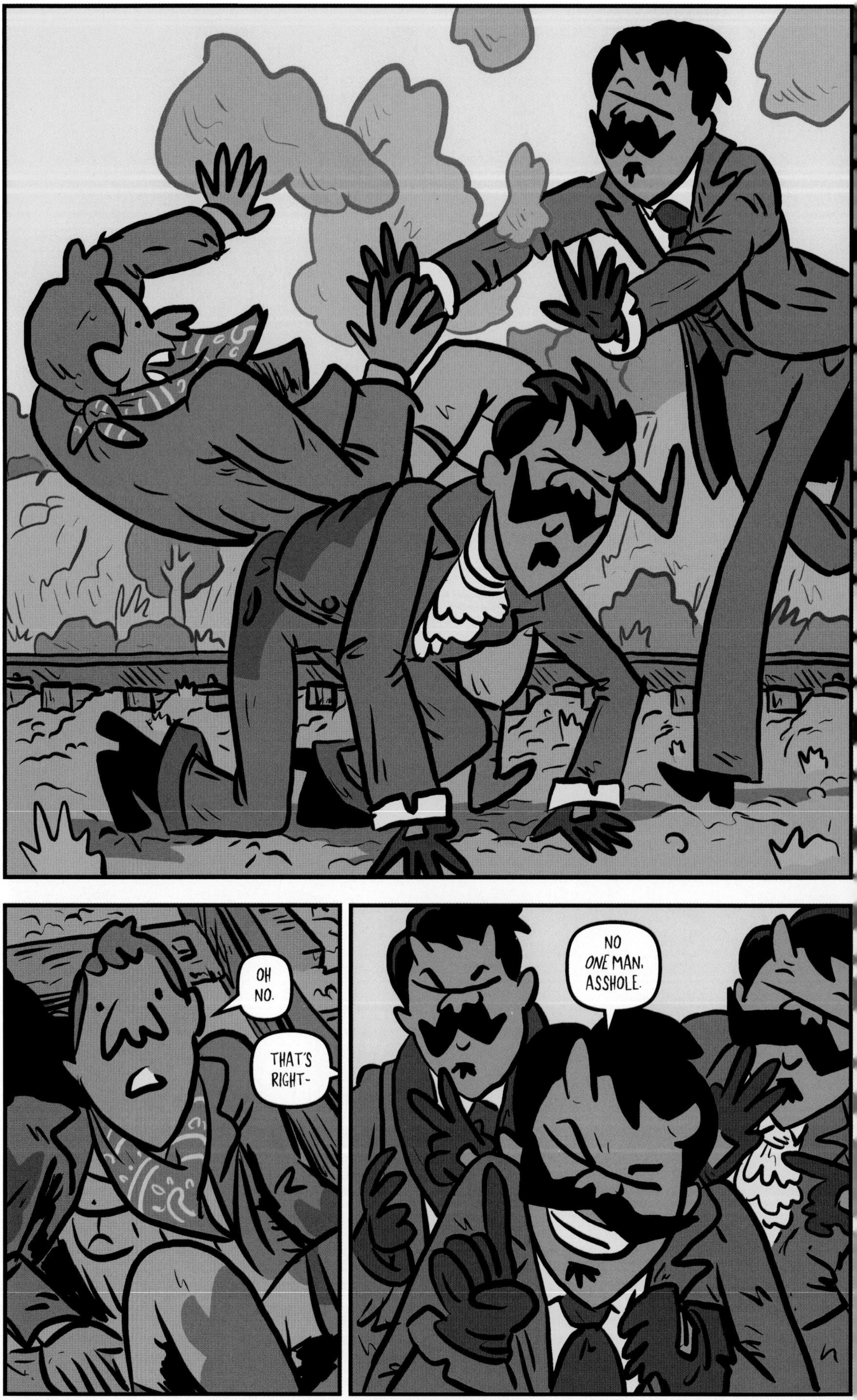
OH NO.
THAT'S RIGHT-
NO ONE MAN, ASSHOLE.

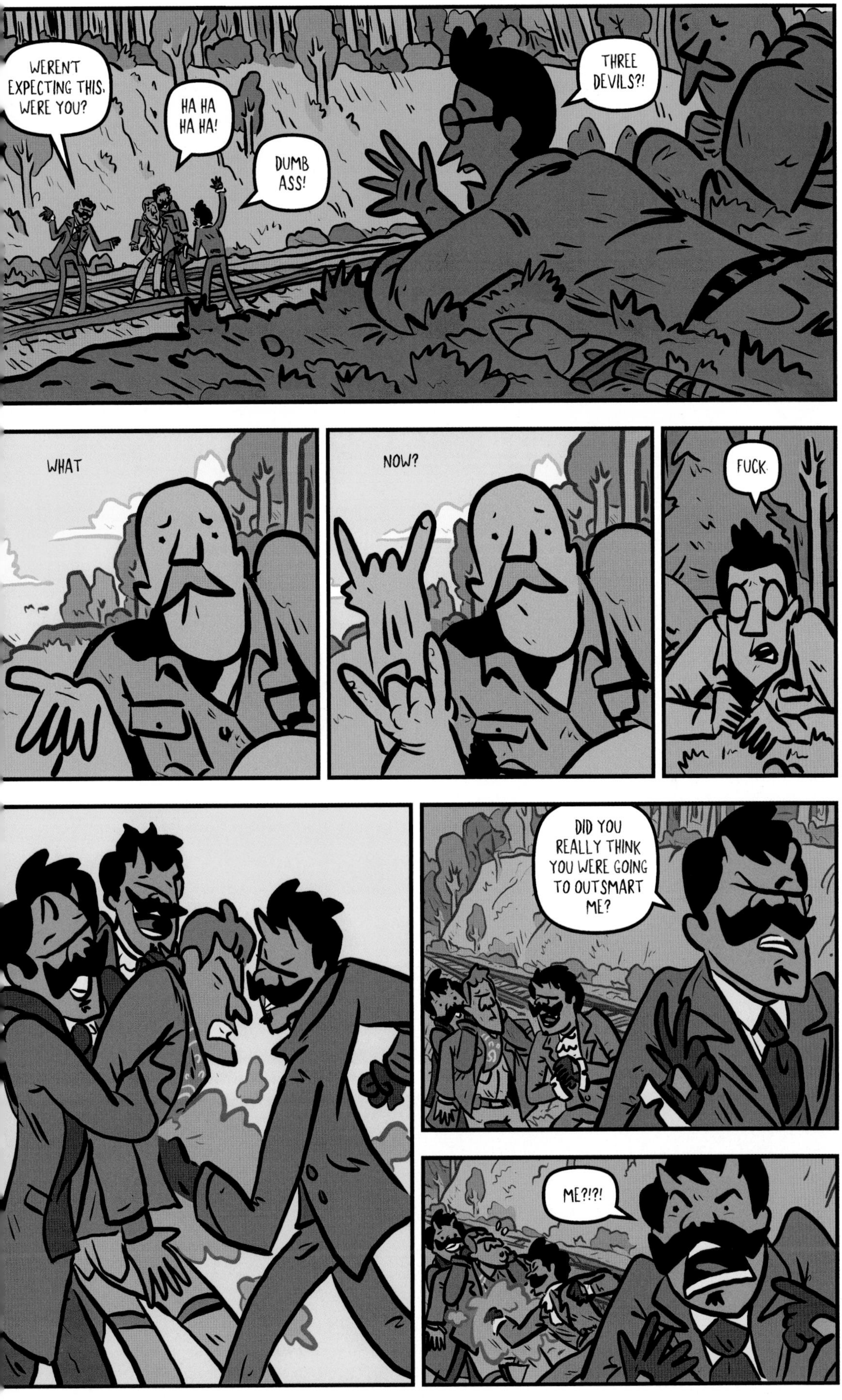
WERENT EXPECTING THIS, WERE YOU?
HA HA HA HA!
DUMB ASS!
THREE DEVILS?!
WHAT
NOW?
FUCK.
DID YOU REALLY THINK YOU WERE GOING TO OUTSMART ME?
ME?!?!

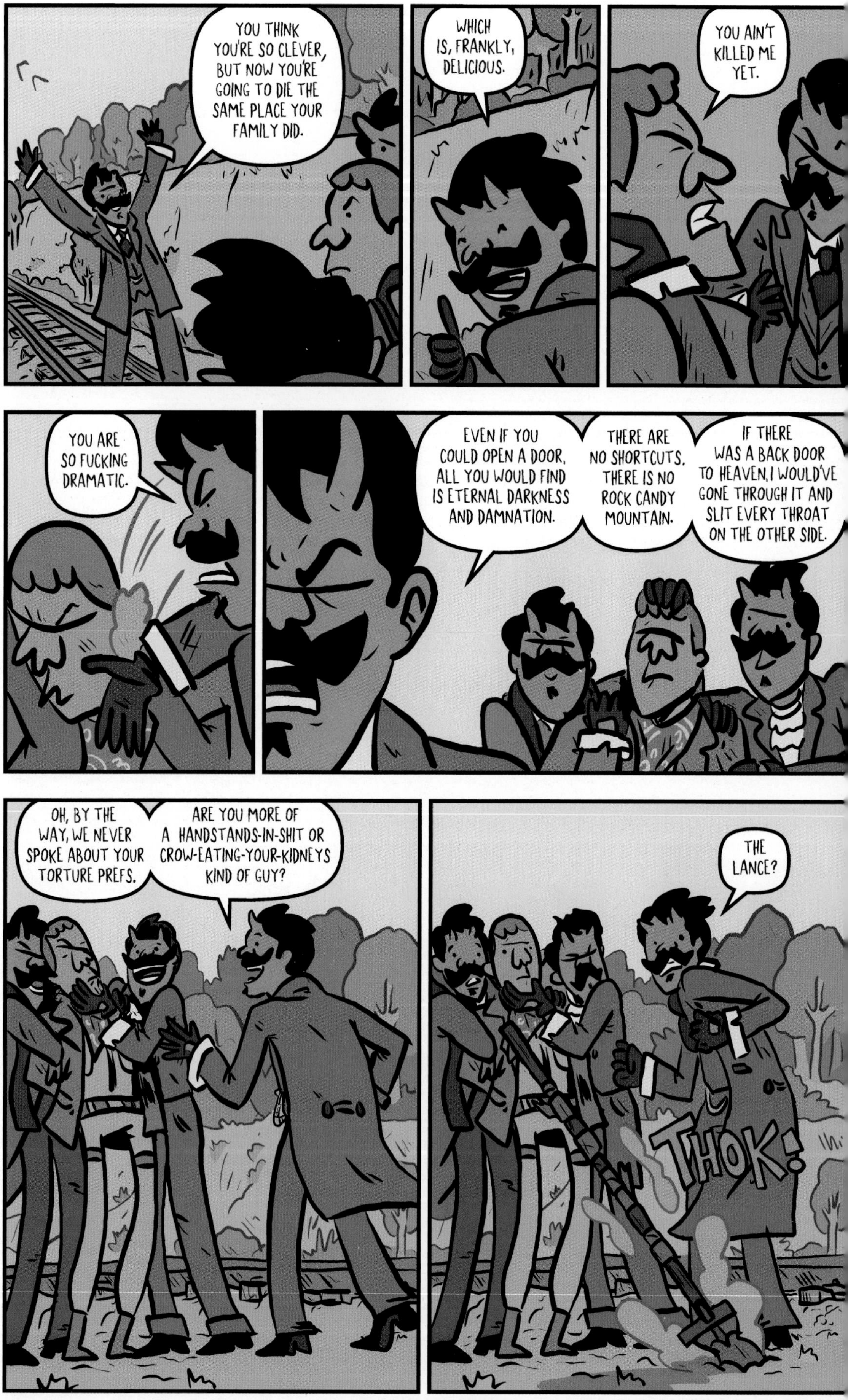
YOU THINK YOU'RE SO CLEVER, BUT NOW YOU'RE GOING TO DIE THE SAME PLACE YOUR FAMILY DID.
WHICH IS, FRANKLY, DELICIOUS.
YOU AIN'T KILLED ME YET.
YOU ARE SO FUCKING DRAMATIC.
EVEN IF YOU COULD OPEN A DOOR, ALL YOU WOULD FIND IS ETERNAL DARKNESS AND DAMNATION.
THERE ARE NO SHORTCUTS. THERE IS NO ROCK CANDY MOUNTAIN.
IF THERE WAS A BACK DOOR TO HEAVEN, I WOULD'VE GONE THROUGH IT AND SLIT EVERY THROAT ON THE OTHER SIDE.
OH, BY THE WAY, WE NEVER SPOKE ABOUT YOUR TORTURE PREFS.
ARE YOU MORE OF A HANDSTANDS-IN-SHIT OR CROW-EATING-YOUR-KIDNEYS KIND OF GUY?
THE LANCE?
THOK!

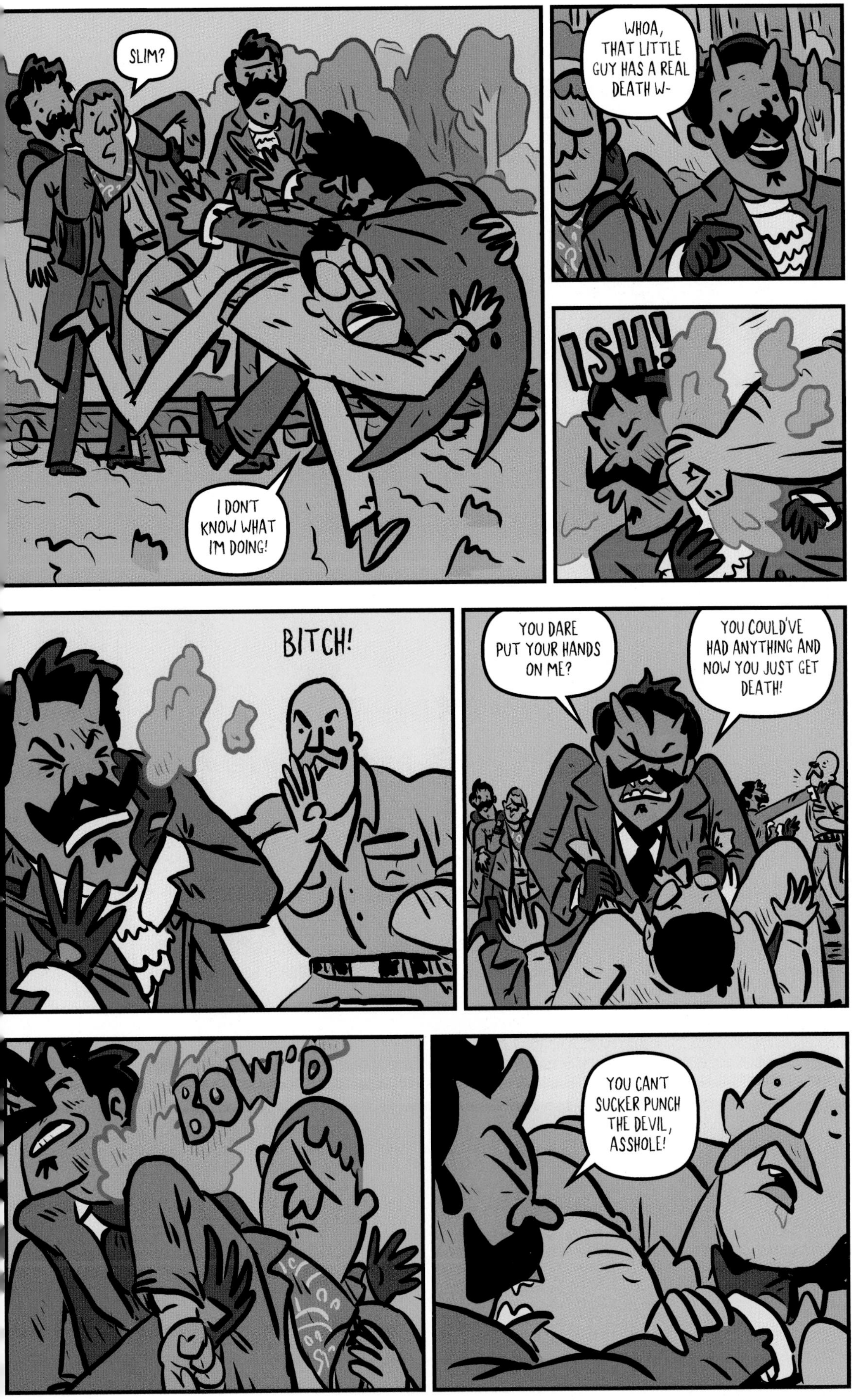
SLIM?
I DON'T KNOW WHAT I'M DOING!
WHOA, THAT LITTLE GUY HAS A REAL DEATH W-
ISH!
BITCH!
YOU DARE PUT YOUR HANDS ON ME?
YOU COULD'VE HAD ANYTHING AND NOW YOU JUST GET DEATH!
BOW'D
YOU CAN'T SUCKER PUNCH THE DEVIL, ASSHOLE!

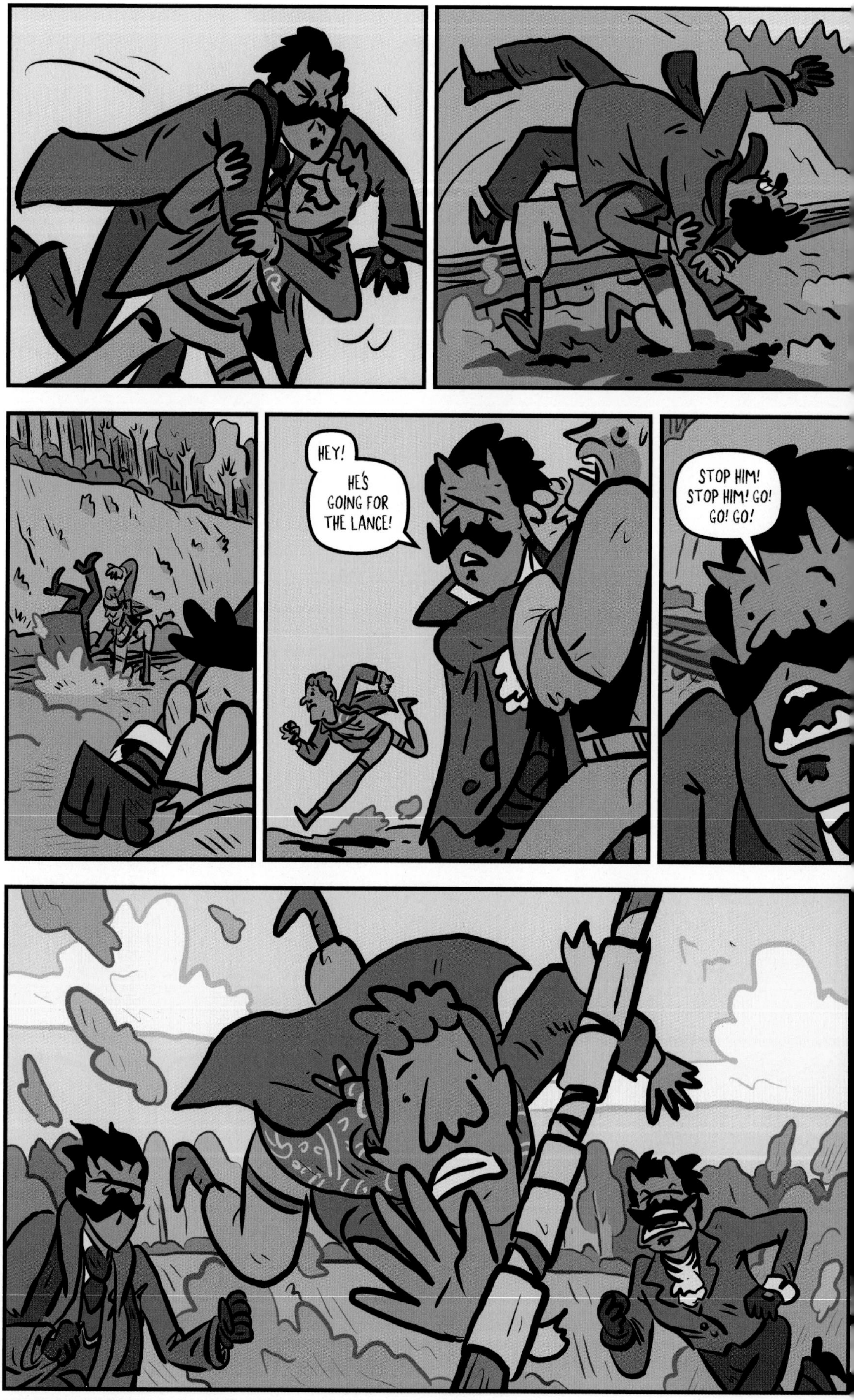
HEY!
HE'S GOING FOR THE LANCE!
STOP HIM! STOP HIM! GO! GO! GO!

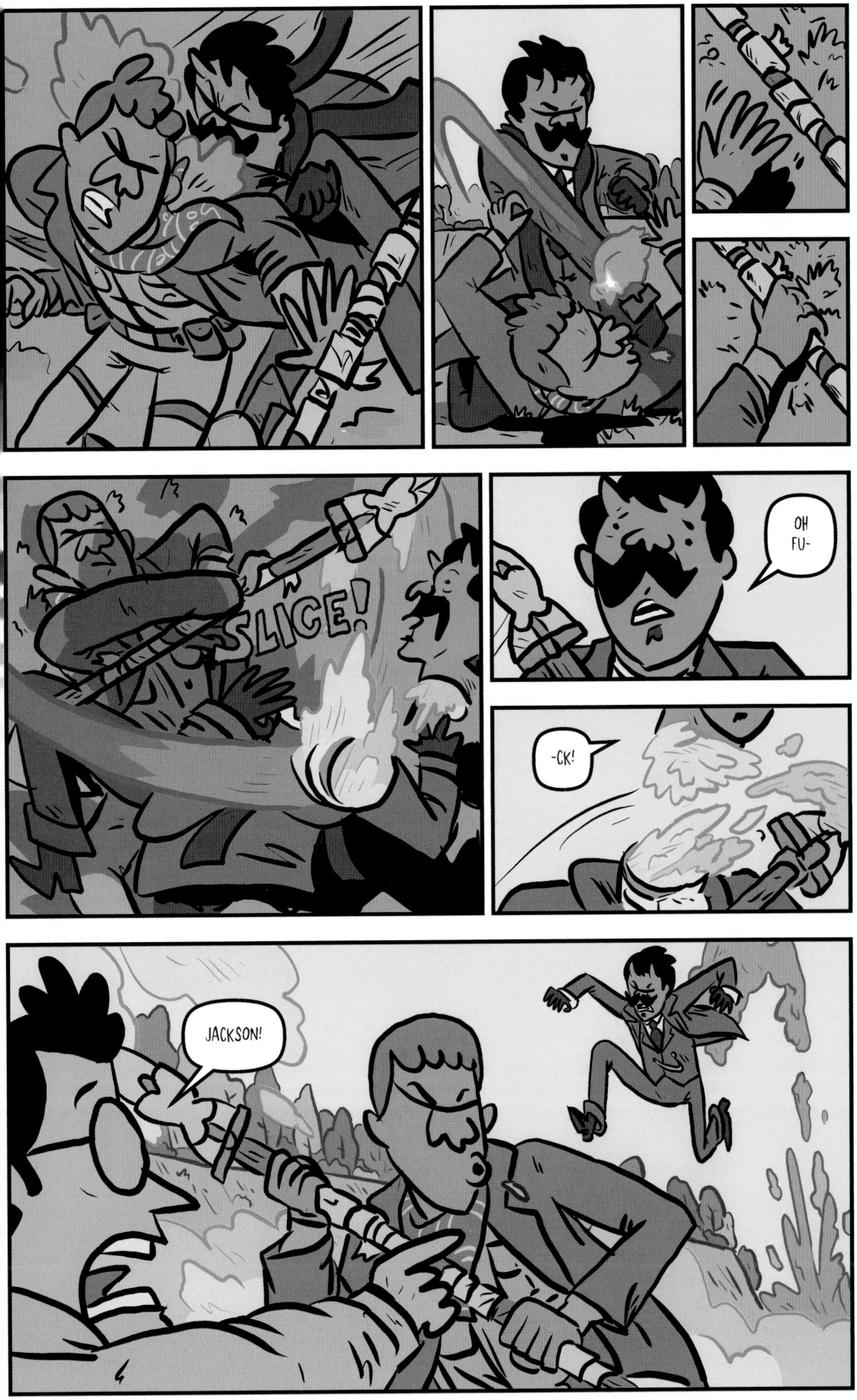
SLICE!
OH FU-
-CK!
JACKSON!

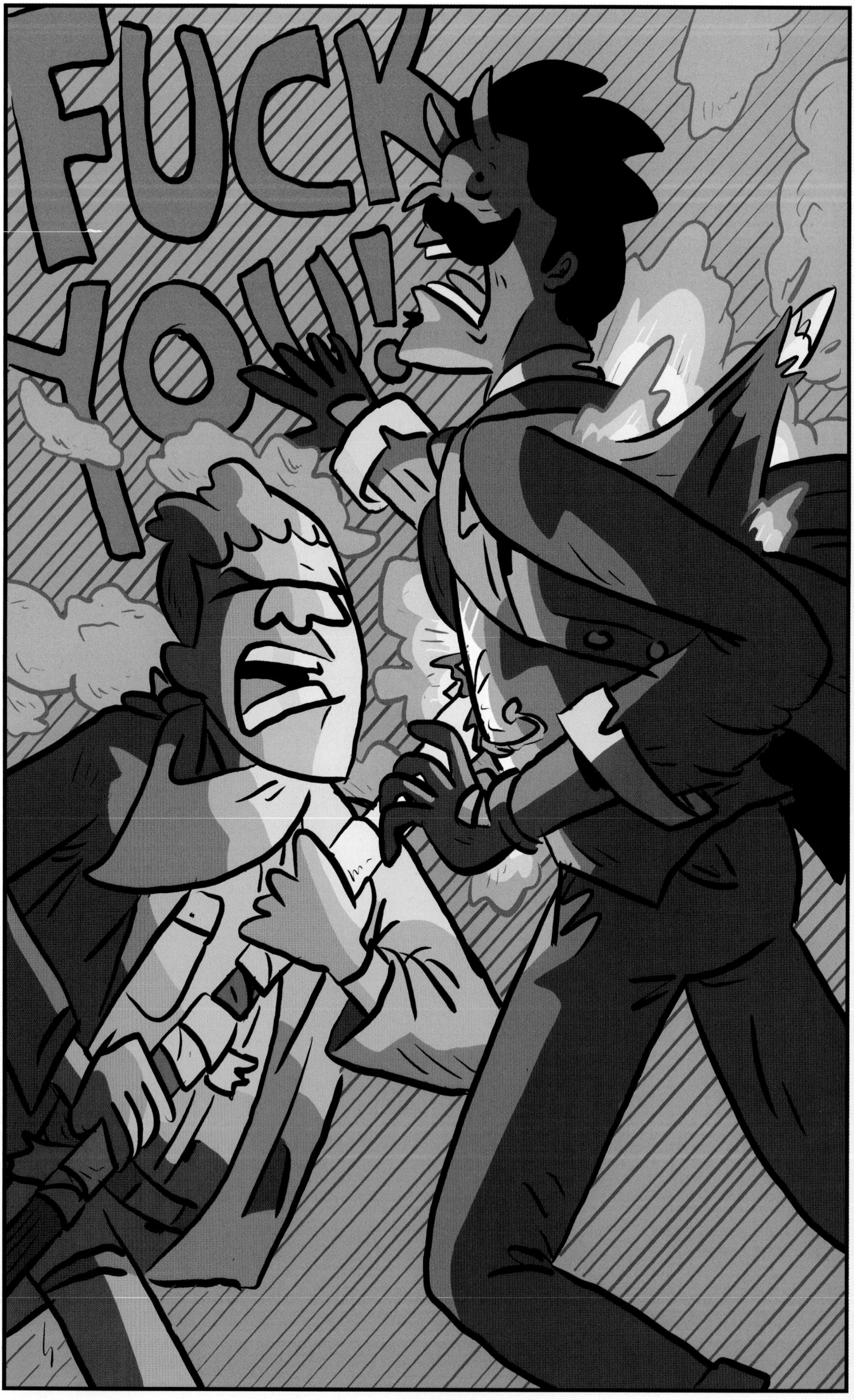
FUCK YOU!!!

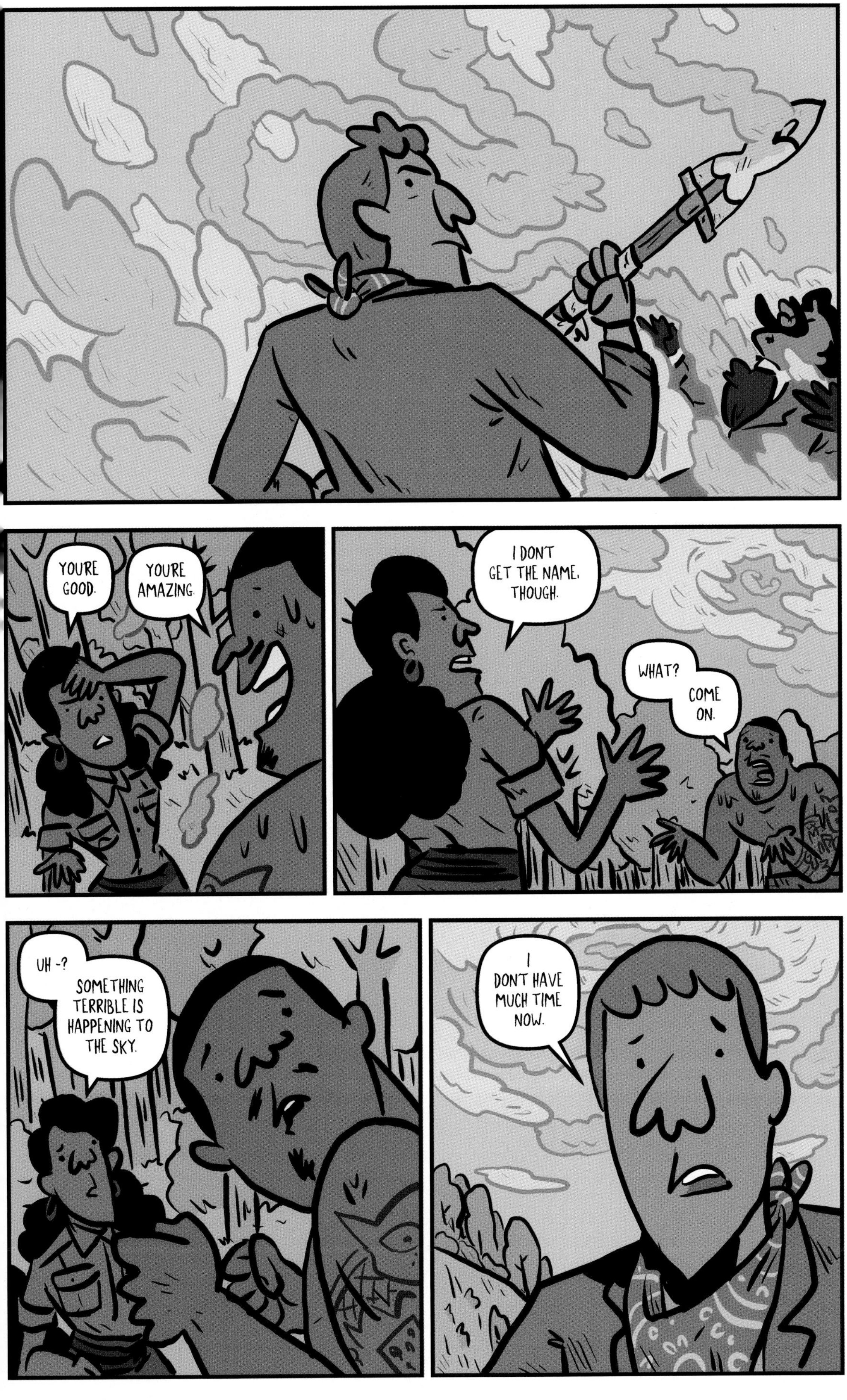
YOU'RE GOOD.
YOU'RE AMAZING.
I DON'T GET THE NAME, THOUGH.
WHAT?
COME ON.
UH -?
SOMETHING TERRIBLE IS HAPPENING TO THE SKY.
I DON'T HAVE MUCH TIME NOW.

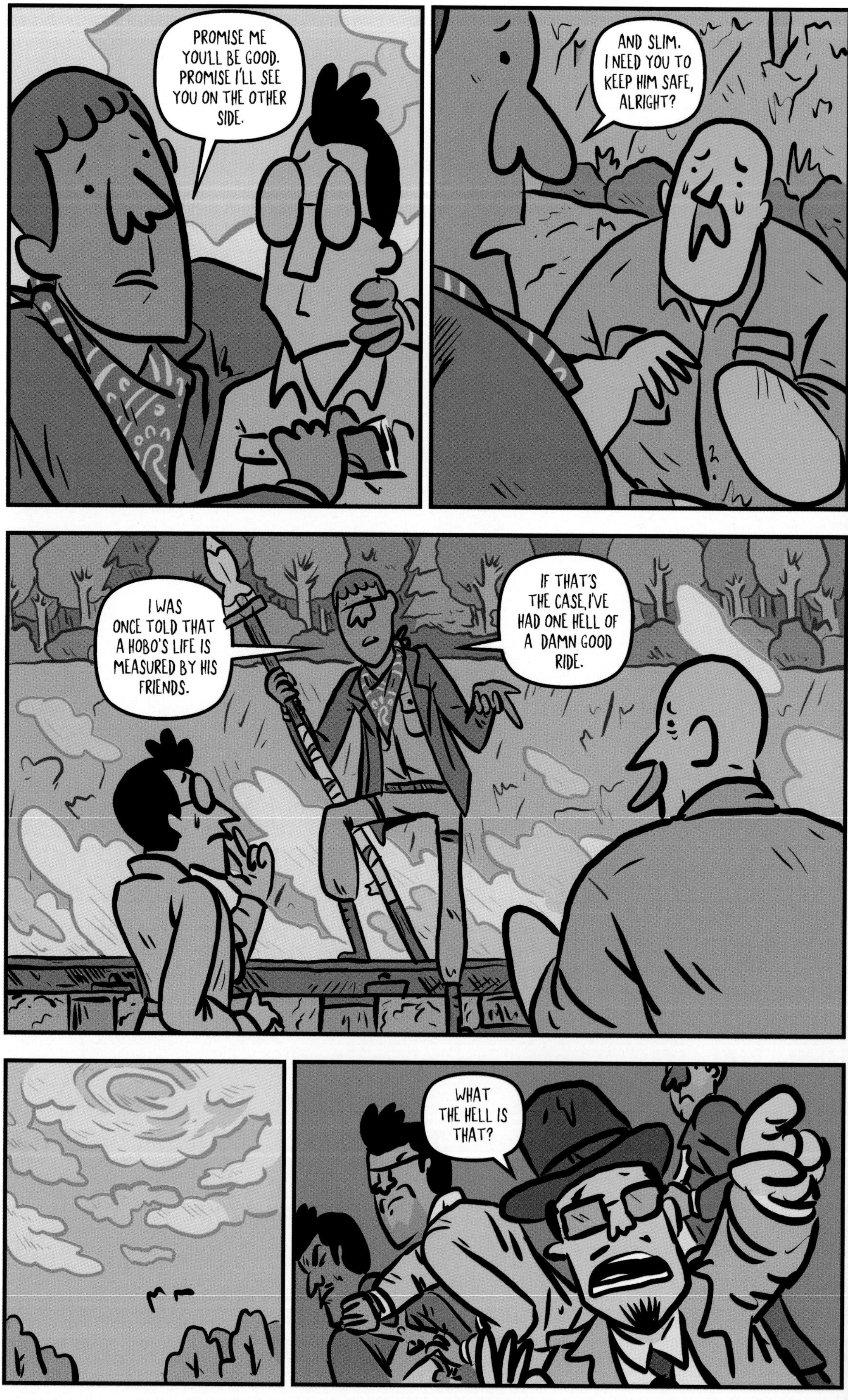
PROMISE ME YOU'LL BE GOOD. PROMISE I'LL SEE YOU ON THE OTHER SIDE.
AND SLIM. I NEED YOU TO KEEP HIM SAFE, ALRIGHT?
I WAS ONCE TOLD THAT A HOBO'S LIFE IS MEASURED BY HIS FRIENDS.
IF THAT'S THE CASE, I'VE HAD ONE HELL OF A DAMN GOOD RIDE.
WHAT THE HELL IS THAT?

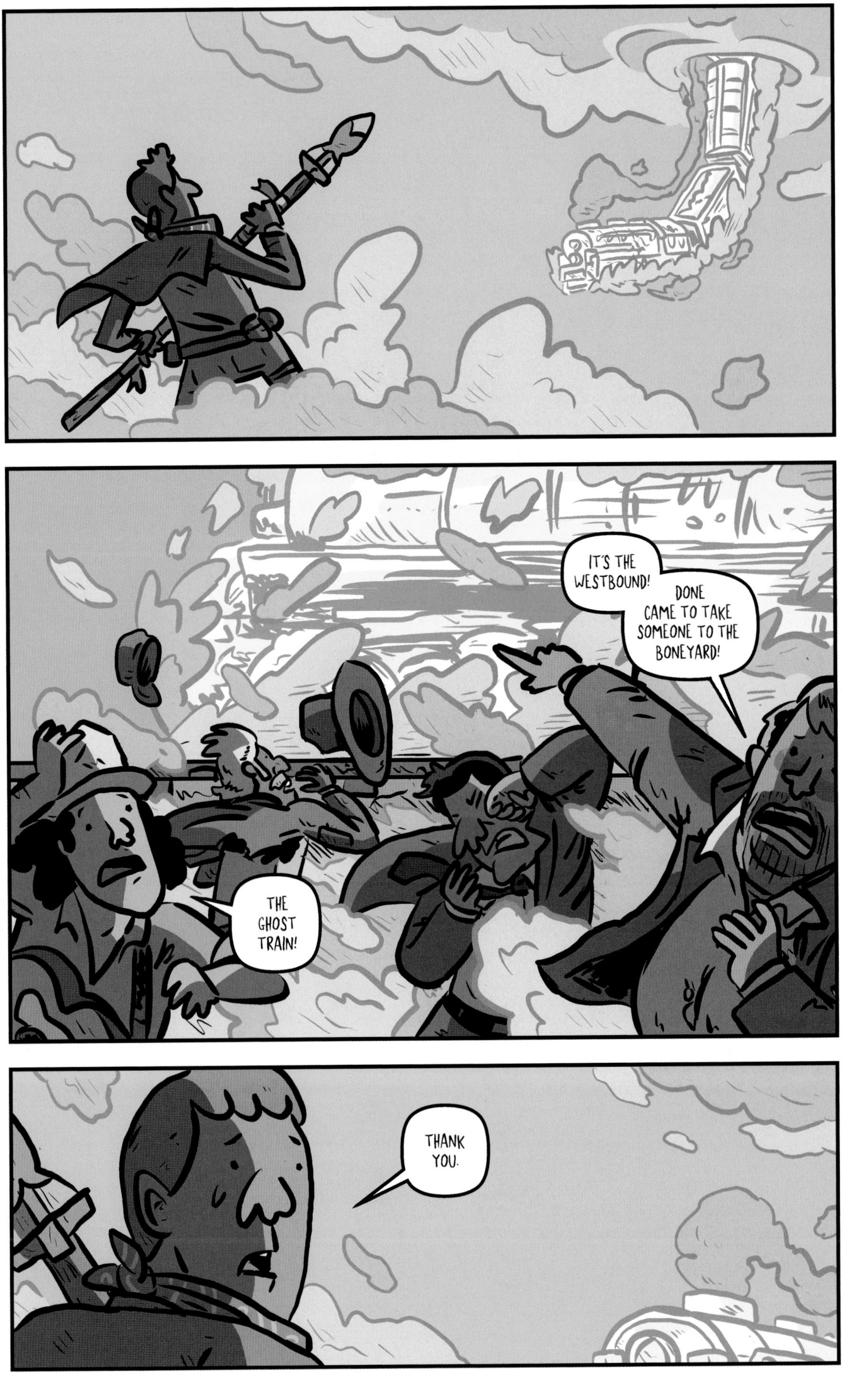
IT'S THE WESTBOUND!
DONE CAME TO TAKE SOMEONE TO THE BONEYARD!
THE GHOST TRAIN!
THANK YOU.

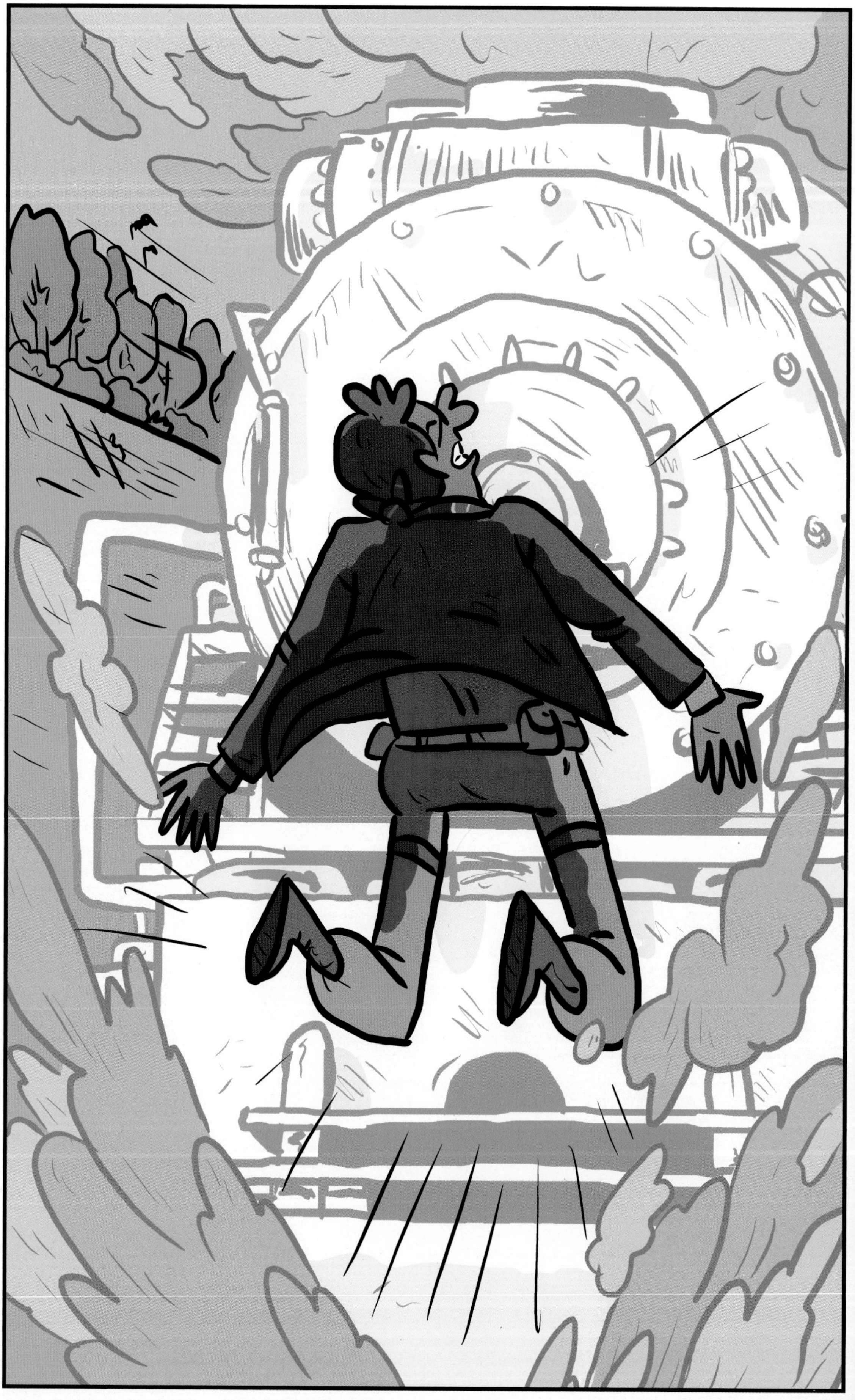

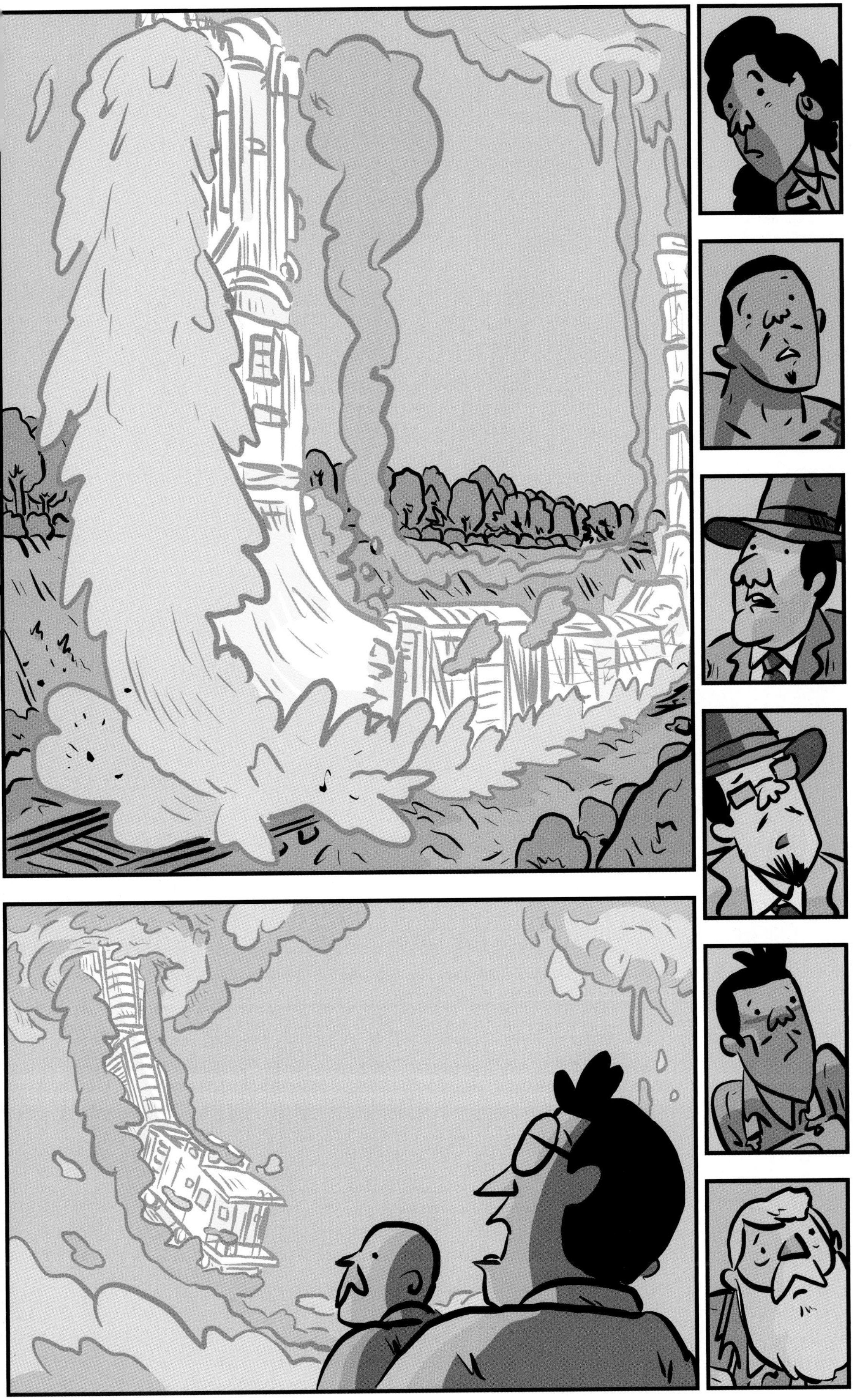

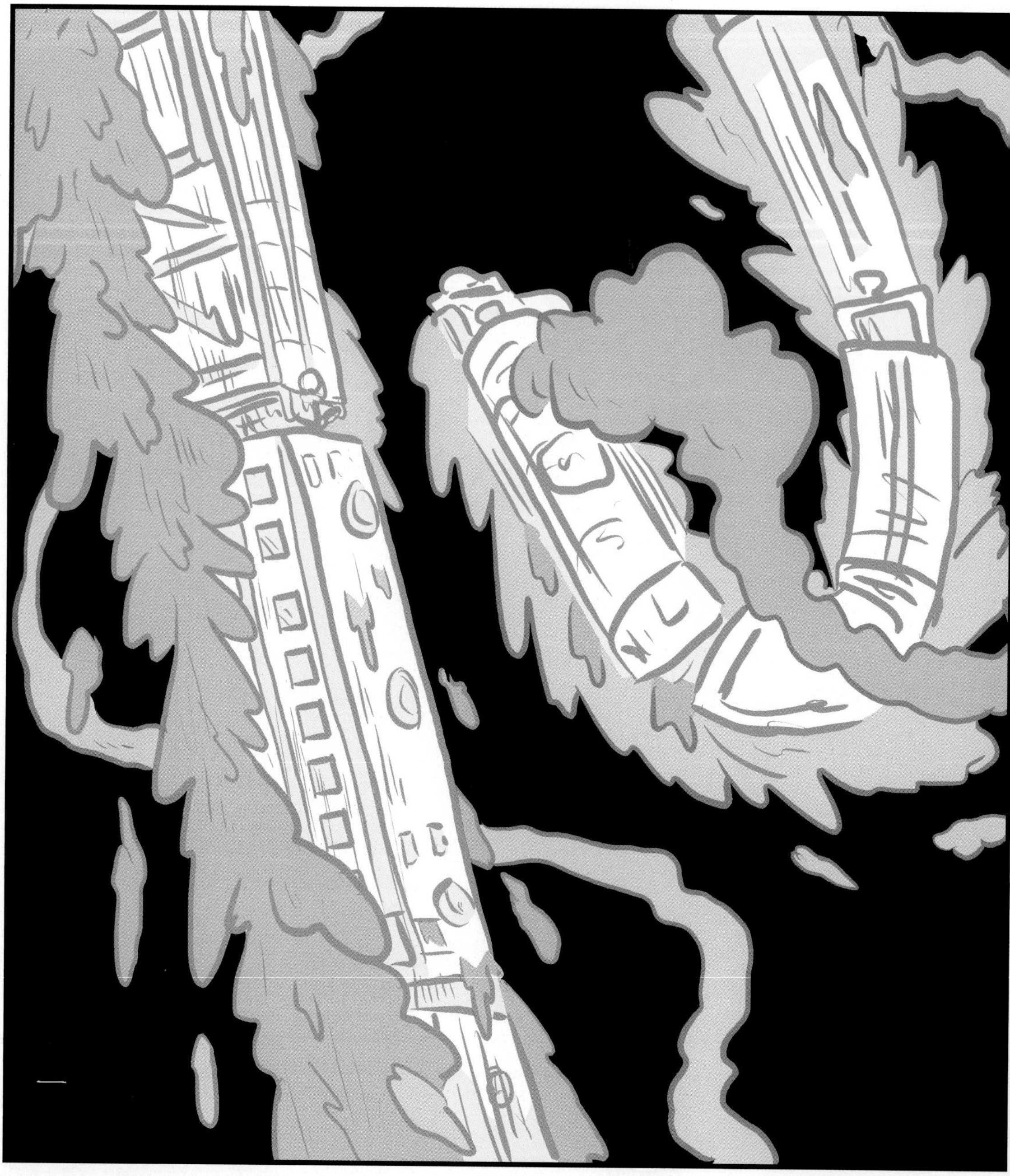

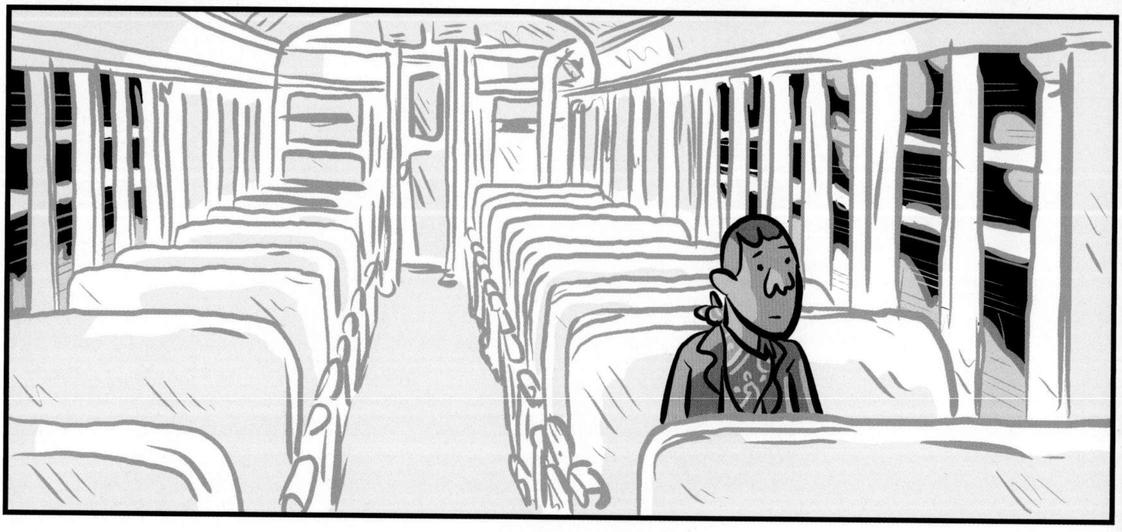

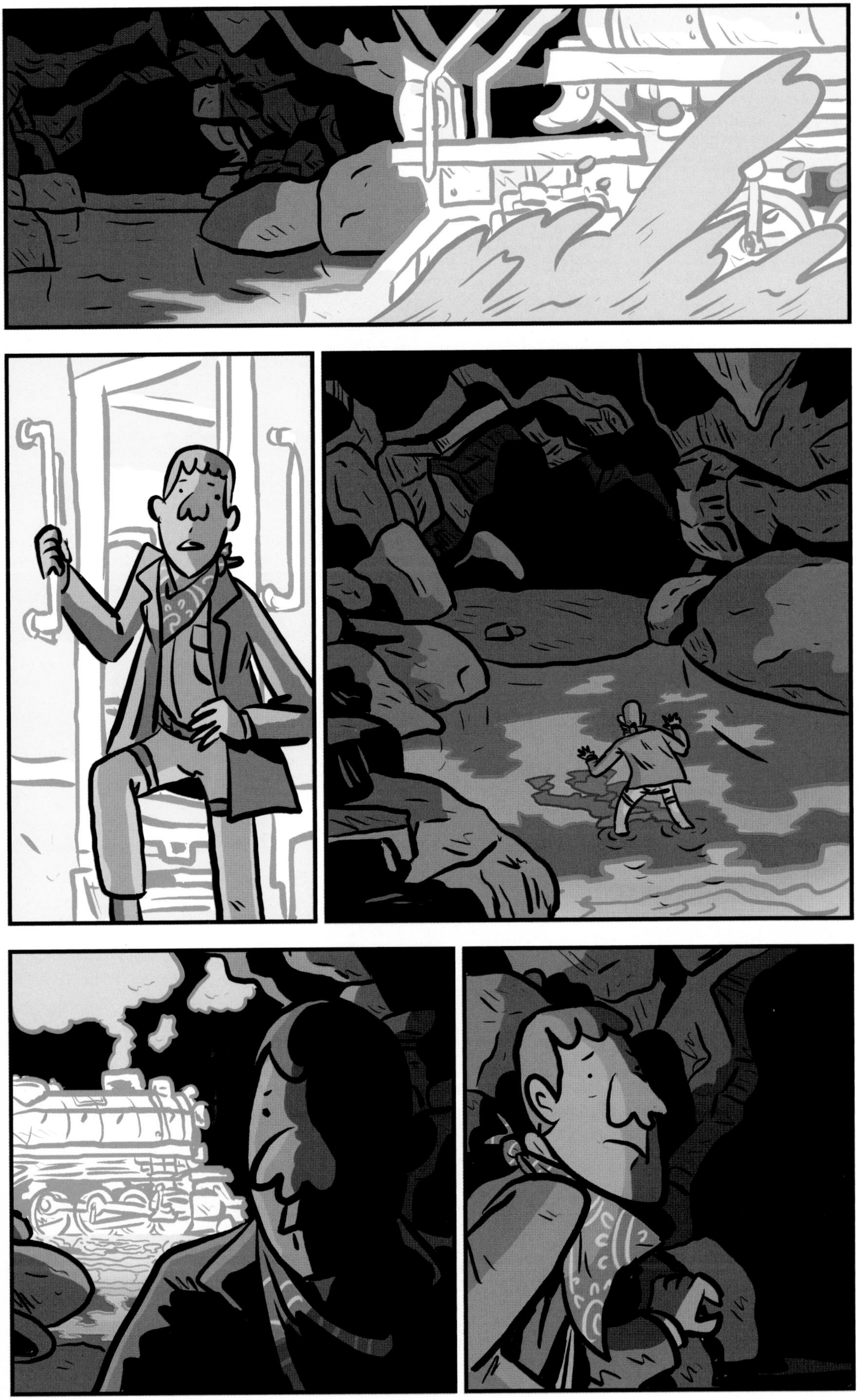

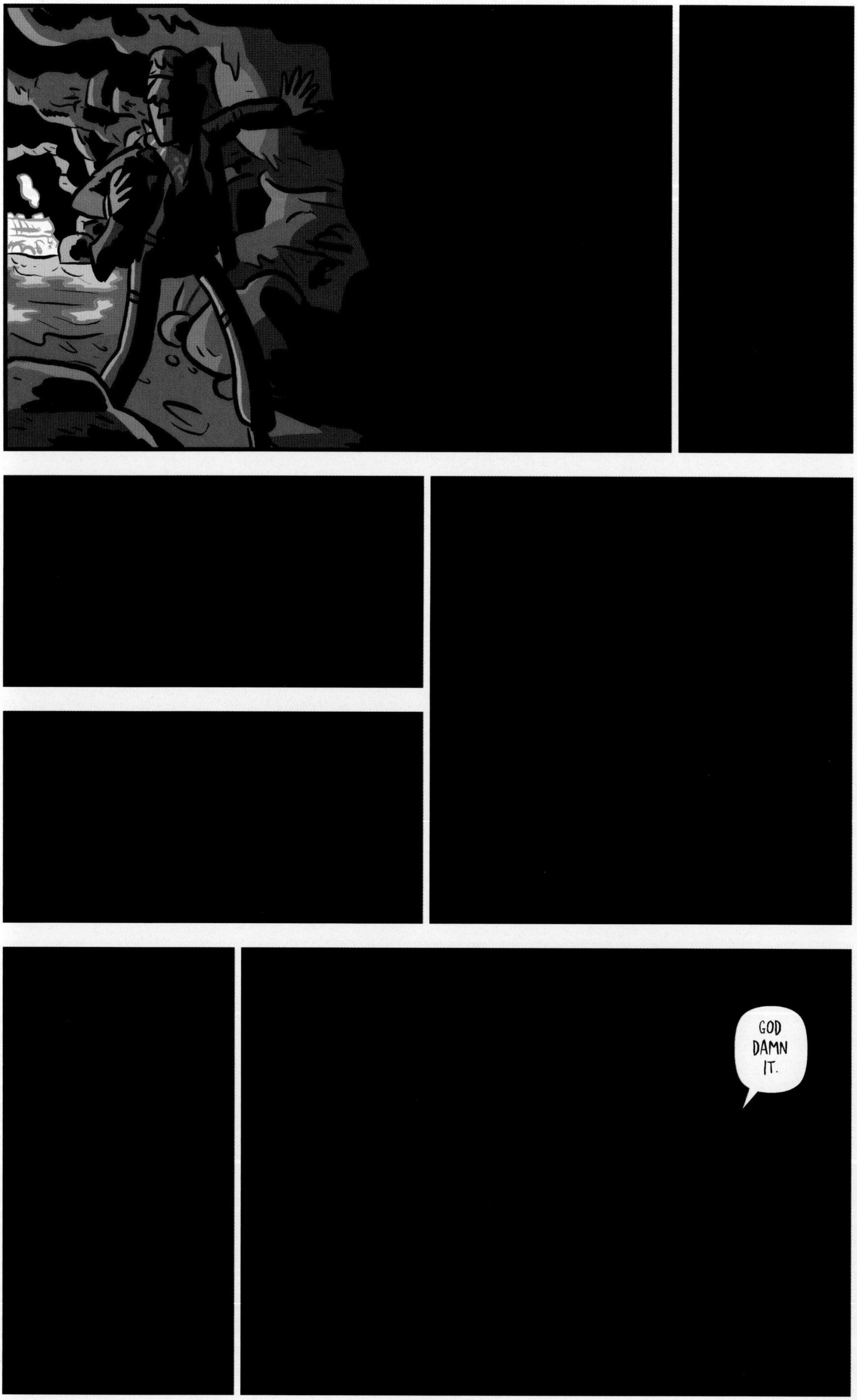
GOD DAMN IT.

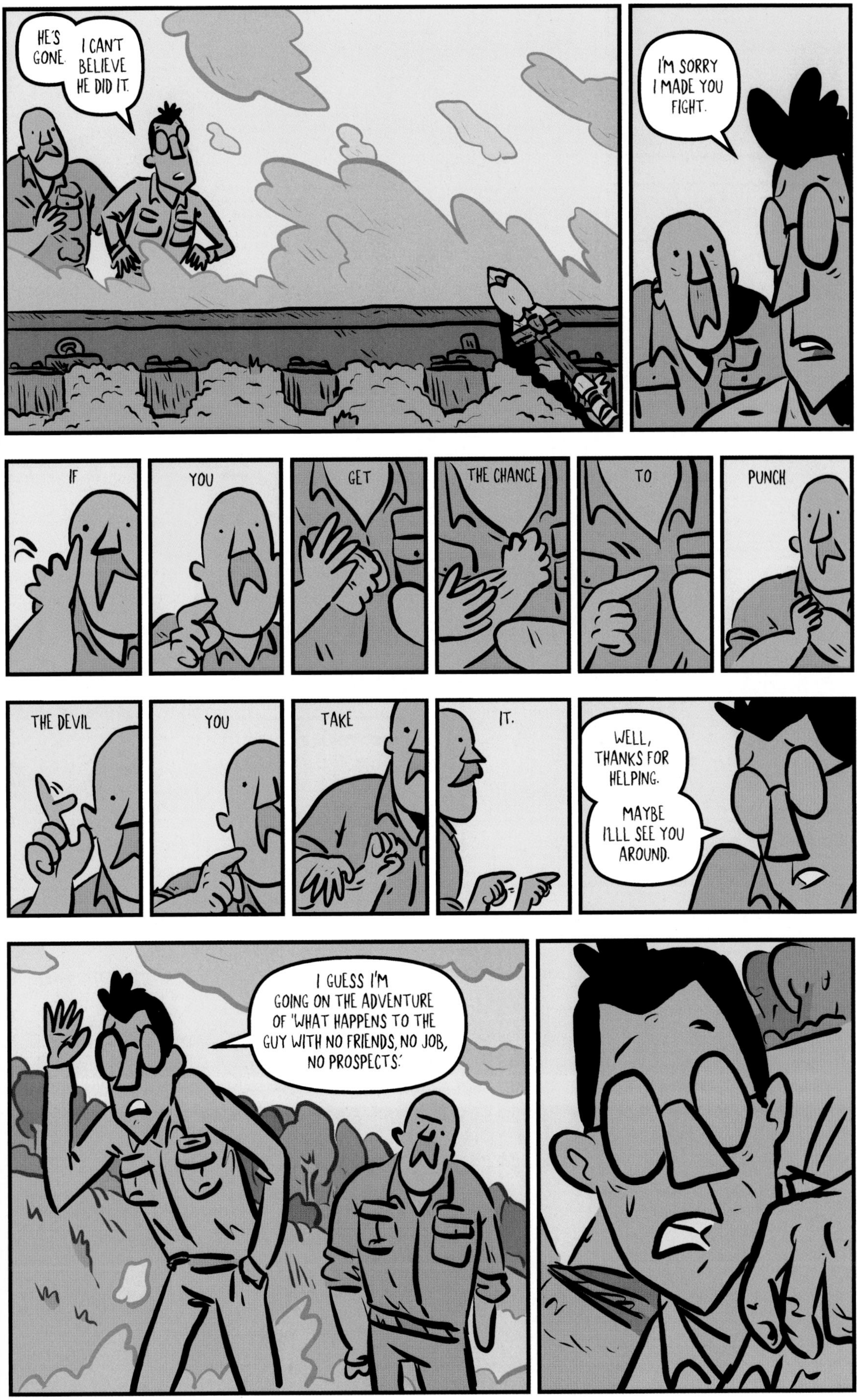
HE'S GONE.
I CAN'T BELIEVE HE DID IT.
I'M SORRY I MADE YOU FIGHT.
IF
YOU
GET
THE CHANCE
TO
PUNCH
THE DEVIL
YOU
TAKE
IT.
WELL, THANKS FOR HELPING.
MAYBE I'LLL SEE YOU AROUND.
I GUESS I'M GOING ON THE ADVENTURE OF 'WHAT HAPPENS TO THE GUY WITH NO FRIENDS, NO JOB, NO PROSPECTS.'

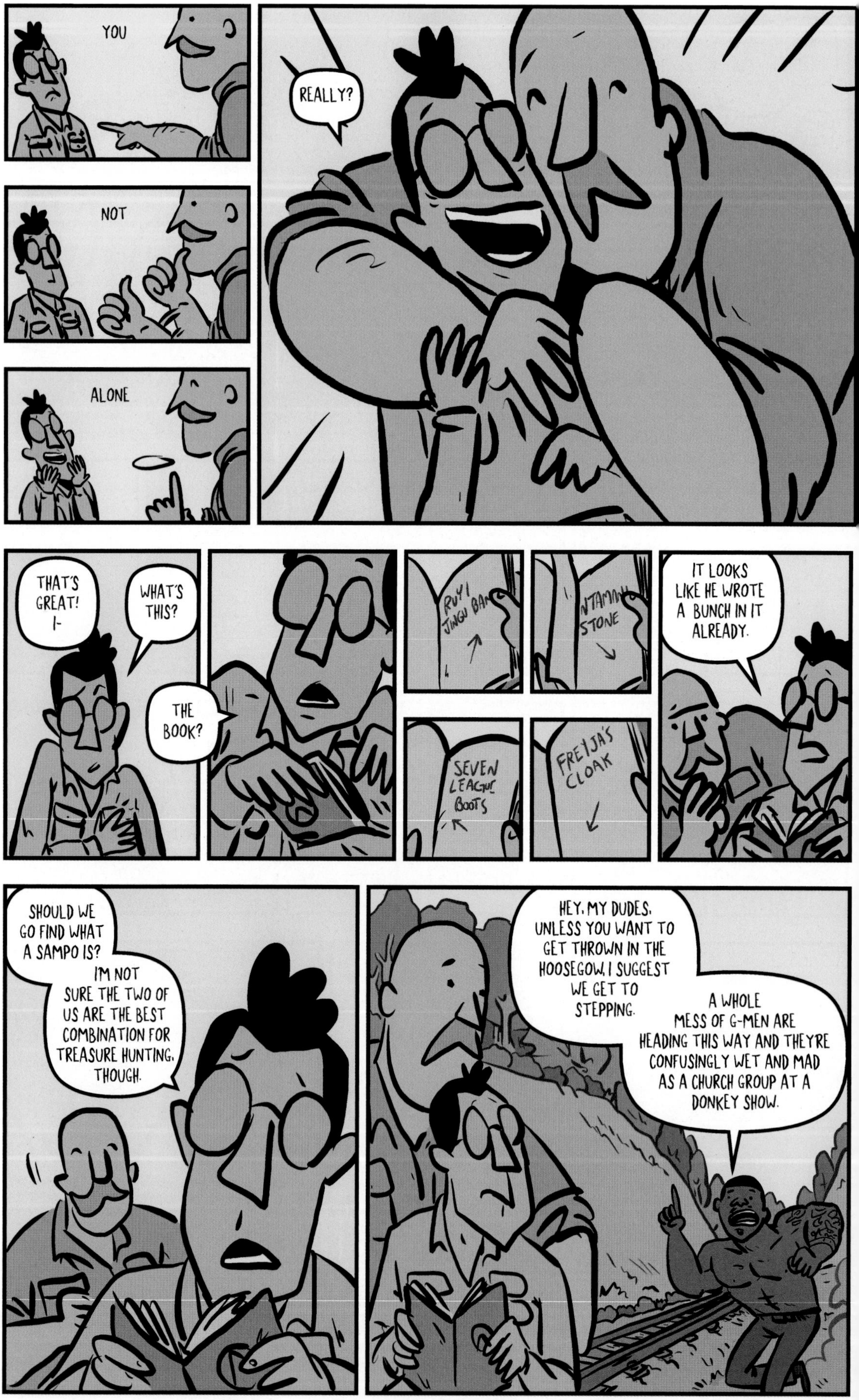
YOU
NOT
ALONE
REALLY?
THAT'S GREAT! I-
WHAT'S THIS?
THE BOOK?
RUYI JINGU BA
STONE
SEVEN LEAGUE BOOTS
FREYJA'S CLOAK
IT LOOKS LIKE HE WROTE A BUNCH IN IT ALREADY.
SHOULD WE GO FIND WHAT A SAMPO IS?
I'M NOT SURE THE TWO OF US ARE THE BEST COMBINATION FOR TREASURE HUNTING, THOUGH.
HEY, MY DUDES. UNLESS YOU WANT TO GET THROWN IN THE HOOSEGOW, I SUGGEST WE GET TO STEPPING.
A WHOLE MESS OF G-MEN ARE HEADING THIS WAY AND THEY'RE CONFUSINGLY WET AND MAD AS A CHURCH GROUP AT A DONKEY SHOW.

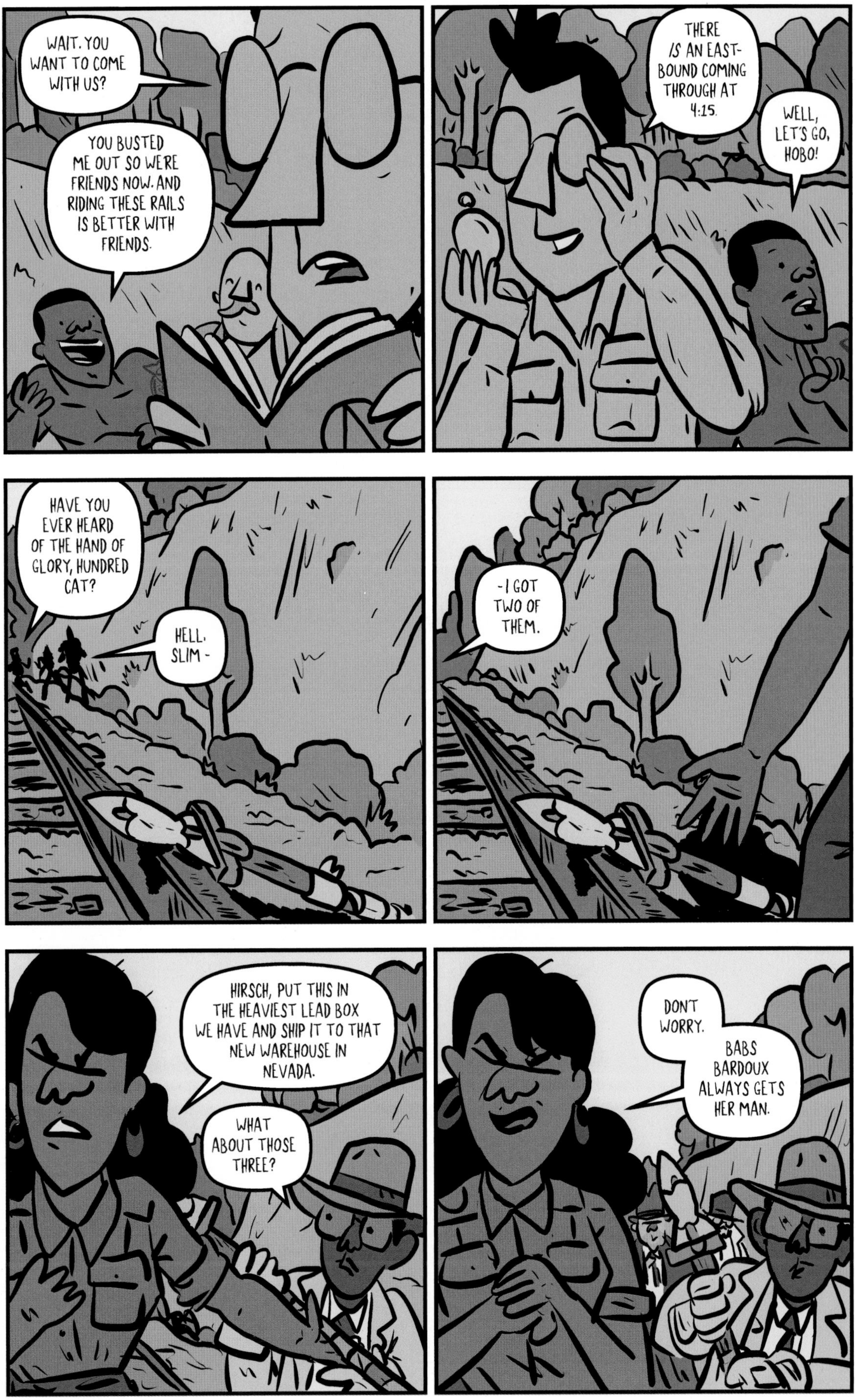
WAIT. YOU WANT TO COME WITH US?
YOU BUSTED ME OUT SO WE'RE FRIENDS NOW. AND RIDING THESE RAILS IS BETTER WITH FRIENDS.
THERE IS AN EAST-BOUND COMING THROUGH AT 4:15.
WELL, LET'S GO, HOBO!
HAVE YOU EVER HEARD OF THE HAND OF GLORY, HUNDRED CAT?
HELL, SLIM -
-I GOT TWO OF THEM.
HIRSCH, PUT THIS IN THE HEAVIEST LEAD BOX WE HAVE AND SHIP IT TO THAT NEW WAREHOUSE IN NEVADA.
WHAT ABOUT THOSE THREE?
DON'T WORRY.
BABS BARDOUX ALWAYS GETS HER MAN.

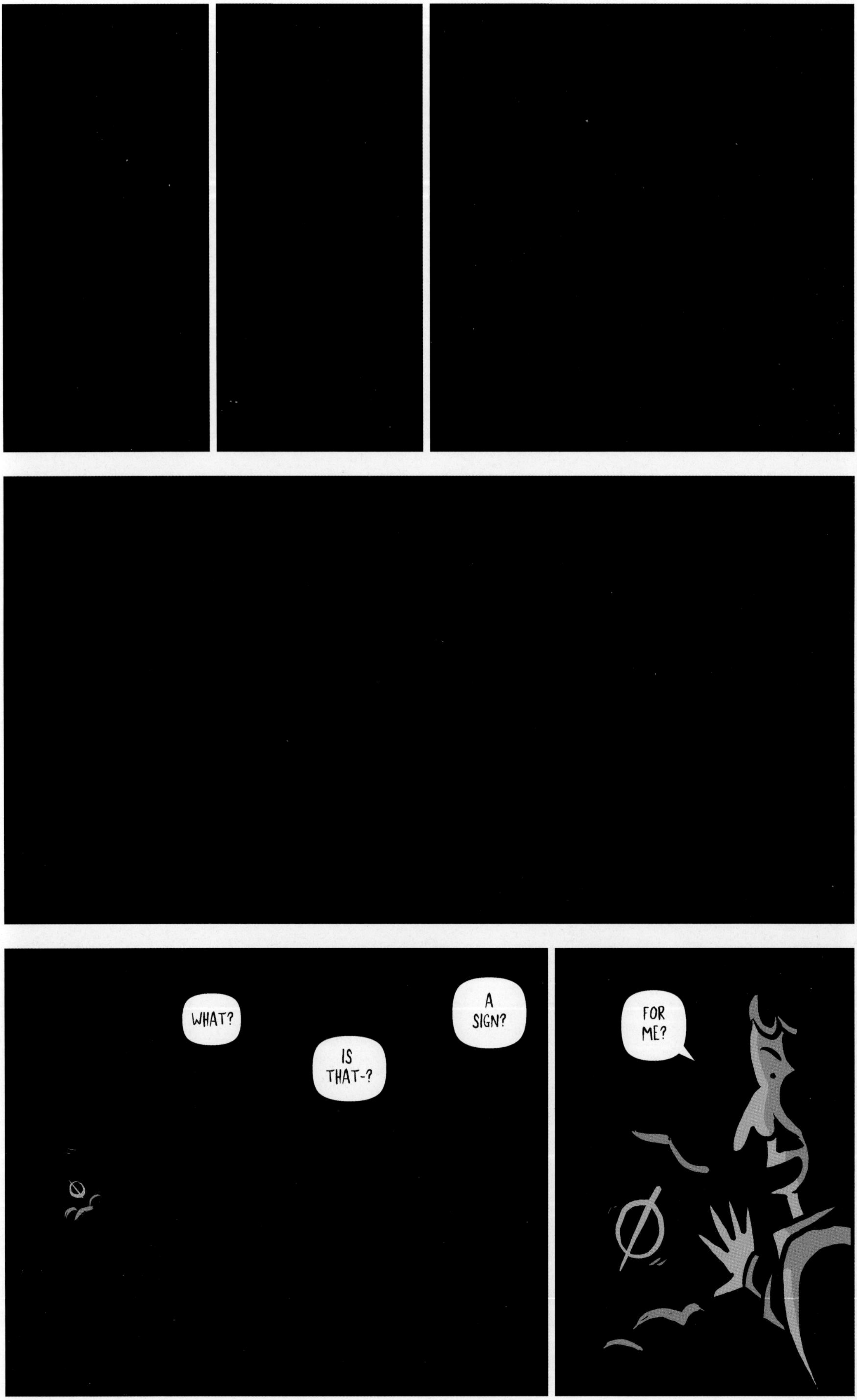
WHAT?
IS THAT-?
A SIGN?
FOR ME?

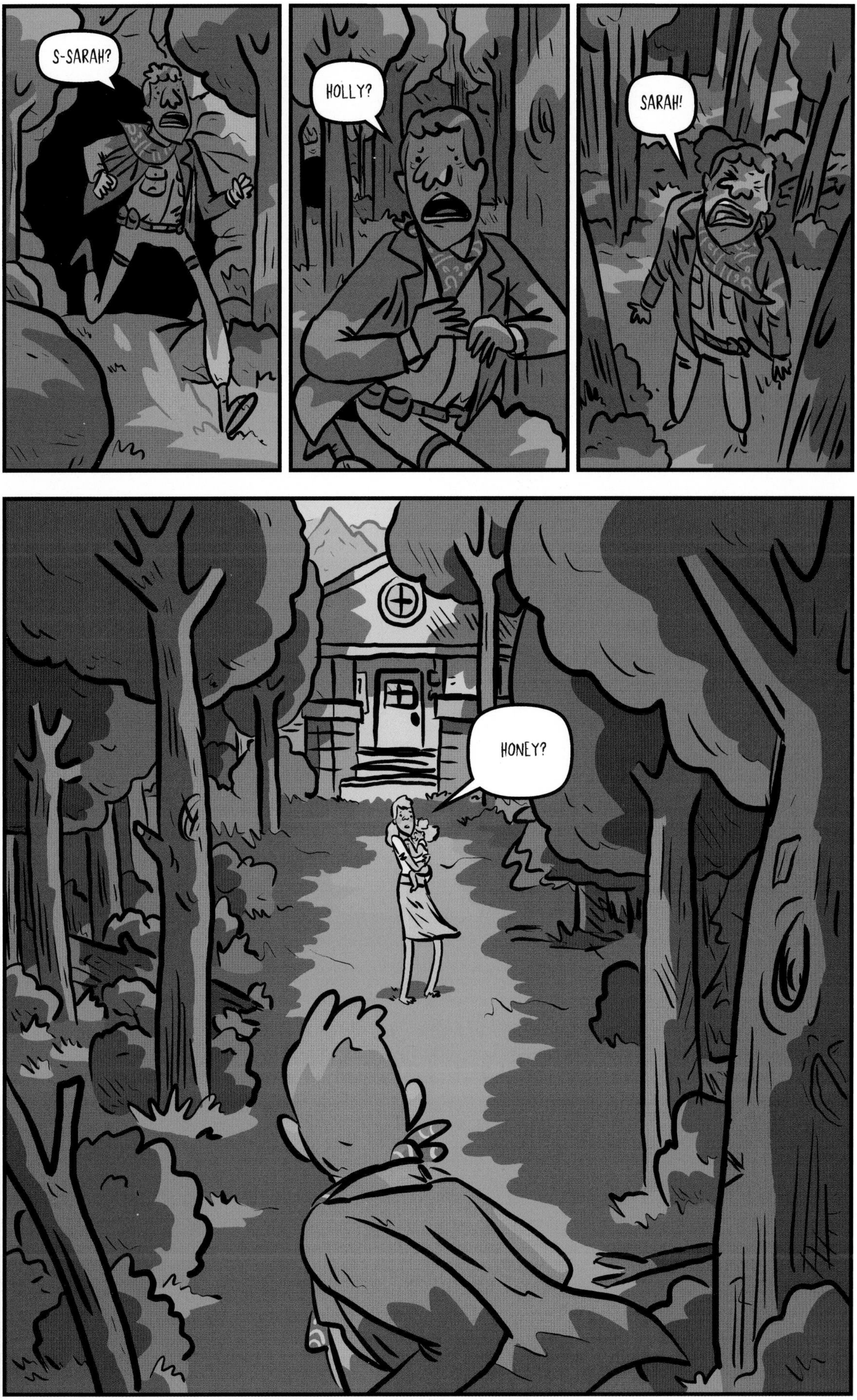
S-SARAH?
HOLLY?
SARAH!
HONEY?

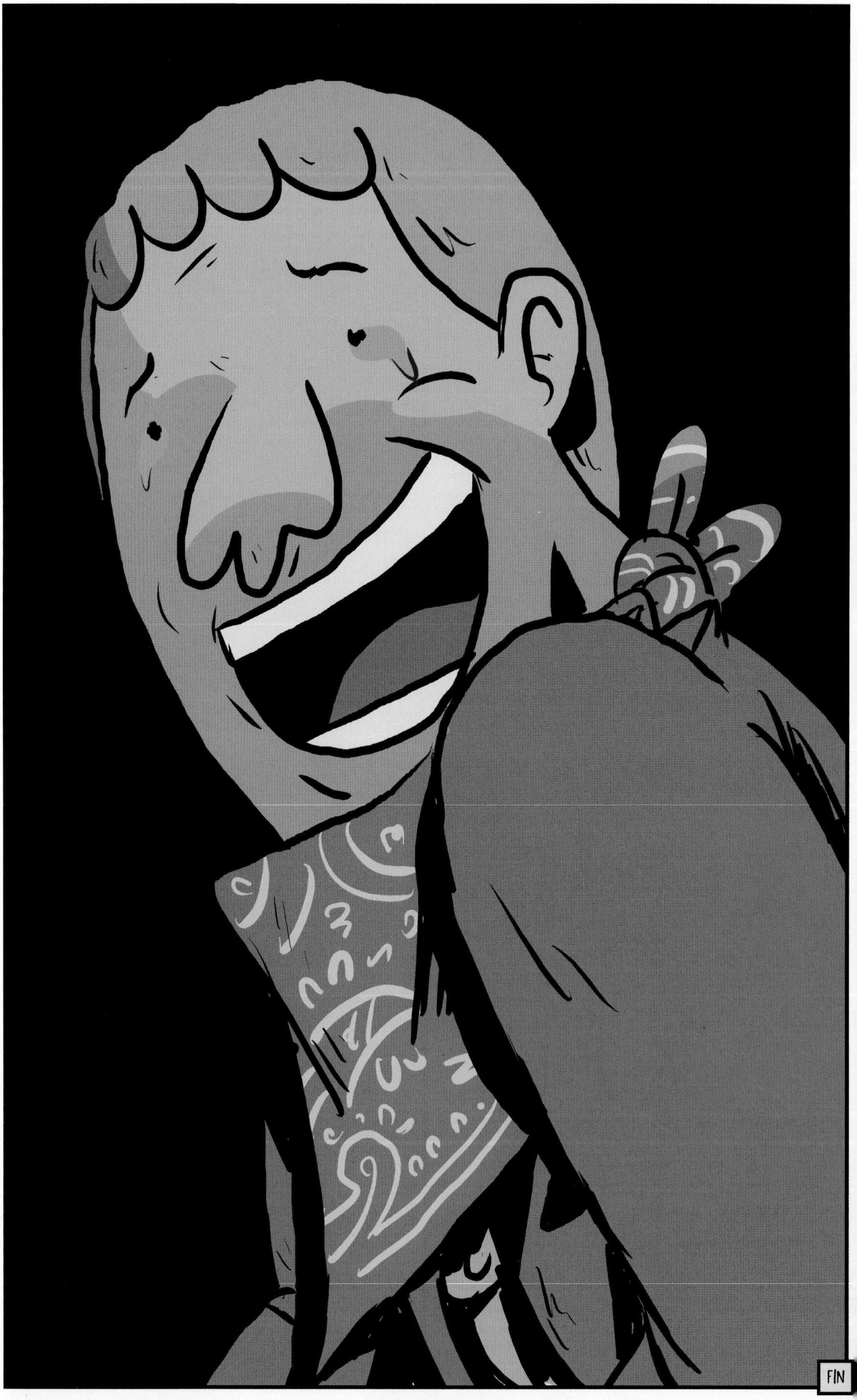

FIN

# I'M WRITING THIS ON THE FIRST OF JANUARY, 2018...

a full two years after the 140-year-old company I was working for – my presumed career – closed its doors. My wife bravely agreed that it was worth the chance to try to make a career in comics and if it didn't work out, well, at least, it would be an interesting year. I'm writing this today, two years to the day that I technically became a professional comic creator.

A few months later in South Carolina I spoke loosely about the growing idea for *Rock Candy Mountain* to some peers. It was the first time I had spoken of it outside of my head and I did it excitedly, nervously, and with enthusiasm. It was important for this plan that my wife so unselfishly allowed that I get a series, and the idea for that series needed to be a good one for that to happen. It was critical. That weekend was the first time I had spent extended time with Chris Schweizer and I remember, clear as day, him loudly proclaiming that it was a mistake to not have it set during the Great Depression, "the Golden Age of Hobos," and I told him that I had a plan. It had to be World War 2. It was important to the story. He cheerfully relented.

A year later, Chris Schweizer – America's Secret Best Cartoonist – would agree to color this book. More than once before the book came out he pleaded that his name not be on the cover. It was my book and his name being on there, just as the colorist, would distract and blah blah blah. He had already colored enough pages to see that his contribution was elevating. It was going to make the book great. It was our book now. He cheerfully relented again. Not long after, Dylan Todd, who I've wanted to work with since I started making comics, came on and elevated the book again.

It's funny to me now, the themes of *Rock Candy Mountain*, as I look at it from the end. It's about how far a man will go for his family as I entered a challenging career with no guarantees. A career very few people are blessed to get to do as their sole income.

Or about how new friendships are formed along that adventure – while I was friendly enough with Chris before, I now consider him one of the most important people in my life and my dearest friend.

Or about how no matter how big or small, how grand or simple that adventure might be, you absolutely can't do it alone. No matter how selfish the venture you can't do it alone. And that's where all of you come in. For supporting my work, for reading this book – for telling of and sharing it. You, dear reader, made this all possible. So I'm saying to you all what Jackson said to those who made his dream possible:

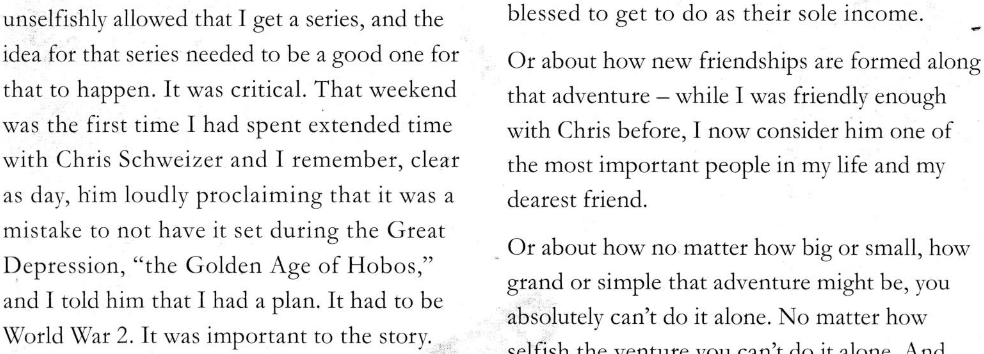
THANK YOU.

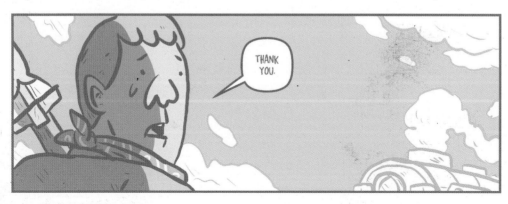

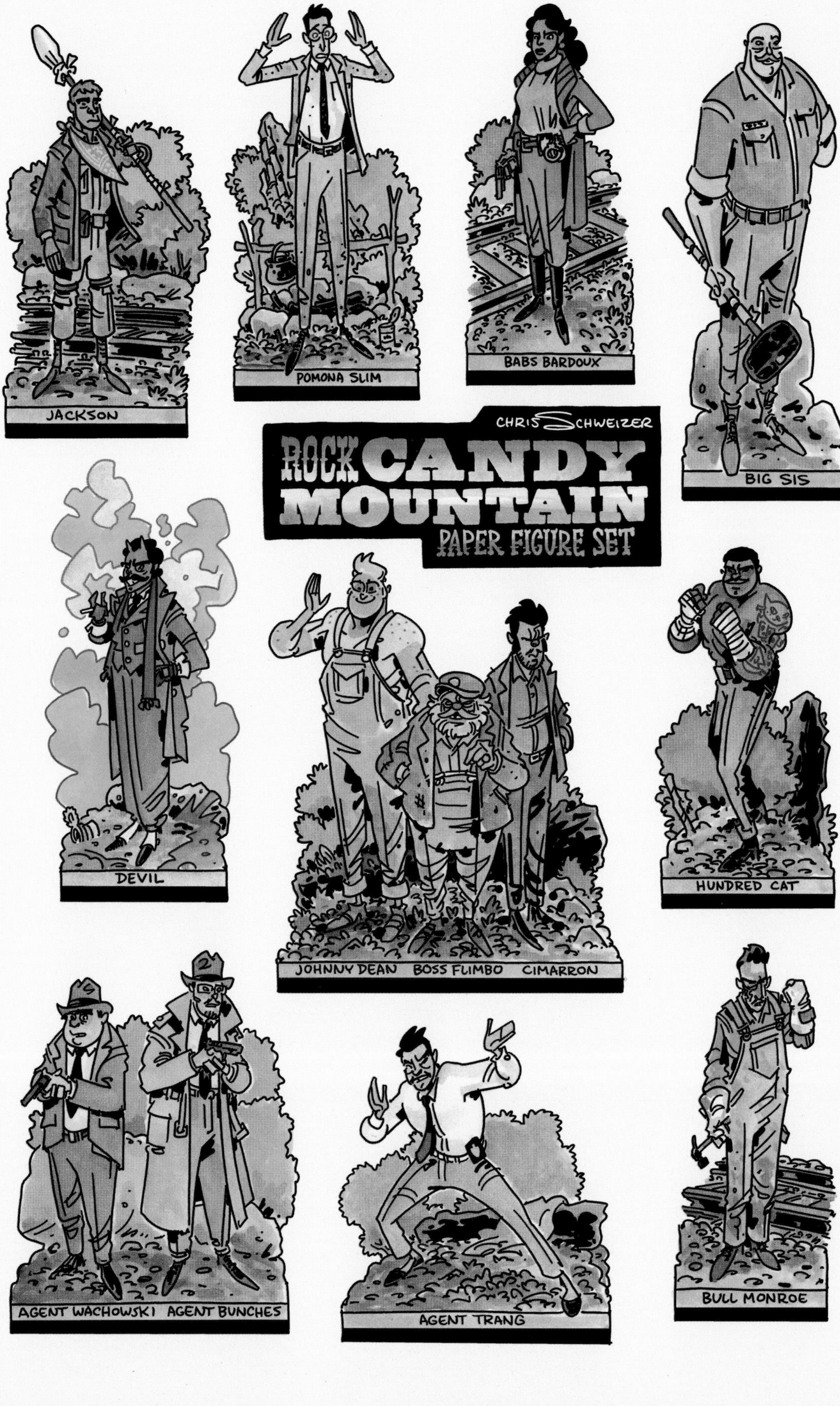
CHRIS SCHWEIZER
ROCK CANDY MOUNTAIN
PAPER FIGURE SET
JACKSON
POMONA SLIM
BABS BARDOUX
BIG SIS
DEVIL
JOHNNY DEAN
BOSS FLIMBO
CIMARRON
HUNDRED CAT
AGENT WACHOWSKI
AGENT BUNCHES
AGENT TRANG
BULL MONROE

## KYLE STARKS

Kyle Starks is an Eisner-nominated
cartoonist from Southern Indiana.

His hobo nickname would be "That City Slicker Isn't
A Hobo At All" and they would be right.

This book is dedicated to my wife and children who inspire
me daily and to the thousands of brave men and
women who rode our countries' rails.

Please do not try to hop on any trains.
Trains are nothing to fuck with.

If you are interested in reading more about hobos,
check out Roger Bruns' *The Knights of the Road*,
or Jack London's *The Road*.

## CHRIS SCHWEIZER

Chris Schweizer is an Eisner-nominated cartoonist
who's written and drawn *The Creeps, The Crogan Adventures*,
and some nonfiction books about car maintenance and historical
mysteries for First Second Books. He's from Western
Kentucky, only a fifty-mile boxcar ride from Kyle.

His hobo nickname would be "Uncle Inky,"
because that's what his niece calls him and
he's often avuncular and ink-stained.

This is the first time he's colored someone besides himself
because he loved *Rock Candy Mountain* so much.

## DYLAN TODD

Dylan Todd is a writer, art director and graphic designer.

When he's not reading comics, making comics, writing
about comics or designing stuff for comics, he can
probably be found thinking about comics.

He likes Star Wars, mummies, D-Man, kaiju and
1966 Batman. He's the editor of the 2299 sci-fi comics
anthology and, alongside Matthew Digges, is the co-creator of
*The Creep Crew*, a comic about undead teen detectives.

You can find his pop culture and comics
design portfolio at bigredrobot.net.

He ain't never hopped a train, but he has eaten
himself a lukewarm can of beans a time or two.